Bookstagram Reviews for for *The World's End*

'I LOVED this book from the moment I started. Gripped from the first chapter!'

'A page-turner and if you like crime fiction, this one's for you.'

'What a fabulous read by Limerick-based author. Couldn't put it down.'

'Brilliantly written debut novel. From the first page I was totally immersed!'

'A fabulous read and I had absolutely no idea how it was going to end. You need to READ THIS BOOK.'

'I devoured *The World's End* in one sitting on the train from Bergen to Oslo – utterly captivated!'

'A must-read for fans of psychological thrillers who enjoy suspenseful storytelling and complex characters.'

'A brilliant thriller that kept me in suspense to the end. I really like the private investigator Lana Bowen as we see her own life and her own struggles as well as how she works.'

'Fitzgibbon's richly atmospheric setting and masterful plotting create a tense, gripping thriller. Lana's battle with panic attacks added emotional depth, and the web of lies and betrayal kept me guessing until the jaw-dropping conclusion.'

'Fitzgibbon certainly knows how to do tense writing. I felt such a sense of unease in the first half of *The World's End*. If you love twists and turns, this would be a great choice, especially if you like authors like Lucy Foley.'

NEVER LOOK BACK

KAREN FITZGIBBON

POOLBEG
CRIMSON

This book is a work of fiction. References to real people, events, establishments, organisations, or locales are intended only to provide a sense of authenticity, and are used fictitiously. All other characters, and all incidents and dialogue, are drawn from the author's imagination and are not to be construed as real.

Published 2025 by Crimson, an imprint of Poolbeg Press Ltd.

123 Grange Hill, Baldoyle,Dublin 13, Ireland. Email: poolbeg@poolbeg.com

A catalogue record for this book is available from the British Library.

ISBN 978-1-78199-675-1

www.poolbeg.com

Printed by L&C Group, Poland

About the Author

Karen Fitzgibbon is a theatre practitioner and filmmaker based in Limerick city. She has been co-writing, co-producing, acting in and directing plays and short films with community groups and professional groups for over twenty years. She holds a Licentiate in Theatre Studies with Trinity College London. Karen lives in Limerick with her family and much-loved springer spaniel Major. Her debut novel *The World's End* was published in May 2024. *The World's End* is the first in a series of novels introducing Private Investigator Lana Bowen.

Acknowledgements

During the early months of the pandemic, my daughter was living abroad. I worried about her incessantly but she refused to return home. This was probably a good decision in hindsight. Our house was full and we were all living on top of each other! But, at the time, there was uncertainty in the world and I couldn't stop fretting. I dreamed a lot during those months, sometimes two or three vivid dreams a night about plane crashes, trains derailing and chases in dark woods and of course, my daughter was in all of them! In one such dream, I paid her a surprise visit and discovered she had a baby. We decided to travel home to Ireland but at the airport, she just disappeared into the crowds. I remember waking from the dream in a cold sweat and writing down the details. And so was born the premise for my second novel!

I would like to thank you, my two dearest friends Stephanie O'Keeffe and Niamh Bowen, who read this book not long after my first draft. You are both always there for me, to offer advice and support and to brainstorm plot holes and incongruities (and there were many)! Sincerely and unequivocally, thank you both so much.

I want to thank my wonderful sisters, Marie and Carmel, who read an early draft of this book and gave me ingenious and candid advice. Every day I treasure you both. To my brother, Ger, who lives in Arizona, returning every other year completely unchanged – the four siblings reverting to our childhood years. Thank you Della, Brendan, Michael, Ciaran, William, Chris, Lorcan, Seany and Mia.

To Ger Nichols from the Book Bureau who said wonderful things about *The World's End* and gave incredible comments and encouragement for me to continue writing.

I would like to thank St. Saviour's, the Northside Misfits, Southill Community Drama Groups, Headway, Adapt Services and Thomond Studio who have allowed me to write with them for theatre and film for many years. For allowing me to be creative and have lots of fun, and for trusting me. Every one of you supported the publication of my debut novel. You told your families and friends and said wonderful words of encouragement and I am forever indebted to you all.

To writers Donal Ryan and Patricia Gibney, thank you for your kindness and incredible quotes for *The World's End*. I will never forget your benevolence! Thank you to Roisin Meaney for all your support.

To my daughter Lauren who worried me sick during those early Covid months and provided me with a dream! To my son Peter who is a rock of knowledge when I'm feeling out of my depth. Thank you to my son Jonathon who always has a twinkle in his eye and a warm hug. You all mean the absolute world to me.

To my husband, Pat, who always has my back. He still passes the living room every now and then while I type away on my laptop commenting, "Are you writing your second book, you are?" Yes, I was, and I did!

To my dear friends Joy Ferris, Martina McDermot, Louise Campbell, Brídín Ryan, Sharon Kiely, Dawn McCarthy, Helena Enright, Eileen

Nevin, Richard Lynch and Anne Fitzgibbon. Thank you for believing in me.

A huge thank-you to my adorable, moody and cracked springer spaniel Major who still sits beside me with an even more worn-out tennis ball in front of him while I write. You never judge, only love.

To my editor Gaye Shortland who continues to surprise me, pointing out new discrepancies and inconsistencies in the storyline, even when I think there are no more. Location, location, location – not my strongest point! Your attention to detail is astonishing and I think, hand on heart, working with you has been the most precious part of this whole experience. And terrifying, of course! To have someone who is ridiculously skilled poring over my novel with a fine-tooth comb. How lucky am I?

I will never be able to thank Paula Campbell enough for taking a chance on me. Paula has been such a solid support for me before and after the publication of *The World's End*. I will never forget what you have done for me. You believed in the character of Lana Bowen and the stories that shape her life.

To everyone at Poolbeg for making this happen.

Finally, thank you, the reader. No matter the platform, theatre, film, books, TV – the audience is where it's at. Always and forever. Thank you.

Dedication

Dedicated to Pat, Peter, Lauren, Jonathon and Major xxxxx

PROLOGUE

The baby was crying again. The girl had begun to hate that noise, and it was a noise. It began as a whimper, soft and meagre, but its intensity grew into a whining, whinging, piercing wail. It stabbed her ears, it hurt her head, and it made her want to scream.

The girl made her way towards the exit. Passengers, tired and weary, surrounded her, dragging their bags and scrolling through their phones as they moved slowly along Platform 5. She watched the security guard behind the Perspex screen as she shuffled along with the crowd. Lost in the repetition of the daily grind, his eyes barely glanced at the passengers as they trudged past him.

The baby had stopped crying, but the girl knew it wouldn't be long before she started again. She arrived at the exit and the guard hardly noticed her as she walked past him. The throng continued to move forward, pushing through the barrier. She watched as a tiny hand reached out over the woman's shoulder, the little one wanting to come to her. She kissed the tips of her fingers and gently touched the hand.

Fear gripped her, tears stung her eyes and her heart ached with pain. She was getting closer now. She knew she was leaving, she knew she had to. It wasn't what she had originally planned, but it was safer. For both of them. Safer for everyone. She caressed the baby's cheek one last time, the soft skin warm to her touch.

Then she moved in reverse through the crowds, smiling as the tears flowed. The baby started to cry again.

"*Goodbye, my sweetheart,*" the girl whispered.

And she began to run.

CHAPTER 1

Lana scooped coffee granules into the stainless-steel coffeepot, poured in boiling water and placed the plunger on top to rest. Tucking her laptop under her arm, she grabbed an empty cup and carried the pot out to the patio. Carefully placing them on the wooden table, she settled into her mother's favourite recliner. She wrapped her mother's fleece blanket around her shoulders even though it was unseasonably warm for March. The sun lingered in a clear blue sky and she felt sure she could hear a lawnmower starting up somewhere nearby.

It had been ten months since her mother died and Lana had moved out of her rented apartment and back into her old family home on O'Callaghan's Strand. Even though she had grown up in this house, she was struggling to get used to her surroundings as an adult. Everything appeared much smaller than she remembered, and the memory of her mother was everywhere. Having said that, being here, surrounded by her mother's things, helped with her grief.

She had given up her small office in the centre of town and set up a space in the side room here so that her assistant Ella could wade through the mounting paperwork. Her relationship with Ella hadn't got off to a very good start. She had found the young woman's enthusiasm irritating but Ella had proved her worth in recent months and Lana had grown quite fond of her. They had a similar work ethic: get the job done no matter how long it takes, then you can relax. However, they were quite different in their approach to downtime. Ella was big into health and wellbeing. She preferred yoga to a fast walk, lentil soup to Subway sandwiches, fruit-infused water to wine – but they got on very well nonetheless. Lana enjoyed the girl's company in the house. With her mother gone, it had become very quiet and it was nice to have someone around every day. The weekends were lonely though. Up until recently, Lana had been spending them down the coast with Peter, but now all that had stopped.

She carefully pressed down on the plunger and poured herself a cup of coffee. Sipping, she sat back and despairingly scanned the expansive garden. To say it was neglected was an understatement. All her mother's careful planting and pruning had been invaded by weeds, the hedges badly needed to be trimmed back and the grass was far too high. But Lana was too busy to take care of it – apart from the fact that gardening had never been her forte. She had asked Norman, her mother's neighbour, if he knew of anyone that could help and Norman said he would put out feelers, but in the meantime Lana would have to put up with it. She could always do a bit of tidying-up herself, she thought, glancing down at the tufts of weeds coming up through the wooden decking – a couple of hours would make a significant difference, right? However, work was too demanding, she told herself – she just didn't have the time. She could see her mother towering over her, disapproving, a frown creasing her forehead. *You work too hard, Lana!*

Opening her laptop, she keyed in her password. She clicked on the file she had been working on the previous night. She was just coming to the end of a big case and there were still a few loose ends to tie up. It had been an intense couple of months. Her client, Sally Moran, had been beaten to within an inch of her life by her estranged husband. When Lana first went to visit Sally in her home, the woman had been in a terrible state of distress. Even though Lana believed, without a shadow of a doubt, that the husband was responsible for the attack, Sally had no proof, no eye-witnesses, not a shred of evidence. She had endured years of coercive control, but the bastard had never laid a finger on her. Even the night she told him she wanted him to leave, that the marriage wasn't working, he had remained calm, even agreeing with her that the relationship was over. He had packed his things and left the house. The following day, Sally changed the front and rear door-locks and set about moving on to the next stage of her life – as a single woman. And she'd marvelled at how easy the whole process had been. She'd wondered why she hadn't asked him to leave years before.

A few months went by and Sally was gaining confidence in her new life as a single woman. She had started to go out more. She knew that she had a lot of healing to do but slowly the emotional trauma was beginning to ease. Then, one night, six months after her husband had left the house, Sally went out for dinner with her colleagues from work. When she returned home he was waiting for her outside the house and that's where the beating took place. He attacked her from behind and she hit the rough pavement on her driveway face first. She was caught completely unaware. She didn't even have time to react, or call out for help. He proceeded to kick her body repeatedly until she stopped moving, leaving her lying unconscious. A dog-walker had found her. Even though she hadn't seen her attacker, she knew who it was. "*I could smell him, Lana.*"

When Lana read through the Garda report, she noticed that her client's next-door neighbour hadn't given a statement. Sally told her that the house was a rented property but was now leased to a young family who hadn't been living there during the time of the assault. Lana had called to the house, got the property owner's contact details and phoned him to find out who had been renting it previously. However, during their conversation, he revealed that the house had been burgled a few months before, after which he'd had hidden cameras installed front and back. The ones to the front were in a tree at the end of his one-car drive and one of them covered Sally's drive also. He hadn't heard about the assault and was shocked when Lana told him, so when she asked to see the footage for the relevant date he was eager to oblige.

Lana could hardly believe it: the investigating Gardaí had missed the cameras and the previous tenant must have neglected to tell them. When she viewed the footage, she could clearly see Sally's husband kicking her repeatedly on the night in question. When he began his attack he was wearing a dark mask but, when he'd finished beating her up, he'd pulled the mask off and smirked at her as she lay there unconscious. No doubt he was thinking that he couldn't be identified. You could have heard a pin drop when the image was shown in court.

The case had been messy. Her client was fragile and facing her husband in court daily had taken every bit of strength she had. But face him she did. Every single day of the trial Sally Moran stood a little bit taller, growing in confidence. Lana was still processing the paperwork while Sally prepared her victim-impact statement and the accused awaited sentencing. Hopefully he would go down for a long time. *Hopefully*.

The doorbell rang, breaking her concentration. Lana re-entered the house. Reaching the hall, she saw a shadow through the frosted glass of the front door. From the person's stance, she was sure her caller was a male. Her heart skipped a beat. Could it be Peter? She told herself to breathe normally. She hadn't had a panic attack in months. But she wasn't naïve. She knew it could happen again any time. She waited for the familiar symptoms as she continued to inhale, hold and exhale. No – this time she was going to be OK.

She quickly checked her appearance in the hall mirror. She had started to part her shoulder-length brown hair in the centre and she still wasn't sure if it suited the shape of her face. She straightened her fitted black sweater over her blue jeans.

Then she opened the front door to find a young man standing on her porch, a sheepish grin on his face. *Not Peter*. He held a clipboard against his chest as he presented his ID. Selling something, no doubt. Lana's heart sank. She silently cursed herself for opening the door.

"Don't worry! I won't keep you more than a minute," the young man assured her as he glanced at the flower bed outside her front door. "I was going to pick some of your flowers for my mother but that would be stealing, right?" He proceeded to laugh at his sales pitch.

Sweet Jesus. Lana didn't react.

When he noticed the look on her face, he sobered up. He cleared his throat. "Do you know what gas company you are with?" he asked, attempting a smile.

Lana shook her head.

"Right, well, I represent –"

Lana held up her hand. "Let me stop you right there." She smiled. "I don't actually live here. I'm house-sitting for a friend."

His mouth opened and closed. He nodded. "Oh, I see." He continued to shake his head. "Well, do you know when your friend gets back?"

Lana shrugged. "No clue, probably the end of the summer. He's having surgery in Sweden, a sex reassignment." Where did that come from? Oh – an article that had popped up on a newsfeed the night before.

The young man stopped nodding. He glanced down the driveway, looked back at her, cleared his throat. "Right, well, I'll call again at the end of the summer." He held up his clipboard. "I'll, *ah*, make a note of it."

"Do. I'm sure my friend will be delighted to see you when he comes back. I mean, when *she* comes back." Lana smiled pleasantly and closed the door.

Bloody hell! She felt momentarily guilty for lying. The poor guy was just doing his job and it couldn't be easy trying to sell door to door. But he needed to change his sales strategy or he wouldn't last long.

She could hear her phone ringing as she made her way back out to the garden. When she reached the patio, she saw Peter's name flash across the screen. Her heart did that funny *flip* again. Her finger hovered over the answer button until it rang out. Why was he calling her? And why didn't she answer?

She thought back to the last time she had seen him, the look on his face. They had first met while she was working on another case the previous year. Her mother died towards the end of her investigation and Peter had been there for her. They had grown close, very close. Until that weekend when everything fell apart. They hadn't spoken since, not as much as a text. And now he was ringing her out of the blue.

The phone pinged that she had a new voicemail. Lana tapped the screen to hear what Peter had to say.

"*Lana? It's me ... em ... can you call me back when you get a minute? I have a friend who needs your help.*"

Lana could picture Peter standing on his boat, the wind whipping strands of his wavy dark hair around his tanned face as he concentrated on his voice-recording. Lana glanced out at her mother's overgrown garden. *I have a friend who needs your help.* Not exactly the message she had been hoping for. She pressed delete.

CHAPTER 2

"I lost her."

Nyah heard the words but he didn't register their meaning. He half opened one eye and spotted the beer can on his bedside locker. His mouth was dry and he was very tempted to drink whatever might be left inside.

The woman on the phone was crying, her breath coming in short, sharp gasps. Who was it? It sounded like his mother but why would she be crying like that?

"Nyah? Are you there? Did you hear what I said?"

OK, it was his mother. He closed his eyes. "Yeah, sorry, Mam. Who did you lose exactly?"

He wasn't sure when he had last spoken to his mother. A few days before, he thought.

His job with the social-media app as a content moderator was always so busy – he was way past shutting down his laptop following a shift, as per his contract. That was an absolute joke. His boss had other ideas about the working hours of his staff. The man never took time off and he expected the same from his employees. Nyah often grabbed a bowl of noodles or whatever he could put together quickly in the kitchen for dinner and worked late into the evening. Of course, when he did eventually call it a day, there was always one of his housemates looking to go for a pint, or a friend calling to the house for a few drinks and a smoke. Sometimes other stuff. Nyah would crash out late and start work early the next morning, feeling like shit and promising himself that he would get a couple of early nights. Until the same thing happened again. Rinse and repeat. The days and nights were slowly running into each other. But he was young, right? That's what people his age did. Work and play, with little to no sleep. He would have plenty of time for sleep later.

"I lost your sister."

Nyah sat up in bed. Narrowing his eyes, he slowly glanced at the other side of the bed. It was empty. Relieved, he leaned back against the headboard. He wondered where the hell his mother was. He could hear a lot of background noise, lots of people talking all at once. Had she mentioned something about visiting Clara in Belfast? Yeah, that was it. She'd said Clara had been a bit vague these past few months about college and stuff, acting a bit strange and communicating less and less. She was worried something was wrong, that maybe Clara was lonely. Nyah didn't agree. Every now and then he would look up his sister's stories on Instagram and she seemed to be out as much as he was. In fact, her social life appeared a little too full-on. His sister was having a whale of a time in college – a far cry from the life she'd led while living at home. Although, now that he thought about it, maybe she had been a little quiet lately, with him at least. He tried to think when he had last spoken to her. It couldn't have been less than a couple of weeks ago – he was pretty sure of that – but that didn't mean anything, did it? His head hurt.

"You lost Clara?"

His mother was crying more freely now. Christ, he wasn't able for this. Their mam was going through the menopause and he and Clara had started calling her *MenoMam* the previous summer. Not to her face, of course. She could be very irritable and a normal everyday conversation could turn into a shouting match in seconds. And then she would apologise, explaining she was going through "the change" and to ignore her. Until the next time.

"Sorry, Mam, I'm a bit confused. How did you lose Clara exactly?"

"Here at the train station. She was behind me one minute and the next she was gone. She just disappeared, Nyah!"

Nyah shook his head in frustration. Sometimes he felt he might murder his little sister. Now what had she gone and done? Had she travelled to the train station in Belfast with their mother, and not bothered to say goodbye? Why would she do that? He grabbed his watch from his bedside locker. It was one thirty. *Shit.* Had he slept through his alarm? He was on a later shift today but he should be logging on at two. Otherwise his boss would do his nut. Throwing back the duvet, he eased himself out of bed. The room began to spin, and he sat back down on the edge of the mattress. *Jesus, his head hurt!* What had he been drinking last night? Had someone brought out a bottle of whiskey? He gagged at the thought of the strong golden liquid burning the back of his throat. He could hear movement downstairs, which meant that one of his housemates must be making lunch, or maybe it was the cute girl he had met in the bar. Had he brought her home? He peered over his shoulder at the unmade bed again. But the other side looked like it hadn't been slept in. No, they must have parted ways in the pub.

"Nyah?"

"Sorry, Mam, thought I lost you there."

He could hear dishes rattling downstairs – there was probably a mess from last night's gathering. Maybe if he stayed upstairs for a little while longer, whoever it was down below would have cleaned it up. But first he had to quench his thirst. Grabbing the half-empty beer can, he downed its contents. The beer was completely flat and tasted a little sweet, but it did the job. He crushed the empty can and fired it into the bin across the room. Hole in one! It made a clanking sound as it hit another container. He was getting sloppy, he thought, and he made a mental note to empty the bin and tidy up his room.

"Nyah? Are you there?"

"She went with you to the station to see you off, did she?"

"No, no – we're in Limerick, Colbert Station. We've just arrived. She was coming home with me."

"*Coming home!* Why?"

He entered the en-suite bathroom. As he took in his appearance in the mirror over the sink, a pair of bloodshot eyes stared back at him. His dark hair was pressed into the side of his head. His mother hadn't replied. Had he lost connection?

"Mam?" He wondered if he had time for a quick shower.

"Did you know?" She sounded calm now, her tone flat.

He put the phone on the small shelf under the mirror and pressed the speaker button. Running the tap, he splashed cold water onto his face.

“Know what, Mam?”

And then he heard a sound, a sort of cooing sound, followed by his mother’s soothing tones. “There, there, it’s alright, there, there ...”

What the hell? Frowning, he grabbed the towel from the rack and wiped his face.

“There, there, my love ...”

He threw the towel on the floor and took the phone off speaker, pressing the device to his ear. “Mam? Who are you talking to?”

“The baby.”

“What baby?”

“Your sister had a baby, Nyah.” Her voice was quieter now, almost a whisper. “Clara had a baby.”

CHAPTER 3

Jenny held the three-month-old infant close to her chest as she tucked her phone back into her pocket. What was she going to do? She looked around the crowded station as trains arrived and departed, passengers embarking and disembarking. But there was no sign of her daughter anywhere. The baby began to stir. With her free hand, she rummaged around in Clara's baby bag, hanging from the back of the buggy, in search of a bottle. She noticed there wasn't that much milk left. But it would have to do for now. She shifted the weight of the infant so that she lay cradled into the crook of her arm as she teased open her lips with the teat. The baby hungrily guzzled the lukewarm liquid, her eyes blinking under the bright fluorescent lights of the train station. A few minutes later, the same eyes rolled as she fell into a drunken sleep. She fed just like Clara had when she was a baby, Jenny thought – she hadn't needed much, just a couple of ounces and she was satisfied. She carefully placed the baby into the buggy, covered her with the knitted pink blanket and adjusted the back so she could lie comfortably.

The question milled around in Jenny's head as she watched the little baby sleep. What was she going to do? The truth was, she didn't know. She hadn't a clue. A baby had been thrust at her, a baby she hadn't known existed twenty-four hours earlier, and she felt immobilised.

The loudspeaker sounded as passengers were informed of arrivals and departures. A thought came to her. Maybe she could request a call-out for Clara. Her daughter was probably somewhere in the station, looking for her and the baby. Relief flooded through her – that is what she should do. Why hadn't she thought of it before? She had been too hasty calling Nyah. He had seemed genuinely shocked about the baby and she couldn't blame him for that. She was pretty shocked herself.

She spotted a security guard standing outside the public toilets – she would ask him to direct her to the information desk. Colbert Station had undergone a complete refurbishment in recent times and everything had been moved around. She secured the baby's bag over the handle of the buggy, hung her own overnight bag on the other side, and made her way across the busy platform.

As she approached the security guard, she noticed him lean his head forward to talk into his mouthpiece. Then, frowning, he raised his head as he looked around the station.

"Excuse me?" Jenny said.

"Yes, ma'am?" The guy looked distracted as he scanned the crowds.

"Can you tell me where the information desk is?"

The security man looked down at the baby sleeping soundly in the stroller. He smiled. "They haven't a care in the world at that age." He gestured at the throng around them. "They'd sleep through all this noise and then have you awake all night when there isn't a sound!"

"Yes ..." Jenny gave a small smile, though she felt like crying. She wasn't able for small talk right now.

"At least my new-born does! She's only a few weeks old and already she has our world turned upside-down. How old is your little one?"

"No ... this is my ..." Jenny couldn't say the word *grandchild*, but that is what this baby was, her grandchild. At the ripe old age of fifty-three, Jenny Doyle had become a grandmother. "She's my daughter's baby. She's three months old."

"OK, Granny," the security man pointed through the crowds, "just up there on your left. A blue-and-white desk."

She could hear a voice on his earpiece as he strained to listen, moving on to his next task. Thanking him, she pushed the buggy through the crowd until she found the information desk. Luckily, there was no one else waiting there. A well-groomed young woman was sitting on a stool behind the counter, squinting at the screen in front of her. She sported an earpiece and seemed to be in the middle of finding someone's missing luggage. Jenny waited as the girl assured whoever it was on the other end of the line that everything possible was being done to trace the suitcase.

The girl sighed as she ended the call. She looked up at Jenny and immediately placed a smile on her face, though it didn't quite meet her eyes. "How can I help you?" she rattled off in a singsong voice. No doubt she spent her days saying these exact words, repeatedly, to disgruntled travellers. Eventually, it would wear her down.

"Yes. I lost my daughter. Can you call out her name or something? Ask her to come to this information desk?"

"No problem, madam. Can you give me some details about her?"

Jenny frowned, confused by the question. "What kind of details?"

The girl continued to smile. "Just her name, her age, a brief description of the clothes she is wearing, hair colour – that sort of thing?"

"I don't see why that matters." And then it dawned on her. "Oh, you think she's a child? No, no – my daughter, she's nineteen years old." She pointed at the buggy. "This is her baby."

The girl's smile changed into the shape of an O. "What's her name?"

"Clara. Clara Doyle." She looked around the station. "It was so busy on the platform, we got separated somehow."

The girl nodded. She leaned forward and spoke into a microphone. "*Would Clara Doyle please come to the information desk? Clara Doyle, please come to the information desk.*"

Jenny thanked the girl and stood back to watch the crowd. She glanced down at the sleeping infant who was blissfully unaware of what was happening around her. Jenny pushed the buggy back and forth, shifting her weight from one foot to the other – a movement you never forgot, she guessed.

Minutes passed.

She turned to the girl behind the counter who was staring at her desktop screen.

"Excuse me, can you call my daughter's name again? She may have been using the toilets or something."

The girl smiled, her eyes resting on Jenny, probably a little bit longer than she intended, a look that Jenny couldn't quite read. "Sure."

"Sometimes she has her headphones in, can't hear a thing." Jenny managed a smile. "Bane of my life, headphones."

The girl repeated her announcement and Jenny waited. She watched as people made their way in and out of the busy station, but there was still no sign of Clara.

She glanced back at the girl.

This time, the girl couldn't hide behind her smile. She leaned over the counter, a look of concern on her face. "Is everything alright?

Tears stung the backs of Jenny's eyes. She couldn't speak.

The girl came out from behind the desk and gently laid her hand on Jenny's arm.

"Come in behind my desk and sit down. I'll get you some water."

Jenny let the girl lead the way. She pushed the buggy behind the counter and sat down.

The girl handed her a plastic cup of water. "Here, drink this."

Jenny accepted and drank the cold water down in one long gulp, not having realised how thirsty she was. She was also exhausted. She had barely slept the night before.

The girl replaced the empty cup with another and Jenny gratefully accepted.

"Is there anyone I can call for you?" The girl's smile had changed, there was more warmth in it now that she wasn't trying to please difficult customers. Assisting Jenny was a distraction, no doubt.

Jenny shook her head. "I already called my son and he's on his way to meet us." She sipped some water. "My daughter, she was behind me in the crowds as we came out past the barrier, and I was in front of her with the baby in my arms pushing the buggy but when I turned around, she wasn't there. That was about forty-five minutes ago now, I think, and

I haven't seen her since. She wouldn't just leave me. She wouldn't leave her baby. This doesn't make sense."

The girl nodded. "I guess you've tried her phone?"

Jenny's expression said yes.

"Why don't I call the Gardaí?"

Jenny shook her head. "I really don't think there is a need for that. She has to be here somewhere. I don't want to get the Gardaí involved."

The girl gently placed a hand on Jenny's shoulder. "Just in case she has hurt herself or something? Or her phone might be out of battery. The Gardaí will find her." She pointed at the monitor on her desk. "There are cameras everywhere here now, since the renovations. Don't worry, everything will be fine." She turned and picked up the desk phone.

Jenny couldn't hear what she was saying as she mumbled instructions to whoever was on the other end of the line. She glanced down at the sleeping child and, for the first time since she had arrived at Clara's apartment in Belfast, she felt a prickle of fear settling in the pit of her stomach. Something was terribly wrong.

CHAPTER 4

Lana watched from the top of the steps outside the courthouse as her client, Sally Moran, answered questions from the press. Her mother and sister stood there protectively, without invading her space – this was her moment. The victim-impact statement that Sally had delivered in court in front of the accused had been brutal and emotional, to say the least, and Lana had to muster up every bit of professionalism she had to remain impassive. She observed her client now, her shoulders straight, her head held high, as she stood and made her final statement to the half dozen journalists who had been following her case from the outset. Her husband had been given a sentence of ten years. Not much for trying to murder someone, his own wife. Because that is what he had tried to do that night. But at least her client could claim some degree of victory – long sentences were extremely hard to come by when it came to domestic violence convictions. Sally had done well.

Sally thanked the press and took a step back before turning to Lana. She smiled, reached out and shook Lana's hand. "I can never thank you enough, Lana. If it wasn't for you ..." She shook her head.

Lana returned the smile. There was nothing more to say. The handshake was a good deal stronger than the first time they had met.

Sally turned and descended the steps with her mother and sister, their arms wrapped around her, all smiling through tears of relief. The victory was bittersweet. It would never take away the pain Sally had endured by the hands of her husband. The physical scars had healed but the emotional ones would take a long time.

Lana checked her phone – there was a second missed call from Peter. This time he didn't leave a voicemail. She sighed as she put her phone back in her briefcase. Did she want to talk to him? Yes. Was she prepared to talk to him? No. It was easier not to.

She tucked her brown hair behind her ears, descended the steps of the courthouse and walked the short distance to the car park beside the potato market. She had been letting her hair grow in recent months and she somehow felt protected with the longer length.

A memory of a sunny afternoon on Peter's boat came to mind. He had pushed a loose strand away from her face and smiled at her playfully. "*Your hair is hiding your cheekbones.*" When she'd asked what was wrong with that, he'd replied "*Nothing at all – it's just, the shape – symmetrically you're perfect, Lana, like a painting.*" She had pushed his hand away, laughing, telling him that he was a weirdo. She shook the memory aside.

It was a warm sunny day and the streets were busy with people shopping or grabbing a quick bite before making their way to the boardwalk to eat outside. Lana was glad she hadn't worn a coat over her navy pinstripe trouser suit. She couldn't wait to get home and change into jeans and a sweater.

Limerick city wrapped itself around the River Shannon, the longest river in Ireland. For decades, offices, shops, restaurants and apartments had faced inwards, away from the water. Until a few years back when someone in the planning department had the initiative to shift the focus around to face the river, so that people could get a sense of the city and enjoy spectacular views of the river along the Three Bridges walking route. Money had been invested in a boardwalk and people were beginning to enjoy the fruits of that decision.

Lana's phone rang in her pocket. She checked the caller ID, expecting to see Peter's name again. But this time she saw a different name, a name that she'd hardly thought about since college. *Nyah Doyle*. Nyah had been in her media course during her first year in university before she had shifted gear and decided to move to Law. The two had been quite close in First Year but, after she had changed her course, they only bumped into each other every now and then. Inevitably, the friendship had fizzled out after graduation. Why would Nyah Doyle be calling her? She remembered their first conversation when he'd introduced himself. She had teased him about his name. "*Mam had been hoping for a girl when she was pregnant with me and she was going to call her Nyah, the name of a character in a book that she'd been reading at the time.*" He'd shrugged. "*I kind of like it actually – it means 'brilliant' – so it suits!*" She was surprised that she still had his number saved in her phone.

She pressed answer.

"Nyah Doyle?" She smiled into the phone. "Now there's a blast from the past? How are you?"

"Lana, I wasn't sure if I still had the right number for you. How is everything?"

"Good, I guess." Nyah most likely didn't know anything about her life during the last few years and probably didn't know about her mother's death. "And you?"

"Well, not too good actually. I need your help with something."

"Oh yeah? Is everything OK with your mum?" Jenny was her name, wasn't it?

"Yes, she's fine. Well, not exactly. There's a problem about my sister, Clara. Do you remember her? You met her that time you visited. Eleven years younger than me?"

"Yes. She was really sweet, though if my memory is correct you said she was annoying."

He half-laughed, and then he went quiet.

Lana thought she had lost connection. "Nyah? Are you there?"

"Yeah, yeah, I'm here."

"What's wrong with your sister? Is she in some kind of trouble?" A memory came to Lana about a conversation she'd had with Clara that weekend when they were alone, and the warning she had given at the end, "*Don't tell Nyah ...*"

Nyah let out a long sigh. "Yeah, it seems so." He cleared his throat. "She's been studying in Belfast for the last year, well, since last September. She's in First Year and she hasn't come home since – you know, because of the distance, and she has a part-time job. But she keeps in regular contact with both myself and Mam. Mam mostly. Until recently."

Lana reached her car. She took the parking ticket from her pocket and placed it on the dashboard. "Go on."

"Lately she hasn't been in contact as much as usual. I hadn't noticed so much. Work has been busy, you know how it is, but Mam did notice. She decided to pay Clara a visit yesterday, a surprise visit."

"And?" Lana switched her phone to Bluetooth and started the engine, turning the steering wheel so her car was facing towards the exit. Then she heard Nyah's sharp intake of breath.

"She found that Clara had a baby. I don't know when, but fairly recently."

"Right." She reached the barrier. Rolling her window down, she scanned her ticket. The barrier slowly lifted. "Well, it won't be the first time a girl got pregnant in First Year."

"Yeah, I know, I know that." He paused. "Mam persuaded her to come home to try figure out what to do about college, so they took the train back to Limerick with the baby. The problem is – now Clara is missing."

Lana indicated as she made the exit out on to the busy street. "Missing?"

"Yes. Mam lost Clara. Mam was holding the baby while they were walking along the platform at the train station and Clara was behind her. Then, when Mam looked back, well, she wasn't there. She'd just vanished. Now, she's not answering her phone and none of her friends know where she is. This is completely out of character for her. Lana, I need your help."

"Have you tried the hospital? In case she's had an accident or something?

"Yeah. Well, not me but the Guards came and they checked the Emergency Department in UHL – and their own accident and emergency records of course. No trace."

"Though, if she'd had an accident and was in a serious condition, the hospital would ring the recent or frequent contact numbers on her phone – I'm presuming she had a phone with her."

"Yes, but neither Mam nor I would be among her recent or frequent contacts. She's been a bit out of touch in recent months. Now we know why."

"I see." The question was, Lana thought, did Clara want to be found?

"Lana? Can you help?"

"Tell me, Nyah – what made you think of me?"

"A friend of mine, Peter Clancy, suggested I call you. He said you would know what to do. Well, he's not really my friend, but we have a mutual acquaintance. Peter said, if anyone can find my sister, it's you. I didn't know you had moved into private practice – that's pretty impressive, Lana."

And there it was, the reason Peter had been calling her.

The sky had changed as she drove over the bridge and away from the city. Dark clouds now hung low, making visibility difficult. A moment later, the first speckles of rain hit her windscreen.

"Lana, you there? Do you think you can help me?"

Could she help him? What she knew about Clara, she could never tell Nyah. She had made a promise. Though that was years ago, and probably not related.

"Where do you want to meet?"

CHAPTER 5

Standing in the queue in Dunnes department store, in the suburbs of Limerick city, Jenny started to perspire as she listened to a woman at one of the busy checkouts chat to the cashier about her upcoming trip to one of the Greek islands.

"I have to take at least seven new beach items with me, you know, one for each day of the week. I take everything home and try everything on, you know. I mean that's part of the vacation, isn't it? The detail is in the preparation. Oh, I just want to get to the airport and have that first drink! At six in the morning if I have to! I mean, your vacation starts at the airport, right?"

The woman roared with laughter as she droned on and on about her holiday, the second this year by all accounts, and it was only the end of March. Jenny wanted to knock her head off. Vacation? Irish people used the word "*holiday*", not vacation. Some people had gone very American. Beads of sweat formed along her hairline and she forced herself to breathe as the queue shuffled along slowly, her body burning with the heat. She eased herself out of her cardigan and folded it into the bottom of the buggy.

The baby was sleeping peacefully. Clara had told her that she was born on New Year's Eve, so she was now about three months old. Which made it very odd that she still didn't have a name. When Jenny asked what her name was, Clara said she didn't have one. Jenny had almost laughed. "Why would you not name your baby? It's the first thing anyone does!" she said, astonished. Clara said she couldn't make her mind up. She liked Rebecca but was still deciding. Meanwhile, she just called her 'Baby'. She had been so defensive in her response that they hadn't discussed it further. They had more important issues to deal with.

It was twenty-two hours since Clara had vanished at the train station, and Jenny had little to no sleep since. When she'd finally drifted into a fretful slumber, she'd dreamt that she was walking along a cliff edge, holding on to Clara beside her. Clara lost her footing and slipped, grabbing Jenny's ankle as she rolled over the side, pulling her along with her. Jenny desperately tried to free Clara's hand from her ankle while Clara was screaming for help. Jenny had woken to the sound of screaming, but it wasn't Clara. Instead, it was the little baby with no name.

Now she could feel her body begin to cool down. The dreaded hot flush had gone. But the next one could start up any minute. She needed to get out of the shop. The flushes had begun a few months back. Initially, they would wake her up during the night. A surge of heat would creep up her body until it reached her jawline, until the prickly heat became unbearable. It felt like she had opened a hot oven door and stuck her head inside. All she could do was throw the duvet back and just lie there until it passed. And then she started experiencing the hot flushes during the day. She worked outdoors in a garden centre so she was lucky that she spent most of her day in a cool environment, but there were times when a flush crept up on her when she was inside a supermarket or a coffee shop, and she really had to improvise to cool her body down. Like now, when she was stuck in a queue with a baby in a buggy. There was nowhere to escape. She had to remain in line between the chrome barriers, as she had no choice but to buy some supplies for the child – vests, babygros, nappies, bottles and formula. Clara had packed plenty of supplies for the baby but she had either taken the bag with her or left it at the station somewhere. If the latter were the case, it could be anywhere by now. It was a fallacy to say a baby did not want for much – food and plenty of love were pretty much at the top of their essential needs but there was all this other stuff as well.

Finally it was her turn at the checkout and she quickly scanned her card as the young girl bagged her items.

A minute later she was leaving the sticky department store. Outside the building, she welcomed the cool air. She checked her phone for missed calls, but there was nothing new. No texts, no voicemails, nothing. This complete lack of communication from a girl who normally kept in touch throughout the day, albeit not so much recently. This was very unusual behaviour from her daughter. Jenny had met the Gardaí at the train station the day before but, because Clara was a nineteen-year-old woman, they hadn't seen any reason for concern, especially when Jenny told them about the baby. Once they had checked that she hadn't been brought into A&E at the hospital, they had assured Jenny that her daughter most likely wanted a break, to let off a bit of steam, and that she would be home in no time. They said they would call the hospital again later, to check that Clara hadn't arrived in the meantime, and would let Jenny know immediately if she had. If not, they would call her the following day to check in, but they said Clara would probably be home safe and sound by then. Jenny wasn't at all sure.

When Nyah arrived at the station to meet her, he had undertaken another search of the building, but to no avail. They had reluctantly left, the little baby propped up on Jenny's lap in the back seat of her car, which she had left parked in Colbert Station.

But Clara hadn't come home, and she hadn't called. Jenny had to ring in sick at the garden centre and, on top of taking the previous two days off to visit her daughter in Belfast, her boss wasn't too impressed. Nyah had picked up a baby's car seat, complete with a rain-cover, in a charity shop and dropped it in to her that morning. He'd looked like he hadn't slept in a week. No doubt the news about his sister had left him shaken. The siblings had always been very close, particularly as they had grown older, but Clara clearly hadn't told him about the baby. He had to go back to work but he promised to call out to the house that evening. In the meantime, he was going to continue to phone Clara and try to get in touch with some more of her friends.

Luckily for Jenny, she lived in a remote area – there would be no nosy neighbours asking questions about a baby suddenly appearing in the family home.

Jenny rounded the corner and walked straight into Megan Carmichael. *Shit*. Megan was the last person she wanted to see right now. Jenny and Megan had been in school together. While growing up, material things had impressed Megan. She wanted the house, the car, the educated husband who was going places, the two-point-two children and the decking, and she did everything she could to get all that. She had achieved four out of five: her husband Ned worked for a car dealership selling second-hand cars. He spent his days warding off time-wasting customers and window-shoppers. But if you asked Megan what he did for a living, she would say he worked in business development. The man was kicking tyres with punters day in day out but, according to Megan, he was extremely successful and some big-noise company was always headhunting him. The Carmichael's daughter, Alexis, had been in the same class as Clara at school and the last Jenny heard the girl was in Second Year doing Science in University College Cork, having skipped transition year at school. Clara and Alexis had been good friends once upon a time, until a tragic event had changed that.

Whenever Jenny bumped into Megan, the other woman loved to compare the two girls. It drove Jenny mad. *Comparison is the thief of joy*, her mother used to say.

Right now, Megan was looking into the buggy, a bemused expression spreading across her face. She looked a question at Jenny.

Damn, thought Jenny, of all the people to meet today. She had to think up a story, *fast*.

"Hi, Jenny. It's great to see you. Are you on a day off? And who do we have here?" Megan quick-fired off each question on the same breath.

"Lucy. This is Lucy." Jenny smiled. *Lucy?* She glanced down at the child and thought it suited her.

"Lucy? What a nice name! Lucy who?"

"Lucy ... *em* ... she's my boss's niece." Jenny's employer lived in the next town, in County Clare, and it was doubtful Megan knew him and, even if she did know of him, it was unlikely she knew anything about his family. The man had moved over from Scotland five years before. "He asked me to take her to the shops with me." She rolled her eyes as she waved her hand in the air. "It's a long story."

Megan smiled sweetly. "I'm sure it is."

Jenny knew that Megan didn't believe her, that the woman could tell she was lying, but, in fairness to her, she didn't push the fact.

"Actually, how is your Clara doing? Alexis said she had left college? Pity, but I'm sure she will find her way in time."

What? Clara hadn't left college! She hadn't mentioned anything about leaving her studies. They just said they would figure out a plan for the baby's care when they got home. And, anyway, how did Alexis know? The two girls hadn't been in touch for years, had they?

Megan fixed her long blonde hair behind her ear – Jenny could see the clips where she had attached her extensions. *Jesus*.

"Alexis is in Second Year now and the pressure is on. She'll be going to Galway for her Co-op experience. It's exciting." Megan beamed, her brilliant white teeth vaguely grotesque, almost too big for her small face. And, as for the lips, the pout was far bigger than Jenny remembered.

"It is." Clara had left college? Megan must be mistaken. But there was no way she could risk challenging the woman. After all, she didn't really know what was going on in Clara's life.

"Where is she now? At home, is it?" There was an edge to Megan's tone.

"Ah, yes. She's at home." What else could she say?

Megan laid her hand on Jenny's arm. "Don't worry about Clara – she'll find something that suits her. Maybe your boss will take her on at the garden centre?"

Jenny was about to respond sharply when Megan glanced at the very large gold-encased watch on her wrist. It looked ridiculous on her skinny arm.

"Oh, would you look at the time! I have to meet the girls for lunch. You should join us some time, Jenny, when you get a day off. It can't be easy working full-time." She looked down at the baby then.

Jenny thought she was about to add something further, but she seemed to change her mind.

"Right, I'll be off." She pursed her lips together and blew a kiss. "See you!" And with that, she took off up the road, barely able to walk in her six-inch heels, her lavender perfume wafting in the air behind her.

Megan was quite funny really, when she wasn't being so tragic. At least, she bought into her explanation about the infant's origin. *Little Lucy*. Jenny's grandmother had been called Lucy, and Jenny had always liked the name. She had wanted to use it instead of Clara, but Clara's dad wouldn't hear of it. "*You gave our son a stupid girl's name. So I'm naming this baby.*" A darkness came over Jenny as an image of her husband came to the forefront of her mind. She forced herself to breathe slowly: in, out, in, out. She seemed to be doing a lot of that lately. *Don't think about him*, she warned herself. *Not now, you have enough to contend with.*

She checked the time – it was almost one in the afternoon, nearly coming up on twenty-three hours since Clara had left her and the baby at the train station. She decided she would go to the Garda Station and see if someone would speak to her. The Guard she had met at the train station said that Clara would need to be missing, with no contact, for at least twenty-four hours before she could be listed as a missing person. It was ridiculous. She knew in her heart that something was very wrong. And the longer they waited, the worse the situation could be. She pushed the buggy and her new purchases along the path towards the carpark. She would drive to the Garda Station in the city. It worked a broader demographic and that meant there was a better chance of finding an actual detective. She would find someone who knew what they were doing and hopefully they would take her seriously. And, besides, she didn't want to risk bumping into Megan again or anyone else.

She quickened her pace as she hurried up the street.

CHAPTER 6

Nyah tried Clara's number again. Now the phone seemed to be powered off. An automated voice informed him that the number was out of service and to please try again later. Yesterday, at least, it had been ringing. He leaned back in his chair and pushed his hands through his hair. He had surfed through all of her social-media platforms, but there had been nothing new in the last twenty-four hours. He had left several messages with Clara to get in touch – texts, direct messages on her Facebook, Snapchap and Instagram accounts and he was long past being nice in his exchanges to his little sister at this stage. The pleasantries were well and truly over. His last message to his sister read: **Get the fuck in touch NOW!**

A baby? His sister had a baby and never told him. Never mentioned being pregnant either for that matter. Jesus, he had become an uncle and he had no idea. But what bothered him the most was that Clara hadn't confided in him. They were close, very close, a few years apart in age but it had just been the two of them and their mam and they were a team. *No secrets*. When Clara had chosen Belfast as her choice of university, he was kind of devastated because of the distance and he knew that the dynamics of his family unit would change, but he was so happy for his sister at the same time. She wasn't the most confident person on the planet and he had thought that living away from home would really build up her self-esteem. Standing on her own two feet, buying her own groceries, cooking her own meals, washing her clothes, all these day-to-day routines would be Clara's responsibility. And she would either sink or swim. And he thought that she had been swimming. She appeared very happy on her social-media stories, always smiling, or dancing, or just goofing around. She'd got a job in a bar in Belfast and she looked like she was loving it.

Nyah was livid.

He thought back to when he had last seen her. It was September, wasn't it? When she left for college. Clara hadn't come home for Christmas and Nyah had been a bit annoyed with her about that. Even though he had moved out a few years back, he always spent a few days with his mam over the holidays. But Mam had said to leave Clara alone, that she was building a life for herself and gaining independence. Mam had brought Nana to stay from the nursing home and they had a hectic time making sure she didn't escape. It was fun in a chaotic kind of way. They took turns in keeping watch and they set an alarm every night in case she managed to open one of the doors. They figured that, between the two of them, at least one would wake up if the alarm went off. They had a good time. They ate lots of food, drank lots of wine. Well, come to think of it, he had drunk lots of wine. His mam hadn't. But she had been on high alert with Nana for those few days.

What was the reason for Clara staying in Belfast? Something to do with one of her flatmates, wasn't it? The girl's family had gone away for Christmas and Clara didn't want to leave her on her own. She'd promised to come down for New Year's Eve. He didn't know if that happened –

he was back in his own flat by then. It had been a normal Christmas like any other, albeit spent without his little sister.

Nyah scrolled through his sister's photos on Instagram for probably the hundredth time that day. He felt sure he was looking for something new each time, something that just wasn't there. He hadn't met any of her friends in Belfast, though she mentioned the two girls she shared a flat with. Emily and Becky, wasn't it? She would talk about them when she called. He remembered she said the two girls were from Belfast and already knew each other before they met her. They had advertised for a flatmate on the university website and Clara saw the notice online and made contact. It all seemed so easy. It had not been like that for Nyah when he went to college in Dublin. He had come across some dodgy flatmates during his four years there and he had to move a couple of times. But things were different for his sister: the two girls liked Clara and Clara liked the two girls. There were other photos too, with another girl that looked familiar to Nyah. He was sure he had seen her before but couldn't put a finger on where. He hadn't been to Belfast since his sister moved up there. She had asked him repeatedly to come visit in the early months but he hadn't taken her up on it. She hadn't mentioned it in recent months.

Clara's friends – their names popped up on most of the photos she had posted. They seemed to be using different Instagram handles but that wasn't unusual. She had tagged a few on her photo post. There were many images – Clara eating dinner in her kitchen with girls he assumed were her flatmates, drinking shots in a bar, dancing on tables at the local nightclubs. He had sent a few of the friends that she had tagged private messages, but they hadn't replied to him yet. He guessed they were still in classes in college, and would come back to him later in the evening. He hoped so.

He scrolled down through the photos again, stopping when he noticed a couple from a night out at Christmas, judging from the decorations in the background. He opened the photo and zoomed in. Again, Clara was with Emily and Becky. The three girls appeared to be in great form, their arms wrapped around each other, all dressed up for their night out, beaming into the lens. Seemed a bit off, considering what Clara was going through at the time. Nyah squinted at the screen. He zoomed in a bit more. Clara's dress was a short skimpy red one with thin straps. His mam had mentioned that she'd bought her a red dress as part of her Christmas present. Clara had sent her a link for a list of items on one of those online websites, Boohoo.com or Pretty Little Thing or Shein. He remembered his mam fretting about whether the parcel would arrive in time for Christmas. He checked the date on the photo, December 23rd – just over three months ago. And then it struck him what was really jarring about the photo. Clara's stomach. It was completely flat.

CHAPTER 7

The rain was coming down hard as Jenny found a parking space close to the Garda Station. She glanced back at Lucy who was staring at the deluge pelting against the windows, her big eyes open wide in fascination. The noise in the car was loud enough to drown out the sounds of traffic outside. Jenny drummed her fingers on the steering wheel while she decided what to do. It might clear up, but then again it could take hours and sitting in a car with a small baby was not a good idea. Lucy would eventually get bored watching the rain, and then she would need attention.

She remembered Nyah had brought a plastic covering for the baby's car seat. Jenny had no idea how to attach the cover but she could just drape it over the seat and make a run for it. She pulled her hood up over her head before stepping out of the car. Running around to the boot, she found the plastic cover. She slipped into the back seat, unclipped Lucy's belt, tucked her blanket around her little body and carefully covered the car seat with the cover, making sure there were no gaps. Then she saw there was a little groove in the plastic so the chair handle could push through. My God, she thought, they think of everything. She lifted the chair out of the car and, closing the door, ran across the street, the edge of the seat banging against the side of her knee. When she reached the Garda station, she pushed open the front door and stood inside, dripping from head to toe. But at least Lucy was bone dry. Jenny pulled back the wet cover and the baby's eyes stared up at her in wonder. As she slipped out of her wet coat, she tried to imagine what was going through the little girl's head and felt a flood of warm affection for the child. In her short little life, she had already been through a great deal of upheaval. The poor little mite must be desperately confused by everything that was going on.

The reception area was empty except for one woman standing at the counter talking to a female Garda sitting behind a glass screen. The woman seemed to be African, with shoulder-length dark braided hair. She was wearing a long red coat, her spotless white trainers peeping out from underneath the hem. She was pushing paperwork through the hatch towards the Garda.

There was a row of plastic chairs attached to a wall behind Jenny and she lifted the baby chair and walked over to sit. She took a tissue out of her pocket and patted her wet face as she listened to the exchange between the woman and the Garda.

"But I was told to bring this document here and that you would sign it for me." The woman's deep throaty tones filled the small space.

The Garda pushed the form back through the hatch. "Well, you were given the wrong information – we don't sign forms without a witness."

"I have travelled on the bus for an hour and a half to come here. My daughter is in school. I have arranged for someone to collect her because I will not be back on time. Please, if you could just sign? I need one signature so that my paperwork can be processed." She spoke slowly and clearly, though she didn't need to – her English was very good.

The Garda shook her head from side to side, a clear no. She closed the glass screen.

"*Please?*" the woman pleaded again, but the Garda left through a door behind her desk.

The woman turned towards Jenny, tears brimming over her eyes. She spotted the baby in her chair and, wiping her tears away, she smiled.

"Your baby is sleeping good?"

"Oh, this is not ..." Jenny hesitated. "Yes, she is." She looked up at the woman. "How old is your child?"

"My daughter is five years old. I have another child, a little boy. He is only two. I am an asylum seeker. I do not have a passport for my little boy so they would not let me take him with me when I left Africa. He is being cared for by relatives in my village until I can get his passport documents processed. So I only have one child here with me in Ireland. I am trying to get him over here to be with me, but ..." she waved her hand at the reception area, "nobody will help me. Everywhere I go, someone tells me the job is not their job." She checked her watch. "I must go for my bus." She gave a warm smile, despite her plight. "Look after your child. Fight for her, she is precious."

Jenny nodded as the woman left, a sadness creeping over her for the little boy who must be missing his mother and sister.

A few minutes passed and the Garda returned to her desk. She opened the screen and beckoned Jenny to come forward.

Jenny approached.

The Garda raised an eyebrow.

"Ah yes, my daughter. She's missing. Since yesterday. Almost twenty-four hours now."

"Name?" The Garda began to scribble on a notepad.

"Clara Doyle. She's nineteen years old."

"Your name?"

"Jennifer Doyle."

"Date of birth?"

"I just ... me?"

"Your daughter's date of birth."

"February 25th 2005."

"When did you last see or hear from her?"

"Yesterday. Around this time. At the train station – Colbert Station. We had travelled down from Belfast together."

The Garda looked up. "She was with you at the station?"

"Yes, she got off the train with me and her baby. And she was behind me as we walked along the platform towards the exit. You see, it was really busy and I was walking ahead of her. When I turned around she was gone."

"Please take a seat." The Garda closed the glass screen and once again left through the door behind her desk.

Just like that: *take a seat*.

Jenny stood where she was for a moment before realising the discussion was over. She sat and waited. Her phone vibrated in her pocket. It was Nyah checking in. She texted him back that she was at the Garda Station waiting to speak to someone about Clara's disappearance. He sent her back a thumbs-up, followed by another message asking if she had managed to post that red dress to Clara at Christmas. She tried to think. Clara had sent so many links for gifts and some of the sizes weren't available. Jenny had to get back to her a few times and suggest she find something else. But she had managed to get the red dress, hadn't she? She had sent it up in a parcel with other items a week before Christmas. She messaged this to Nyah, wondering why he wanted to know. He messaged back but didn't say why he had asked – instead he said that he had contacted an old college friend who worked as a private investigator. He was on his way to meet her and he would let her know what she suggested.

Jenny glanced down at Lucy in her little chair. She was fast asleep again, just like Clara. As a baby, Clara would sleep just about anywhere. Nyah, on the other hand, hadn't been a sleeper. He would wake on the hour, crying and looking for milk in the early months and Jenny had been exhausted trying to keep him fed. He never seemed satisfied.

The Garda returned to her desk. She didn't make eye contact with Jenny.

Another fifteen minutes went by before a door opened and a tall middle-aged man, dressed in a dark suit, called her name. Jenny stood, grabbed her coat and picked up Lucy's chair.

The man in the suit pushed the door open and asked her to follow him. She found herself walking down a dimly lit narrow corridor with closed doors on either side. The man stopped halfway and extended his hand into an empty room.

Jenny entered the small space, taking in her surroundings. The area was sparse except for a table with two chairs on each side of it. What looked like a camera was mounted in the corner of the wall behind her and a black recording device sat on the table. Jenny was pretty sure she was in an interview room. The man held a chair for Jenny. She placed the sleeping Lucy's seat on the floor and sat down. He sat opposite her and put a file on the table.

"Now, Jennifer. Jennifer Doyle?"

Jenny nodded.

"My name is Detective Bart O'Neill." He opened the file and started to write on a blank sheet of paper. "I believe you haven't seen your daughter in twenty-four hours?"

Jenny cleared her throat, sitting forward in her chair. "That's right, yes."

"Can you tell me what happened yesterday?"

Jenny repeated what she had told the Garda at the train station the day before and what had happened since. She explained how Clara had moved to Belfast to study and that everything was going well for her initially, and then how quiet she had become recently, prompting her to pay a surprise visit. She finished her story with the discovery that she was a grandmother. Detective O'Neill listened without interrupting, taking notes every so often. When Jenny stopped talking, he sat back and dropped his pen on the table.

"Have you checked the hospitals?"

"The Guards who arrived at Colbert Station called the hospital. You mean A&E?"

He nodded. "Yes. Just to rule out that something might have happened to her."

"But she was with me at the station ..."

"She might have fallen somehow, sustained a head injury."

"Oh ... I see."

He scribbled something on his notepad, "I'll check UHL again. She may have arrived since the Gardaí made their enquiries yesterday."

"They said they would call the hospital back and –"

"I'll check again."

"Thank you." Though Jenny felt that her daughter wasn't in hospital.

"Is there anything else you can tell me?"

Jenny shook her head.

"What about her husband or boyfriend? The father of the baby?"

"Well, she's not married, you see – and if she was dating someone she didn't tell me. Or her brother for that matter. And the two of them, they're very close. It makes no sense that she wouldn't confide in him."

"What about drugs?"

"Clara doesn't take drugs."

He raised an eyebrow at that.

"No, honestly, she barely drinks alcohol. She doesn't like the taste. It's just not her thing."

"Have you spoken to her friends in college? Her flatmates maybe?"

"Nyah, my son, has sent messages to the two girls she shares with."

"And?" He picked up his pen and started to write.

"They haven't replied yet."

"I will need their names."

"Becky and Emily. I don't know their surnames but they should be on the rental agreement. I can get that to you, it has their addresses.

Both girls are from Belfast and they knew each other before they started university. Clara told me this. They are all First Year students at Queen's."

"What about work? Did she have a part-time job somewhere?"

"She got herself a job, yes, part-time in a local bar. I think she had a couple of shifts a week. I'd been sending her an allowance for food, clothes, that sort of thing – she has a grant, you see, an educational grant – but recently she asked me if I could increase the amount a little bit, if I could spare it."

O'Neill nodded, writing away. "So, when was this? That she asked you to increase her allowance?"

"A few months ago."

He sighed as he dropped his pen again.

Jenny leaned forward. The look on his face disturbed her.

"I will look into your daughter's disappearance, Jennifer, but honestly, she is most likely to be with friends somewhere. Young people your daughter's age, they go missing all the time and more often than not they just turn up."

More often than not? What the hell did that mean? Jenny couldn't believe what she was hearing.

"No, you have to understand, this is not normal. Clara wouldn't just take off and go off grid like this. I am telling you something is very wrong." She pointed at the baby. "She wouldn't leave me with this. She just *wouldn't*."

O'Neill formed the shape of a steeple with his fingers, his expression one of sympathy. "Can you tell me what happened, Jennifer, after you arrived in Belfast, at Clara's flat."

Jenny thought back to the moment when she had knocked on Clara's door two days before. Then she began to recount what followed. Clara had opened the door, her expression turning from expectancy to shock, and then she had fallen into her arms. At that same moment, Jenny had heard a baby crying.

Clara had cried a lot as she told her about the pregnancy, how she didn't know until a few months before Christmas that she was having a baby, that there was no father in the picture and that she was exhausted. Jenny had been stunned but, shocked as she was, she'd made a huge effort to comfort and calm her daughter.

Later, between bouts of feeding and attending to the baby, they had talked about Clara's options for the future. However, Jenny realised that Clara was too physically exhausted and emotionally overwrought to make any decisions.

By ten o'clock Clara was fast asleep in her bed. After sitting quietly for a long time, looking out at the night sky, Jenny decided to take control of the situation. She needed to take her daughter home to rest and recover before any decisions could be made.

She booked train tickets online, leaving Belfast at 8am. She woke Clara at half past six and told her she was taking her and the baby back to Limerick. Clara hadn't protested. In fact, she'd seemed relieved. Together they'd packed a few bags for Clara and the baby and had taken a taxi to the station. Clara slept for most of the train journey down and when they arrived in Limerick, she disappeared.

"I'm afraid your daughter is a classic case of a young girl who has had a child she is not ready to look after. I'm sorry to say, Jennifer," an expression of kindness crossed his face, "that she most likely wanted you to take care of the baby. She is probably feeling guilty about that and ..." he waved his hand in the air, "in a few days she will call you."

He closed his notebook and stood, indicating that the interview was over.

"I'll ask one of my colleagues in the North to make a few enquires, question the flatmates. But I expect that Clara will turn up safe and well." He took a small card from his pocket and placed it on the table. "Email me the addresses for the two girls living in Belfast. I'll see you out." He opened the door and waited for her.

Jenny stared at the half-open door, the darkness of the empty grey corridor outside. She didn't want to move, she didn't want to leave the small room. She didn't know where to go or what to do. She had come to the Garda Station hoping they would help her, and yet the detective wouldn't listen. *Nobody* was listening.

She looked down at Lucy – the little baby was awake now, staring back up at her with big innocent, questioning eyes.

Jenny felt completely helpless.

"Ms. Doyle?"

Jenny sighed.

"Come on, let's go, baby girl." She picked up the chair and followed the detective out of the room.

CHAPTER 8

Lana folded her umbrella when she entered the coffee house, before placing it in a bucket behind the door. She found a table beside a window towards the rear, allowing her a view of pedestrians passing up and down the street outside, dashing in and out of buildings to get shelter from the rain. But, more importantly, she would be able to watch the door and hopefully she would catch sight of Nyah before he saw her. A waiter approached and offered her a menu – she politely refused and asked for a coffee without milk. Reaching into her satchel, she pulled out her laptop. It was just after two and the café was quiet after the lunchtime rush. The staff kept themselves busy clearing tables and a lovely aroma of herbs and spices drifted from the kitchen.

Lana opened her laptop and, clicking on her Facebook link, she typed **Jenny Doyle Facebook** into the search icon. There were quite a few Jenny Doyles, it seemed, so Lana scrolled down through the list. But she had to click on each profile to get a good look at the photo and personal details and it was taking far too much time. She had met Jenny before and, though it was quite a few years back, she was fairly sure she would remember her if she saw a photo.

Nyah had invited her down to his house in County Limerick for a weekend when they were both in First Year at college. Nyah grew up in the countryside with a river nearby and, she remembered, the weather had been unpredictably warm for the time of year. Was it late April or early May? Lana couldn't remember, but it was definitely towards the end of their second semester. They had larked around by the river during the day – swimming, sunbathing, and just chilling. Nyah had brought a picnic and a bottle of rum and they had eaten and drunk until eventually Lana had fallen asleep. When she woke, the sandwiches she had eaten earlier had left a dry taste in her mouth and she had a slight throb in her temple. Her head was resting on Nyah's shoulder. He was playing with a strand of her hair, stroking it away from her face. She remembered smiling, still a little bit drunk as she snuggled into his warmth, before falling asleep again. The next time she woke, he was the one in a deep sleep, facing towards her, his hand resting on her waist. She had watched the rise and fall of his chest, every so often his eyes flickering beneath their lids. He was so handsome, his dark hair, sallow skin, full lips and strong hands. She had touched his hand as it lay just above her hip and the movement woke him. He appeared startled for a moment and then his hand had moved up her arm towards her shoulder and around the back of her neck. He began to stroke her skin, his strokes growing in intensity. She had sat up then, a little bit dazed, and he had stopped what he was doing. She remembered taking his hand, looking him in the eye, smiling, and shaking her head. *No.* He had smiled back. "Can't beat a guy for trying, right?" They had both laughed it off and continued with their weekend, no awkwardness between them. A few weeks later, they had finished First Year. Lana changed her course and their paths hadn't crossed that much during the following years. She had graduated and thought no more of Nyah Doyle. Until his phone call.

She decided to narrow her search down to location to see if that helped. She typed **Jenny Doyle Limerick**. This time only a handful of Jenny Doyles popped up on the screen. She got lucky with the third – clicking on the profile picture, Nyah's mother appeared on the screen. The photo, taken in a greenhouse, showed Jenny pointing at a giant orange pumpkin, a big grin spread across her face. She was dressed in an army-green puffer jacket, her shoulder-length dark hair peeking out from under a grey woolly hat. She had piercing blue eyes and her skin had that glowing appearance you get from spending time outdoors. She had aged a little from the last time Lana had met her, but she looked well, far younger than her years, Lana was sure.

When Lana clicked on Jenny's personal details, she noticed the information was sparse. Born in Limerick, went to college left blank, date of birth "**I can't remember**", working at Ryan's Garden Centre, married to "**It's none of your business**". The woman wasn't giving much away. Lana clicked on the photos icon and several images appeared on the screen, mostly Jenny gesturing towards a plant or a tree or a vegetable or, even more boring, a shot of the plant or tree or vegetable on its own. Her life wasn't particularly exciting if these photos were anything to go by. There was not a single post that wasn't related to the garden centre where she worked. She tried to remember what the story was with Nyah's dad. Did he go missing or something? Nyah had always been vague about him during that first year in college together. Had he said something about the man leaving home when he and Clara were very young, and that they didn't know where he was? Something like that? She well remembered meeting Clara that weekend – how could she ever forget? A shy, quiet young girl, aged nine or ten, immersed completely in her own world, her hair like white candyfloss, un-brushed and wild. She wore oversized T-shirts with leggings and walked around in her bare feet. Lana had thought she was such a free spirit – until Clara confided in her – told her a dark secret. Lana had recognised that the young girl had a desperate need to unburden herself by telling someone, but couldn't tell her mother or brother. Yet she still wondered why Clara had chosen her to confide in. But her instincts had been sound: she had chosen well as Lana understood and would never betray her by disclosing her secret.

Lana looked up as the door of the coffee shop opened. A very wet Nyah Doyle stood at the entrance, scanning the interior as he eased out of his jacket. Lana closed out of Jenny's profile. Before Nyah spotted Lana a waitress offered to take his coat. He smiled at the server and said something Lana couldn't hear, causing the girl to blush. Lana smiled – girls had always liked Nyah. He had a charming, easy manner and a warm smile. He handed his wet coat to the girl and spotted Lana. She sipped her coffee and waved him over.

When he reached her table, she stood to greet him. He kissed her on the cheek before holding her away from him, narrowing his eyes as he gazed at her closely.

"You look good, Lana, really good."

Another woman might fall for the intensity of his stare, but not Lana. She laughed as she pushed him away and sat back down.

"You're still up to your old tricks, Nyah?"

He spread his hands, his expression innocent. "I don't know what you're talking about!" He smiled as he sat down opposite her.

The waitress who had taken his coat arrived at their table. She had her notepad and pen in hand but she only had eyes for Nyah.

"A tea, please, and thank you." He looked up at her with his easy smile and she practically genuflected as she backed away.

Jesus, he was smoother than Lana remembered.

She shook her head as she pushed her laptop back into her satchel. "Oh my God, I'm embarrassed for you."

"What did I do? Just being polite." A smile played on his lips.

Lana shook her head and pulled out her notebook.

He glanced at her book as she began to write. "You still take notes?"

"All the time. Taking notes has got me to where I am today." She paused, pen in hand.

"And where is that exactly?" he teased.

She ignored his playfulness. "OK. Talk."

Nyah exhaled as he looked around the café. "I don't know where to start really." He took his phone out of his pocket and rested it on the table. "Mam called me yesterday ..."

"Time?"

"Mid-morning, I think? No, I'm wrong, it was later than that, because I remember being surprised to see her number appear on my phone. Mam never rings me while I'm at work because she knows I'm busy. Here, let me check it." He unlocked his phone and tapped the screen a few times. "13.30, she called me at 13.30. See?"

He held the phone out to Lana and she wrote down the time.

She looked up. “Tell me everything your mother said when she called you.”

“She was upset, crying. I couldn’t understand her at first – she said she had ‘lost her’ – lost Clara. And I was thinking Clara is an adult, how can you lose an adult? I didn’t know what she was talking about and Mam has, you know ...” he lowered his voice as he scanned the café, “*menopause.*” He said the word like it was an infectious disease. “She overreacts a lot of the time over the smallest things.”

Lana stopped writing and raised an eyebrow.

“She can be dramatic at times.”

“Remind me not to come to you for sympathy when I hit mid-life. What happened next?”

“Then I could hear a baby, making sounds, you know, like, baby sounds. And Mam was soothing the baby. That was when I started to pay attention.”

Lana stopped writing, a question in her eyes.

“As I said, Mam is going through menopause, she can cry at the drop of a hat. Clara and I, like, we’re sympathetic, but sometimes she’s over the top, you know? We let her have her rant and then she calms down. But the baby – that threw me.”

Lana continued to write. “Go on.”

Nyah shook his head. “I told Mam to stay where she was and I collected her from the train station and brought her home. Well, I searched the station first. Looked everywhere but there was no sign of Clara so I took the two of them home.”

"Your mother and the baby?"

The waitress arrived with Nyah's pot of tea and set it on the table in front of him along with a cup and saucer. He didn't look up, distracted now by his story. The waitress looked fleetingly disappointed as she backed away.

Nyah poured from the pot and added milk and sugar. "Some girl at the station had called the Guards so Mam could explain that Clara was missing but they said they couldn't do anything about it because she was an adult and that she had probably run off somewhere to let off steam, because of the baby. Mam is beside herself with worry."

"What about last night and this morning? I assume you tried her phone?"

"Yeah, of course, many times. Yesterday it was ringing out, today I can't connect at all."

"You said on the phone she was in university in Belfast?"

"That's right. Queen's. First year. She seemed happy."

"It's what, late March now? When did she start? September?"

"Yeah, first semester starts around mid-September or a bit later – you know that."

"Start dates vary with colleges."

"Oh, right."

"How old is the baby, Nyah?"

"Clara told Mam that the baby was born on New Year's Eve – but get this – she hadn't even named the child. Like, how crazy is that? A three-month-old kid with no name!" He took a sip of his tea.

Lana put down her pen and stared at him. "Nyah, where was Clara living before she went to Belfast last September?"

"Here at home with Mam. Why?"

"Do the maths. Clara left for college mid-September. The baby was born on New Year's Eve – only three and a half months later. So Clara must have conceived the child here, down home. She was already six months pregnant when she left for Belfast."

The waitress arrived back just then to ask if everything was OK. Nyah muttered that everything was fine and she quickly moved away, confused by his change in manner.

"That's impossible, Lana!" Nyah shook his head as he looked around the café. "But that's not the only impossible thing. When I couldn't get through to Clara on her phone I started messaging her on her social media – Snap Chat, Messenger, Instagram. She has a lot of photos on Instagram, with her flatmates, friends on nights out, eating together, sitting around in their pyjama – you know, normal college life?"

He looked at Lana for acknowledgement. She nodded as she wrote.

Encouraged, he continued. "OK. Look at this."

Nyah unlocked his phone again and swiped his finger down the screen until he found what he was looking for. He turned the screen to show Lana a photo.

Lana tilted her head to look. And there she was, the girl Lana had met when she was barely ten years old. She had changed a lot since then. Gone was the candyfloss hair and the oversized tops. Clara was all grown up now. Her hair was long, blonde and sleek. Her short fitted red dress with spaghetti straps accentuated her figure. She and her two friends were smiling widely for the camera. Lana took the phone from Nyah and pinched the image. What was it that Nyah wanted her to notice? The beautiful girl in a little red dress on a night out with her pals – what was significant about it? Then she saw the date and time on the top right-hand corner of the image – December 23 at 22:05 PM – and registered the sparkly Christmas decorations draping the walls in the background. The girl in the photo, Nyah's little sister, with her flat stomach, looked no more pregnant than Lana. How could Clara have given birth to a baby on New Year's Eve?

CHAPTER 9

Jenny pulled into the carpark of her mother's care home, a small building with less than thirty residents and, conveniently, only a ten-minute drive from home. It wasn't long after lunch and there was just a handful of cars parked outside the property, mostly belonging to the staff. The majority of visitors arrived in the evening after tea when the residents were more settled so that there was less of a risk of their routine being disrupted. If there was one thing Jenny had learned about care homes since her mother moved into one, they were all about routine. Medicine run, breakfast, physio, Mass (optional), full three-course lunch, followed by a snooze. Mind you, a three-course lunch laden down with high-calorific ingredients would knock anyone out. Then there was afternoon tea or a sherry for those who fancied it and maybe some music or a game of bingo. The actual tea followed, and then, there was more tea before bedtime or a yogurt, with night-time medication. The residents spent their days consuming, from the minute they woke up in the morning to the minute they turned in for the night. Jenny marvelled at the staff and their patience. There was a lot to remember and, of course, there were always the residents who didn't want to eat the food or drink the tea or take their medication. And that created many challenges for the staff. They had to think of other ways to provide the nutritional intake for the residents, while remaining patient and good-humoured. Unsung heroes, Jenny called them, each and every one of them.

Jenny's mother had been living in the care home for over three years and she had recently decided she didn't want to eat anymore. She had started refusing her food, turning her head the other way when a spoon was put in front of her mouth. The carers would gently try to encourage her with yogurts or drinks brimming with nutrients and vitamins and, most of the time, they were successful. They were keeping her alive, but against her will. Jenny guessed, sadly, that her mother wasn't long for this world.

Sue had started showing the early signs of dementia over ten years earlier. Jenny had noticed a few red flags, but didn't pay too much attention to them at the beginning. It was easy to explain them away. Like, there was the time that Sue had driven into Limerick city to do some shopping and had forgotten where she had parked her car. In a panic, she had called Jenny who was at work at the time, and Jenny, over the phone, had helped her retrace her steps back to Ellen Street. They had laughed about it afterwards. "It could happen to a bishop," her mother had said, and Jenny concluded that she would be capable of doing the same thing herself. Then, there was the time Jenny, Nyah and Clara went to Sue's house for a Sunday roast dinner. Sue served up beautifully presented vegetables and gravy with stuffing and Yorkshire puddings on the side – Nyah loved Yorkshire puddings. But when Sue went to take the roast chicken out of the oven, she found that she had forgotten to turn it on. Again, they laughed about it and Jenny had driven to the nearest supermarket and bought a cooked chicken.

Then, the forgetfulness became more persistent. Still relatively small, but significant to someone who knew Sue well. She often lost track of time or mixed up her days. She would tell you a story and stop mid-sentence, her expression turning vacant, not remembering what she had started the sentence with. She would forget names of people she knew her whole life, or places she was familiar with. She wouldn't turn up for pre-arranged meetings, or would turn up for meetings that hadn't been arranged at all. She would mention a man living in her house, that he had left his clothes in one of the bedrooms and she could hear him moving about upstairs, getting ready for work. Jenny had asked her to describe the man and she said she hadn't met him but she knew he was there. She'd made Jenny go and look around the room. She wasn't afraid of him, she had said, "*not yet anyway*". Of course, there were no strange clothes in any of the bedrooms. All these little events turned into bigger events. They started to happen more and more frequently.

Then one night Jenny got a call from her mother's neighbour to say that Sue was sitting on her front lawn in her pyjamas. The neighbour was pulling his blinds when he spotted her. He had walked across the road to ask if she was OK, and Sue had given him the strangest look.

"It was as if she didn't know how to respond, or how to move," the neighbour had explained.

Jenny had driven over to the house, to find her mother sitting on the wet grass, the neighbour standing close by, a blanket in his hand.

"I tried to cover her, Jenny, but she wouldn't let me. She keeps looking over her shoulder at the house, as if there's someone there, but I went inside and checked and there was no-one."

The man looked baffled, but Jenny knew what was wrong – at least she had a good idea – the strange man who had taken up residence in one of the bedrooms. She had thanked the neighbour, sat down beside her mother on the grass and held her hand, neither of them saying anything for a while. The moon had been high in the sky and the night was warm, the only sound coming from the new flyover that had been constructed close by. Jenny had never been able to get used to the sound.

Eventually, Jenny spoke. "I think you should come and live with us, Mam. For a while at least." Her mother had simply nodded.

Jenny had helped her up and they had packed an overnight bag. The next day, Jenny returned to the house and started to clear it out. It was the beginning of the summer and Clara had been off school and Nyah was home from college, so they would take it in turns to stay with their grandmother while the other helped their mother pack up the house. A few weeks and three skips later, the house was empty, except for some old furniture. With Sue's permission, Jenny put the property on the market and it wasn't long before they had a buyer. Jenny was an only child so there were no siblings needing to be to consulted on the matter. The proceeds from the sale went into a savings account for Sue's future care, in case she needed it, though Jenny never thought the day would come that she would have to sign her mother into a nursing home. Unfortunately, that decision was taken from her.

Sue started randomly leaving the house, and Jenny would search for her and bring her back. Initially it was just during the day, but then it started happening at night. She upgraded her alarm system so that it would alert her to when Sue left her bed, and this did work very well initially. But Jenny soon became exhausted and had to take some leave from her job at the garden centre to become her mother's full-time carer.

Then, one morning Sue left the house and Jenny slept through the alarm. Luckily, a jogger had come across her wandering close to the river and phoned the authorities. The Gardaí brought her back home. They reported the incident to the national health authority, who subsequently made a house call and decided that Sue would be better off in a care home, just temporarily, until Jenny could install a more secure system and get some much-needed respite. Jenny was so exhausted that she didn't even argue. And besides, in her head, it was only for a short time.

However, after Sue had moved into the care home, she had refused to return home. Every time Jenny tried to talk to her about it, she stubbornly declined. "Only Christmas," she would say. "Christmas is for family." It was as if she had given up on her life. So, one month turned into two, and two turned into six, and then a year, and now three years had gone by, and every time Jenny came to visit she felt like she had lost another little piece of her mother. The woman's memory was waning more and more with every visit, to the point that she rarely recognised Jenny anymore.

Jenny sighed as she stepped out of her car. She had decided on the earlier visiting time because she didn't want to meet anyone she knew when the evening visitors shuffled in – after three years the other families had become very familiar. She carefully lifted the child's seat out of the car, the sleeping Lucy tucked up warm inside. The rain had cleared and a splash of blue broke through the grey sky. Crossing the carpark, she entered the building at the reception area. Cliona was on duty today.

"You're early today, Jenny?" Cliona said as Jenny signed the visitor's book.

"I know, Cliona, can't make it later. How are you?"

Cliona rolled her eyes. "Ah sure, it's like *Groundhog Day* in here, you know yourself."

Jenny smiled. "How is Mam?"

"I met her in the dining hall. She wasn't too interested in her food, but sure, nothing new there." She gave a small smile. "She's in good form though, even cracked a joke about married life."

"Oh?"

"She said being married is like travelling down a long and slow road to misery." Cliona laughed.

"Charming." Jenny smiled. Her mother had been married to a wonderful man, Jenny's father, for twenty-seven blissfully happy years until bowel cancer had taken him from them.

Cliona glanced curiously at the sleeping baby in the car seat. "Cute little baby you have there, Jenny! You kept that one very quiet!"

"That's because I'm just babysitting this one for a friend, Cliona! Not mine at all."

Jenny forced a smile and set off down the corridor towards her mother's room.

She gently pushed the door open, finding her mother slumped over, asleep on her chair by the window. She carefully placed the baby's seat on the floor across from her mother. Two sleeping beauties, she thought. Her mother's favourite blue fluffy blanket lay wrapped around her miserably thin legs – her white-grey hair looked like it had been recently washed and set. She was wearing a pale-pink blouse, loosely opened around her neck exposing a rose-gold chain with a dolphin resting against her papery skin. Clara had sent the necklace to her at Christmas and she hadn't taken it off since. She appeared peaceful and rested, just sitting there and not for the first time Jenny thought she was in the right place – even though it broke her heart that she wasn't a part of this new world that her mother inhabited. As if sensing she had company, Sue opened her eyes, frowning as she tried to adjust her focus on her surroundings. She nervously circled the ring on her wedding finger. Sue always circled her wedding band when she was muddled about her surroundings.

"Hi, Mam, how are you today?"

Her mother looked confused. She tilted her head to the side. "Hello, dear."

Jenny nodded sadly. "Hi, Mam. It's me, Jenny, your daughter." She reached forward to touch her mother's hand.

Her mam pulled her hand back towards her chest, a cautious look in her eyes. She fiddled with the button on her cardigan as she looked at Jenny, her daughter of fifty-three years. How did this happen to her mother, the most vibrant, energetic, funny, charismatic woman Jenny had ever known? Her brain had shrunk to the size of a pea, the consultant had told her after the scan – her cognitive brain, reducing her knowledge of her whole life to a fraction of what it had been.

"Did you have dinner today? What did you have, Mam? Let's see, it's Tuesday, so I am guessing pork steak with apple sauce and roast potatoes? Followed by apple tart and custard?" Her mother didn't respond, the cautious look replaced by a confused one, as if the mention of food were a strange thing. Jenny held in the sigh. She adored her mother. They had always been so close. But these visits were difficult. It was hard to think of things to say to someone who didn't remember how to respond. Even though Jenny had long since grieved for her mother and the woman she had been, it still hurt every time she visited.

Jenny moved to the window and looked out at the car park, noticing that a people carrier had pulled up in front of the entrance. A nurse was pushing a wheelchair up a ramp. Billy Jones no doubt, heading to the hospital for his daily dose of kidney dialysis.

"Any news, Mam?" She watched the nurse drape a rug over Billy's legs before sliding the side door of the people carrier shut.

"Well, I was at my brother's funeral. I was the only relative there. From my own family that is." Sue's voice was scratchy from disuse.

"Really?"

"Yes!" her mother answered with enthusiasm. "He was alive when I first got there and then, I don't know, they must have done something to him. He had wives that I didn't know about. They were very kind to me, mind."

"How did you get to the funeral?" Her mother's one and only sibling lived in Phoenix, Arizona.

"I don't remember that now. But I was there."

"In Arizona?"

"Yes! He has other children, you know. Some are only babies."

She often told this story about her brother's funeral. When she first brought it up, Jenny had almost believed her, she was that convincing. Now, she just went along with it. It was a bit like the tale about the man that was living in her house. She heard her mother give a chuckle behind her. When she turned, she saw Sue peering inquisitively down at the sleeping baby in the car seat, leaning forwards to get a closer look. Then she smiled a wide smile.

Jenny crossed the room and sat opposite her mother. "Do you know who this is, Mam? This is Lucy, your great-granddaughter."

Her mother tutted as she shook her head. "Don't be daft. That's not Lucy. That's little Rebecca." She smiled and started cooing at the sleeping infant.

Jenny looked at her mother in astonishment. The woman hadn't shown any interest in another human being for such a long time. And who the hell was Rebecca? Wait ... hadn't Clara mentioned the name Rebecca? Or was she imagining that? "Rebecca is a nice name, Mam."

"Well, that's what I said to Clara. Much nicer than the one she had chosen."

"What are you talking about, Mam? When did you see Clara?"

"Clara wanted to call the baby Jane, but I said she would be called Plain Jane in school and the child wouldn't forgive her for it. Rebecca is a much nicer name and she agreed with me."

"When was this, Mam?"

"Oh, I don't know when. Why are you asking me all these questions?"

A nurse gently pushed open the bedroom door. "Only me. Time for medication, Sue." She glanced at Jenny. "How are you, Jenny?"

"I'm good, thanks, Margaret."

"We're not used to seeing you visit this early ..." She rounded Sue's bed and spotted the baby's chair. She smiled down at the infant. "And who do we have here?" She placed a small plastic cup on Sue's bedside locker along with a glass of water. There were three large tablets in the cup.

Before Jenny could answer, Sue piped up. "Not tablets again. The one from this morning is still stuck in my throat."

"Ah, you're a rogue, Sue! These aren't big at all." Margaret laughed.

"Mam, can I leave Lu ... Rebecca with you while I go to the toilet?"

"Of course you can, I'm well able to mind a baby. Didn't I raise you?"

Jenny smiled at her mother, tears stinging the backs of her eyes. Sometimes Sue had moments of clarity and surprised her, though it was very rare. She glanced towards the nurse who nodded at Lucy, acknowledging that she would keep an eye on her. Jenny smiled gratefully and quickly left her mother's room.

The nursing home was sufficiently staffed yet they always seemed to be run off their feet. She would have to be quick. Hurrying back down the corridor, she passed the visitors' toilets and found the reception desk empty – Cliona must be on her break or using the bathroom. The sign-in book lay open on the desk and she quickly scanned the visitor names for the previous days. The care home was very strict on visitors signing in. Eventually she found it: *Clara Doyle*. Her daughter had visited Sue eight days before, during the morning. It was hard to make out the letters – Clara was very artistic in her writing style, often using loops and curls, but Jenny knew the signature. She had been watching over her daughter's homework all her life. Clara had been here, in this nursing home, eight days ago. But why? Why had Clara come to her mother's care home with her baby? And why had she not contacted her or Nyah?

CHAPTER 10

Nyah shoved his hands into his coat pockets as he hurried down Windmill Lane. It was over twenty-six hours since Clara had disappeared at the train station and they were still none the wiser about her whereabouts. Having spent longer with Lana than he had planned, he was now late for an afternoon team meeting. He was anxious – his highly-strung boss was probably losing his shit right about now. It was just coming up on four and Windmill Lane was a short cut to the main street, and his office block. Limerick was full of lanes and each one brought you somewhere closer to where you needed to be. At one time, the lanes were not the prettiest routes to take around the city, but a few years back someone in the council's planning department had the ingenuity to apply for funding to carry out low-maintenance improvements. Staff were recruited from Back to Work schemes to sweep the lanes and power-wash the walls which they then mounted with planting structures filled with flowers and hanging baskets. Local artists erected murals of the people who had lived on the lanes, modelled from pictures provided from family members. Now, they didn't look half bad. The lanes had a continental vibe about them and, what's more, people were actually using them.

His boss had called him into the office for a *chat.* Nyah was losing focus, what with everything that had been going on over the last twenty-four hours. And the man was going to pull him up on it if he didn't cop the fuck on. He shook his head at how quickly everything had changed. What had started off with a bad hangover yesterday morning had turned into his worst nightmare. How life could turn on a dime, *eh*? What a difference a day makes? So many songs commented on how quickly your life can turn upside down in a very short amount of time. How the hell was he supposed to concentrate on his work when his little sister was missing? Not to mention the fact that he had just found out that he had a niece. Uncle Nyah. *Dear God*. It didn't make sense. None of it did. Clara, his little sister, was now a mother who had managed to hide her pregnancy from her nearest and dearest. The last time they had spoken she had sounded like her normal self. He tried to remember when that was. Maybe a couple of months? But they messaged each other all the time. She had given nothing away. How was that even possible? Was she not worried about her pregnancy, or having a baby? It just did not add up.

Then, Lana had pointed out that Clara must have been six months pregnant before she left for Belfast – or even more if the baby had been born *before* the flat stomach photo but why would she lie about the date of birth? Nothing made sense. And, whatever about his own powers of observation, how was it possible that his mam hadn't noticed her daughter was over six months pregnant?

And who was the father? Not a word out of Clara about that and Mam hadn't pressed her. She hadn't been dating anyone in Limerick, not that he knew of anyway. She would have told him. She never mentioned anything about any guy at all. He had fired off a quick text to his mam as he was leaving the café and she had confirmed what he thought – she was sure that Clara wasn't involved with anyone before she left for college. Of course, it could have been a one-night stand – he flinched at the thought – but that would have been so unlike Clara. It also assumed she was careless about contraception – or the guy was. He flinched again.

His phone rang in his pocket and he whipped it out, checking the caller ID. His boss's name flashed across the screen. **Brad Fulham**. *Damn*. Brad, forty-four-year-old managing director of a relatively successful international multi-media company who designed apps for mobile phones and iPads. Nyah's primary role was to scour social-media platforms, lurking, in a manner of speaking, looking at people's profiles and stories, watching what they were saying, what they were doing, what they were into, what kind of lives they posted about, checking their suitability for whatever app he was working on.

Nyah was slacking off work, with everything that had been going on, and his boss wasn't the most patient man on the planet. Of course, Nyah regularly put in extra hours, seldom took time off and often did overtime on weekends. But yesterday's phone call from his mother had broken his concentration and Brad Fulham was going to go crazy on him.

"Brad? I'm on my way. I lost track of time. I should be with you in five minutes." He dodged traffic as he navigated his way across the busy street. Car horns blared as he held up his hand in apology to angry drivers. "Jesus, what's your rush?" he muttered.

"Where have you been? You've been offline all morning. And you were missing for a few hours yesterday."

His boss didn't sound annoyed with him, more surprised if anything.

"I have some things going on in my personal life, things that I needed to sort out. The problem has been pretty much resolved now and I'm completely focused on the job again. Don't worry."

"You sure?"

Brad didn't sound convinced. Brad wanted only fully committed employees.

"I'm sure." He arrived at the building. "I'm outside now, be up in a sec."

Brad hung up.

As he entered the lobby, the lift was just closing. Spotting the door to the stairs, he took them two steps at a time. By the time he reached the fourth floor, he was out of breath. He was holding on to the wall to steady himself when his phone rang again. *Jesus, could the man not wait two minutes*? Swiping the answer button, he pressed the phone to his ear. *Stay calm,* he warned himself. *Keep your shit together.*

"I'm here."

"Nyah? It's Lana."

Lana? He had just left her. Why was she ringing so soon? Surely she hadn't found Clara already. Hope filled his heart. Clara had come home and he could go back to his old life, the drama was over.

"Nyah? Are you there?"

"I'm here, Lana. What is it? Did you find Clara?" He was breathing hard and he forced himself to be still and calm the fuck down.

"I didn't find her, as such, but I know where she went. Have you a minute to talk?"

Nyah glanced down the hall towards Brad Fulham's offices, the name BRAD FULHAM, CEO, in capital letters plastered on the door. Brad would be on the other side of that door, pacing while he waited for Nyah to arrive.

"Yes, go ahead? What did you find?"

"I have a friend who works at the train station. She was able to show me CCTV footage from yesterday when Clara and your mother's train arrived into the station. The footage is quite clear – you can see your mother carrying the baby, and Clara walking behind them along the platform. She has a purple rucksack on her back and she's carrying a large gear bag. Then Clara slows her pace. She begins to back away as your mother walks on, then she turns around, takes off and disappears from the video clip."

"OK. But we know that she was at the station. That only tells us that she didn't get lost in the crowd."

"Wait. The CCTV footage picks her up outside the station less than a minute later. A black car – not a taxi – pulled up and she got in. I couldn't see the driver or the licence plate. She got in without hesitation. In the clip, she only has the purple rucksack with her so she must have dropped the gear bag somewhere at the station."

"Mam said that Clara had packed another bag with all of the baby's things."

"Judging from her body movements, she seemed confident about what she was doing."

Nyah's heart sank. "So, what does that mean?"

"Wait. There's more."

He heard Lana inhale before she continued.

"They drove straight to the airport. Clara got out of the car and entered through the departure doors. The car drove off."

"How do you know she arrived at the airport?"

"I have another friend who did me another favour."

Lana had a lot of friends doing favours, it seemed. "Let me get this straight? Clara left Mam at the train station, was picked up by a car, driver unknown, and went to the airport. The departure doors, you said?"

"Yes. She got on a plane, Nyah. Clara took the nine-twenty flight to London. All I know is that her plane landed just over an hour later in Stansted Airport. I can only assume she got off the plane. My trace stopped there."

Nyah leaned against the wall as he tried to take it all in. What had taken Clara to London? She had never been there in her life – neither had Nyah, for that matter. She didn't even know anybody there, did she? Except ... possibly ...

"Nyah? I need you to think hard about Clara and her behaviour over the last year. Who was she hanging out with before she left for college? What made her choose Belfast University over the local one in Limerick or closer to home in Cork or Galway? Look over all the recent messages and any videos she has posted. There has to be a hint in there someplace of her mindset, what she was thinking, and who she was spending time with."

Nyah shook his head. He was in complete shock, *again*. He had really begun to think his sister had taken off somewhere to blow off steam like the Gardaí had suggested, and that she would be back in a day or two. But London! And who the hell had picked her up at the train station as if it were all pre-arranged?

"Does Clara know anybody in London?" Lana asked.

"No," he lied. "Definitely not."

"What about her friends from school? Did any of them go to college there? Or take a year out to work there?"

His answer was the same. They had grown up on the outskirts of a small village in County Limerick. Everyone knew everyone else and what they got up to. You couldn't change your brand of tea bags without someone knowing about it. He was sure there was nobody in Clara's circle of friends living in London. She would have said or his mam would have mentioned it.

"Right. I am going to have to travel over there, see if I can follow the trail. I don't have the same connections over there as I do here, but I do know her flight arrived in Stansted. It's a start. Stansted is a much smaller airport compared to the others in London, so hopefully I'll be able to find out where she went once she landed."

"Right, OK. Thanks, Lana. When do you leave?"

"This evening. The sooner I go, the better. Time is critical when ..."

Nyah didn't need her to finish her sentence, because he knew. Time was crucial when a person went missing. And it was already over twenty-four hours since his sister was last seen. He glanced down the corridor towards the door of Brad Fulham's office – he could practically see his boss striding up and down the grey industrial carpet behind the wooden frame.

"I'm coming with you."

"What? Nyah, there's no need. This is my job. This is what I do. Leave the situation with me and I'll report back to you, OK?"

"What time is your flight?" He was already running down the stairs.

"Seven-fifteen, I think. I'm leaving for the airport in about an hour."

"Pick me up at my place. I'll send you the Eircode. It's kind of on your way. I'm just heading back there now to pick up my passport and an overnight bag. I'll see if I can book a flight on the way."

"Nyah? This is probably not a good idea ..."

"Clara is my sister, Lana. She is the only sibling I have. Mam is beside herself with worry and she can't travel with the baby. Clara has to be in some kind of trouble. She would never leave like this. Unless ..."

"Unless what?"

"Unless she's trying to protect us. Mam, me or the baby." He left the building and hailed the first cab coming towards him with a light on.

"Why do you say that?" Her voice was sharp.

"No why. Just a stray thought."

"OK, I'll pick you up. Be ready. Traffic might be heavy."

"Don't worry. I'll be ready." He hung up as the cab pulled in at the kerb and gave the driver his address.

He fired off a drop pin with his address to Lana and then went about booking his flight. There were plenty of seats available on the plane so he clicked on the one-way button and paid with his credit card.

What was he going to tell his boss? The man's reaction wouldn't be good. *Shit*. He decided to send an email – it was easier than calling the man. He would say that he had urgent family business to deal with and could he please have a day to sort it out. A couple of days – max. He typed up the email and pressed send. Then he made a call to his mam.

CHAPTER 11

"So, how do you know Peter?" Lana asked as Nyah secured his seat belt.

She was pulling out of the driveway of Nyah's apartment block. It had started to rain heavily again and the condensation began to creep up the sides of the front windscreen of Lana's old car. She pressed the demister button and it slowly started to clear. Though, even with the wipers on full speed, it was difficult to see traffic, so she slowly edged out onto the road when she saw a gap.

"He's a friend of a friend actually. A guy I was in college with has a holiday home in Castle Cove. Well, his parents do. Jonathon Lyons? Remember him?"

Lana shook her head.

"Anyway, nice guy. I shared a house with him in Dublin during our final year and sometimes we would go down to stay in his parents' place when they weren't using it. For weekends, you know. And Peter was always there, in the pub or whatever. He took us out on his boat a few times – he took us out to an island a few times. Nobody lives there –"

"I know it. Mutton Island."

"You know it?"

"Rocks on one side and the beach stretches out to sea on the other."

"That's it. It's a really cool spot, when the weather is good."

"Yeah, I liked it there." Her answer came out harsher than she had intended.

She sensed Nyah watching her.

"So how do *you* know Peter?" he asked.

She took a moment before she replied. "I was investigating a case last year. A young girl travelled over to the island on a boat with some friends. She was found the next morning by a local fisherman, barely alive. The friends had left her there. It's a long story, for another time. Peter took me out to the island, so I could see where the girl had been that day. It always helps me to trace the last movements of someone, leading up to whatever happened to them."

"Right."

"That's how we became friends."

The city passed them by and once they had joined the motorway it was only a ten-minute drive to the airport. They had plenty of time. Their flight wasn't leaving for another ninety minutes.

Nyah had fallen silent, looking out the window. Lana guessed he was lost in thoughts about his sister so she didn't try to make small talk.

In the CCTV footage, Clara had seemed very confident as she climbed into the black car outside the train station and, likewise, when she entered the airport, a purple rucksack on her back her only luggage. She looked like she knew where she was going. She certainly hadn't appeared frightened or pressurised. Whatever she was up to, the girl was in control of it.

Lana took the exit for the airport and settled in behind the traffic moving slowly towards the small terminal. The rain was easing off and she was relieved about that – the thought of taking off on a wet runway frightened the shit out of her. Lana didn't like flying full stop. She didn't like take-off, landing, cruising in the air. She didn't like any part of it. And if there was any turbulence she was finished. But she found it tolerable if it was a normal dry day – not too hot, not too cold, no wind or snow, just a normal dry day. She worried about the pilots and their field of view if they had to fly the plane through a downpour. The fact that it was getting dark now was already beginning to freak her out.

She gripped the steering wheel and stole a glance at Nyah who was still staring intently out the passenger window. He hadn't spoken since they had the exchange about Peter. *Peter.* She pushed him to the back of her mind. She wasn't going to think about him now. She had to concentrate on the task at hand.

"You were lucky to get a seat on the plane."

"There were plenty free actually."

"Did you call your mother?"

He let out a long breath. "Yeah. I told her about Clara flying to London. She's just as baffled as I am." He turned in his seat. "Like, she said there is nobody in Clara's circle of friends connected to London. She did tell me she went to talk to a detective this afternoon and that he said the same thing as the Gardaí at the train station the day before – that Clara had run off somewhere and would return soon. She also went to visit Nana in the care home." He glanced over at Lana. "My nana has been in a nursing home for the past three years. She comes out some weekends and for the Christmas break. Her memory, it's not so good." He waved his hand in the air. "Anyway, Nana claimed that Clara had been in to visit her over a week ago, with the baby. Nana called the baby Rebecca and Clara had told Mam she was thinking about calling the baby that. Mam was stunned. So she did a bit of detective work – she managed to check the visitors' sign-in book when the receptionist had gone on her break. Clara's signature is there in black and white. So she must have been to visit Nana."

Lana slowed as she approached the barrier. Lowering her window, she pressed the green button and retrieved the printed ticket for the short-term carpark. The barrier lifted and she advanced until she found a parking spot.

Switching off the ignition, she turned towards Nyah. "Let me get this straight. Your sister visited your grandmother in a nursing home over a week ago with the baby."

Nyah nodded.

"I don't get it," said Lana. "What if she had bumped into your mother? Or *you* for that matter?"

"She arrived in the morning, according to the sign-in sheet. We normally don't visit Nana until the evening, hardly ever in the morning. The staff encourage it because there's a lot of activity during the day and the residents like to see their loved ones before they retire for the night. Clara would know this routine and I'm sure she knew there wasn't much risk of meeting Mam."

"But there was also the risk that the staff might tell your mother she had been there."

"True. That's weird."

"Is she very close to your grandmother? Would she have felt a strong need to show her the baby?"

"Well, yeah, we're both very close to our nana. She used to visit all the time when we were kids, or we would stay with her. And then she came to live with us – but by that time I was already in college and busy with study and sports." He shrugged. "Wasn't at home as much. When her memory started to go, she wasn't the same, you know?" He looked over at Lana. "I confess I haven't been as involved in their lives as much as I used to be. Mam, Clara, Nana ... we were always a very tight unit."

Lana shook her head. "All the way from Belfast. With the baby. It doesn't make sense."

"Nothing does."

He turned to look out the window again, his face creased in a frown.

Lana checked her watch. "We better get a move on. Our flight leaves in just over an hour, we still have security to get through and I want a glass of wine in my hand as soon as possible."

He grinned. "Sounds like a plan."

She smiled as she climbed out of the car and popped the boot. Nyah got out and grabbed his coat and bag from the back seat.

Lana locked the car and they made their way to Departures in silence, lost in their own thoughts.

The departure terminal was quiet for this time of day and they moved through security with ease.

"White wine if I remember correctly?"

Lana laughed. "Good memory!" She enjoyed a glass of white wine. Even in her student days. Though what she could afford back then was pretty rancid. "Yes, please. I'll just use the loo and meet you in the bar."

"Up to your old tricks again, Lana? Putting in the order and making someone else pay?" Nyah said as she left.

She turned and gave him the thumbs-up. Who said they would only have the one drink?

She finished with the toilet and, as she washed her hands, checked her appearance in the mirror. Taking her hairbrush from her bag, she brushed her shoulder-length brown hair back into a short ponytail, pulling at a few loose strands to hang over her eyes. Taking her bronzing powder from her make-up bag, she swept the soft brush over her cheeks before topping up her lipstick. She straightened her black blazer jacket over her dark-green T-shirt and blue skinny jeans. One of the laces on her white trainers had come loose and she crouched down to tie the knot. She quickly zipped up her bag and made her way back to the bar, wondering why she was being so particular about her appearance. She was getting on a plane for Christ sake. Generally, that mere thought consumed her, not how she looked.

She spotted Nyah sitting with his back to her as she approached the bar lounge, an untouched pint of beer in front of him. He was scrolling through something on his phone, concentrating hard. She slipped into the seat opposite him and took a sip of her wine. It was deliciously cold. She waited for him to say something.

At last he looked up.

"You know I wasn't concerned at first, when Mam called. I just thought ... Mam worries too much, she can't help herself, she's so protective of us. Sometimes it's like she doesn't want us to grow up or something, you know?"

Lana nodded, wishing she still had that luxury. With both her parents gone and no siblings in the world, it would be nice if she had someone to look out for her. She kept her thoughts to herself. Nyah clearly wanted to talk, so she took another sip of her wine and settled back into her seat. She felt her body begin to relax.

Nyah looked around the bar. Shaking his head, he sighed. "Imagine, she was here twenty-four hours ago! What was she doing here? Who did she talk to? What is she hiding, Lana?" He sighed again. "I've been a crap brother – why couldn't she tell me she was in some kind of trouble?"

"You don't know if she is in trouble, Nyah."

"I would be kidding myself if I thought otherwise, Lana." He took a long drink of his pint. "Clara had a friend in primary school. Alexis Carmichael. Clara spent a good bit of time in the girl's house – you know, play dates, that sort of thing. There was an accident at the house. Alexis had an older brother, Luke. He died in the house. He fell down the stairs and broke his neck. Clara stopped going over there after that. She withdrew into herself for a while. I remember Mam was really worried about her at the time. Like, this happened after Dad was gone ... She started hanging out with me more after the accident. We just chilled together, listened to music, watched movies. We became inseparable really, and our relationship stayed like that, for years ... and now? What

I don't understand is why she didn't come to me? I'm her brother. We have no secrets. Well, we *had* no secrets."

Don't tell Nyah, Lana ...

"But somehow she managed to keep a pregnancy from me," he continued. "And the rest." He started scrolling again, stopping a moment later. He frowned as he leaned towards the device. "*What the fuck is that?*" He showed the screen to Lana.

There was a photo of Clara and another girl, a girl she hadn't seen in any of the other photos Nyah had shown her. The girl had long blonde hair, hanging loosely around her face. Both girls were wearing T-shirts and jeans, not Clara's usual night-out attire. The girl had her arm around Clara's shoulders.

Lana shook her head. "What exactly am I looking for, Nyah?"

He handed the phone to her. "Look closer."

She took the phone and pinched the screen to enlarge the image. Clara was leaning into the girl. They were both smiling, heads close together. They appeared close, very close, but other than that nothing stood out as unusual about the photo.

"What is it, Nyah? I don't see anything significant."

"Look at the girl's arm."

Lana looked at the screen and then back at Nyah. "She has a tattoo."

He took the phone from Lana and pinched the screen a bit more. He held the phone out to her again. "Now, look."

"OK. The girl has a tattoo on her arm. Why is that significant?" But there was something jarring about the tattoo, wasn't there? She felt as if she had seen it before somewhere ...

"I have seen that *exact* tattoo before, Lana. The swan with a hand clutching its neck."

"OK ..."

He threw the phone on the table and ran his fingers through his hair.

Lana caught the device just as it slipped over the edge.

"You need to calm down, Nyah." she said softly. "You are no help to Clara if your emotions are out of control. She needs you to stay calm and focused."

He stared at her. "*You don't get it.*"

"What don't I get, Nyah? Tell me!"

"You've seen that tattoo before. Don't you remember?"

"Where? When?"

"You asked me about it once, when you came to stay in my house." He looked like he had just seen a ghost. "My dad. He had the exact same tattoo. It's an original design. He designed it himself. So, you see, it's not random that Clara is pictured with a girl who has the exact same drawing in the exact same part of her body as my dad." He pointed at the image on his phone. "This girl, she must know my dad. And, so, he must be alive."

Lana frowned, perplexed. "Did you think he was dead?"

"I've never been sure what happened to him. I only knew he was gone. Mam never talked about him."

Nyah's tone prompted Lana to keep quiet, and so she did, for the moment. *Tread carefully,* she told herself. The subject of Nyah's father had always been a sensitive one. Now she remembered seeing the tattoo. She had been looking at some old framed family photos on a sideboard in Nyah's house that weekend. There was this one photo of their mam, Jenny, with a man. He was quite tall with dark hair worn just past his shoulders, dressed in a white vest and black jeans. The photo was faded, probably taken before Nyah and Clara were born. Jenny was looking up at the man adoringly. The man was grinning at the camera, his left hand clutching hers, his right arm draped over her shoulder – a swan tattoo visible down the side of his forearm, rigid fingers clasping the neck. When she remarked on the tattoo and asked Nyah who the man was, he had turned the photo face down and walked away. Annoyed at his abruptness, she followed him and pressed him on it. He said it was his dad, that he was gone and he didn't want to talk about it. Then, another night, when they were back on campus and both of them had too much to drink, Nyah had apologised for being short with her about the photo. He explained he hadn't been close to his dad, that the man had let the family down and he was glad that he was no longer in their lives. She didn't bring it up again and neither did he.

The tattoo looked darker on the girl's arm, a more recent inking, but it was definitely the same image as Nyah's dad's, a swan starting at the elbow and ending just above the wrist. A hand clutching its neck. Actually, a most disturbing image.

Lana was almost finished her drink and desperately wanted another one before they had to board the plane. Glancing around the bar, she noticed the waiter and waved him over.

"Do you want another one?" she asked Nyah.

"Yeah."

She ordered two more drinks.

When the drinks arrived Nyah finished his pint in silence and started into his second.

Lana waited.

At last he spoke. "I remember, in the early years, my dad would take me fishing. There was a river near our house, remember it? You were there – I brought you there that one time you came down for the weekend?" He looked up at her then, a question on his face.

She nodded.

"So, he would take me fishing. In the evenings or on the weekend. We would go out, just the two of us. Mam would pack some food for us. Flasks of tea, sandwiches and some fruit and we would just sit there and fish."

He stopped. Lana sipped her wine and waited.

"Then he changed," he said at last. "I don't know when or why, but he changed. The fishing trips, they stopped. I think he was drinking. I think ... I know he used to hit Mam." He looked at Lana. "I mean, I never saw him hit her, but I heard them arguing, and Mam would cry and the next day she'd have a bruise somewhere. Or bruises." He sipped his pint. "There was this one time ... just before my fourteenth birthday. Clara was about three at the time. She had left one of her toys on the floor, one of her dolls. He came out of the bathroom and tripped, falling over the doll, flat on his face on the carpet. I was in Clara's room with her – the door was open and we saw him fall. He swore when he went down. Clara looked over at me, fear in her eyes. She had our father wrapped around her little finger but even she knew at that young age when to be wary. And she also knew that it was her fault he had fallen. She was the one who had left her doll on the floor. He always gave out to us for leaving our toys lying around, but this particular day he really lost it. He roared for her to come out and see what she had done. And I mean he *roared*, yelling her name over and over. Clara looked petrified. She was clutching one of her dolls, shaking her head. I could see tears brimming over her eyes. I knew I had to do something to protect her." He took a drink of his pint. "So, I went out and said I was the one who had left the doll there. I remember him snarling at me. He grabbed my wrists and started pushing me back towards my bedroom. He kept shouting stuff at me, like, '*You little shit, you like your little sister's dolls, do you? You think this is funny*?' You see, I had this habit, I still have it, where I smirk a little when I get nervous."

Lana knew what he meant. She remembered Nyah in the lecture hall, when he was anxious about an assignment or a presentation – he would give this semi-smile, appearing confident. But inside he would be bricking it.

"Dad just got more and more agitated, until he was practically spitting in my face. '*You're a stupid fucking retard!*' he roared at me and then he punched me, full on the mouth. I fell back onto my bedroom floor. Clara appeared at the door screaming, but he wouldn't stop. He started kicking me, in the knee, the thigh, whatever part of me he could connect with. I curled up in a ball, to protect myself. Then he went for the back of my thighs, my back, my shoulders, he was pounding his foot into me. I was begging him to stop. So was Clara – I could hear her little voice somewhere in the room, but he just wouldn't stop. He would not stop. It was like he was in this haze, you know? Possessed or something."

Nyah took another gulp of his pint. His hand was shaking.

Lana's heart was pounding. She sipped her wine to steady her breath.

"And then he did stop. His leg was mid-air, his fist was raised and he just stopped. I remember him staring down at me, his eyes popping, and then he fell on top of me. I started pushing him off, tried to wriggle out from beneath him. When I looked up, my mam was there. She had one of my hurleys gripped in both her hands. She was furious – I could tell by the look in her eyes. Her mouth had dropped open and she was breathing hard. She dropped the hurley and held her hand out to me, pulling me up. She clasped Clara's hand with her free one and she pulled us from the room. We ran down the hall. She grabbed her handbag and took us out to the car. Then she ran back into the house and reappeared with a gear bag stuffed full of clothes and things. We drove to Nana's house. We stayed there for a while, I don't know how long – it could have been a few weeks, it could have been a few months, I don't know. I was in no rush to go back." He drank some more of his pint. "But we did go back, and he wasn't there. He was gone. The only reminder that he existed in the first place was the picture with Mam, the one with his arm around her shoulder. Mam never spoke about him again. Clara asked from time to time – you know, where her dad was. Kids would talk at school about their dads, stuff they did together, that sort of thing. Mam would just explain it away, calmly. '*Your dad is gone, Clara. He left.*' I never asked. I never asked her what happened to him that day and she never told me. She just got us out of there and she didn't bring us back until it was safe. She simply said he was gone and I started to hope that he was dead, I really did." He finished his drink.

Their flight was called just then.

Nyah looked at Lana, and she saw fear in his eyes.

"Lana, if he's not dead and if my sister is mixed up with him, with my dad, it's not good news. He's an evil bastard. That day he beat me up, it was the first time for me, but not for Mam. Sometimes, before that day, he had attempted to hit me, but Mam put herself in front of me. To protect me. She would send me out of the room and I know she took the blows. He never touched Clara, but maybe that would have changed if we hadn't moved to Nana's. He was definitely losing patience with her more and more."

"You're probably right."

"And, Lana, the swan in his design with the hand strangling it – I think the swan was supposed to be Mam."

Lana shuddered at the thought. She drank off her wine and gathered up her bag.

Nyah caught her arm. "Lana, if Dad has found Clara and is some way involved in her life, she desperately needs our help."

The final call for their flight sounded again over the intercom.

Nyah let go of her arm. He stood, grabbed his jacket and rucksack and strode away.

Lana followed, fear in the pit of her stomach. Both for the flight and what lay ahead when they landed.

CHAPTER 12

The flight was uneventful, with limited conversation, both of them lost in their thoughts. The two glasses of wine had helped to calm Lana's nerves, but thankfully there was no turbulence, which greatly reduced her fear. They landed smoothly and Lana gathered her things into her bag as the plane taxied up the runway. It was approaching eight thirty and she figured it would take them at least twenty minutes to get through passport control and reach the car rental office. All in all, it would be over two hours since she had drained her wine glass before getting behind the wheel of a vehicle.

A short time later they emerged through arrivals to see a sizeable queue in front of her at the car-rental company desk.

Groaning, she turned to Nyah. "This could take a while. Do you want to get us some coffees?"

He nodded. "Yeah, sure, and I need to use the toilets. What will I get you?"

"Just regular coffee, no milk, thanks."

He nodded before shuffling off.

Lana turned towards the desk as the queue moved slowly on. She imagined Clara arriving in this very airport the evening before. Did she make her way into the city on her own, or had someone picked her up?

A couple were in front of Lana, their hands in each other's back pockets as they leaned in for a kiss. The woman was wearing white jeans and she had a visible dark stain at the back – chocolate or something else. When it was their turn at the counter, they both stepped forward and perused the paperwork as the clerk pointed at different sections with his pen.

Lana scanned the airport arrivals while she waited. Where did Clara go? What did she do? Whom did she meet? She turned back to the rental desk. The woman was asking the clerk about the tolls.

"What if we don't use them?" Her accent sounded Scottish.

The clerk shrugged. "It doesn't matter whether you use them or not." He pointed at the form. "It is in your contract. You must have clicked on toll usage."

The woman was shaking her head. "No. Why would I do that?"

The man pulled at her jacket. "Come on, baby. It's just twenty-five pounds."

"I don't care, Ed. It's the principle."

"Oh, come on, sweetheart. Let's just pay it. I want to get you to the hotel." He smiled at her seductively.

Jesus Christ. Just sign the bloody documents already!

They eventually scribbled their signatures and left with a set of keys.

There was still no sign of Nyah.

She offered her passport and driving licence to the clerk. He checked her credentials and started the tedious paperwork.

"I'm afraid the car you hired is not available." He held up his hand before Lana could protest. "Don't worry, I'm going to upgrade you to a

BMW sports. I was going to offer it to the last couple, but she was being such a bitch."

Lana nodded, indifferent to the car he was offering.

He smiled at her reaction. "Not a car lover then?"

Lana smiled back. "I don't really mind. I just need keys to a car. So long as it moves, that's all I care about."

He laughed at her reply as he handed over the paperwork and a key fob. "Well, that I can do."

"Oh, no keys?"

"Nope. You just need this."

She accepted the key fob.

"Have a safe trip."

Turning from the desk, Lana scanned the crowded airport – there was still no sign of Nyah. She decided to send him a quick text saying she would collect the car and meet him outside the arrivals set-down area.

She followed the clerk's directions to the rental garage. A few moments later, she located her upgraded car. She threw her bag into the back and slipped into the driver's seat.

She looked for a slot to insert the key fob but couldn't find one. She stared at the dashboard in front of her, with its buttons and screens with numbers and single-letter symbols. She hadn't a clue what to do. She could feel the slow throb of a headache coming on.

She scanned the park and recognised a guy in the rental company's uniform. He was assessing a car parked nearby. She climbed out of the BMW and called him over.

A moment later, he arrived with his clipboard. "Alright, ma'am?"

"I don't know how to start the car. This key fob ..." She shrugged. She didn't like to admit she couldn't cope.

The guy looked at her, his clipboard pressed against his chest. He failed to hide his smirk.

Smart bastard. Lana glared back. "Where do I insert the key fob?"

"You don't need to. There's a chip in the fob that pairs with the car."

He sighed as he placed his clipboard on the roof of the rental and got in. He pointed at a button with the word *Power* written on it. "Just press this. It's a stop/start system. High tech." He pressed the button and the car purred into life.

He climbed out and took his clipboard.

"You *do* know the car has a paddle control?" he said, in a tone conveying that doubtless she didn't.

What the hell was a paddle control? Lana's phone beeped in her pocket. Checking the message ID, Nyah's name appeared on the screen.

Where you? I am outside arrivals.

She fired back a quick text. **Two minutes. Stay where you are.**

"Ma'am."

"Yes?"

The guy pointed. "Use that right paddle near the wheel to shift into the next gear and the left paddle to shift down. You don't need to use your feet."

With that, he went back to his inspection.

Lana sat in behind the wheel and fastened her seatbelt. Cautiously, she operated the right paddle and slowly accelerated. The car moved off smoothly.

She changed gear again and took the exit for the arrival area. She spotted the woman wearing the white jeans taking photos of their rental. Her boyfriend stood to the side holding their bags, looking bored.

The ride was smooth, very smooth.

As she pulled in at Arrivals, Nyah was standing on the path, his bag slung over his shoulder, a cup of coffee in each hand. He really was a handsome guy, tall and slim with dark hair and deep-brown eyes. He had put his jacket on over his check shirt and black jeans. Lana smiled – from her memory of their days in college, Nyah had never put any effort into his appearance but he still managed to pull off a stylish *I-just-rolled-out-of-bed* look regardless. When she came to a stop and rolled down the passenger window, he gave a low whistle.

"OK, private investigators are well paid then. Kind of sorry I didn't switch from media like you did." He climbed in, his tall frame awkward in the small interior.

"They upgraded me. I couldn't care less what I drive but I don't know where I'm going so I hope this satnav works." She fidgeted around with the device but the screen wouldn't light up, no matter what she pressed. "*Stupid bloody thing doesn't work!*" She slammed the steering wheel with her fist. "*Stupid car!* Why couldn't they have just given me what I booked? We'll never get to central London at this rate!"

The satnav lit up and a smooth, female voice filled the interior. "*Hi, I'm Carly! Do you want to go to Central London?*"

They looked at each other and Nyah started to laugh.

"It's voice-activated, Lana."

"What the fuck is a voice-activated car?"

Nyah laughed harder.

"Well, I'm glad you think it's funny, Nyah."

"*Where would you like to go?*" Carly asked.

Nyah was still laughing.

"Please stop, Nyah. I have a headache."

"I'm sorry, but you're kind of cute when you're annoyed."

"*Would you like to go to Central London?*" Carly repeated.

"She sounds kind of sexy," Nyah said.

"Nyah!"

"*Pimlico,*" he answered the car.

Lana looked at him, a frown creasing her forehead. "Pimlico?"

"My dad was born in England, he spent the first few years of his life here. I don't know for how long. He must have been nineteen or twenty when his family moved over to Ireland, something to do with the dad, my grandfather. My grandmother, on my father's side, died when she was in her forties – a road traffic accident, my mam said, but she couldn't be sure. She'd put small bits of information together from what he told her. So, when she died, my grandfather moved back home with him – my dad. I think they moved around a bit. They lived in Cork for a while, then Galway. That's where he and Mam met. Mam was doing a course in college up there and on one of her many nights out she met Dad. He was a bouncer in one of the student hangouts, a dingy club with a late-night bar. She became a regular and they got to know each other." He shrugged. "So she told us."

"*Turn right and take the second exit onto Route 14,*" Carly announced from the satnav.

Lana did as she was told, her headache getting worse. She needed the coffee Nyah had put in the cup-holder. Once she was away from the airport and out on the road, she lifted the paper cup to her lips and took several sips.

"Keep going, Nyah," she encouraged. "Tell me everything you know."

"I'm trying to piece it all together, Lana. Clara was quite young when all that business happened. Only three years old. It seemed as if she didn't remember anything about it. Mam worried that she was suppressing a memory that would later surface, but she didn't show any cause for concern while she was growing up. Though she did go a bit quiet for a while after the accident."

"What accident?"

"The one in her friend's house. Remember – I told you about it? Clara used to be really good friends with this girl, Alexis Carmichael, when she was in primary school. She was always over at the girl's house."

"Yeah, you told me."

"The friend's brother Luke, he was a bit of a weirdo, younger than me. Anyway, when he fell down the stairs, broke his neck and it was Alexis who found him. Clara stopped going over there after that."

"That's horrible – for the girl to find her own brother dead."

"Yeah."

"In what way was Luke weird?"

Nyah sighed. "Look, the whole family are a bit creepy, to be honest. The mother, she's kind of flashy, the way she dresses. A show-off, boasting about shit. I could never tolerate her bullshit so I made myself scarce whenever she was dropping Clara home from a play date. And the dad hardly opens his mouth. Alexis was quiet too, like her dad. I don't know why Clara was friends with her back in school. But Clara could be like that, you know? She would befriend the kid that nobody else wanted to hang out with. I remember there was this one time I had to collect her because Mam was working or something. When I called to the house, the dad answered the door. He gave me this weird look, I can't describe it. He freaked me out, to be fair. And I remember he just turned and roared up the stairs for Alexis to come down. He went back into the kitchen and closed the door but I could hear him shouting his head off, repeating Luke's name over and over, telling him what a stupid fucking idiot he was. I remember asking Clara about it when we walked into town to meet Mam and she just shrugged, said that the dad was a bit of a bully but that he usually wasn't at the house." He shook his head. "Anyway, that friendship ended when Luke died. I don't know whether it was Clara or Alexis who chose to end it. But ... I think the violent accident might have caused a memory to surface ... a memory of what happened the day Dad attacked me."

Lana glanced at him. "Why do you think that?"

"Well, she never said a thing about it – but, then, last summer, there was this one time she asked me about Dad. She said something like – did I forgive him? It shocked me that she remembered. I just said it had been so long since he was gone that I couldn't remember much about him anymore."

Lana took another sip of her coffee. The pain in her head was reduced to a dull ache now. "How did she respond to that?"

"She didn't say anything. Just accepted what I said. I'm sorry now. I should have had the courage to talk to her about it."

"Last summer, you say?"

"Yeah, before she left for college."

"Strange she asked that question after so many years."

"Yeah – it is."

"But ... maybe she didn't remember. Maybe someone told her."

"Who? Mam?" said Nyah, incredulous. "Never! And no-one else knows."

"Except your father."

He stared at Lana. "You think she was already in touch with him? Last summer?"

Lana shook her head as she took the exit for the motorway. "Look, we can't jump to conclusions. You don't know if he's even alive. I know you say it can't be a coincidence, about the girl with the tattoo, but there may be an explanation for that." She scanned the road ahead. It was busy and traffic moved slowly. "OK, let's change tack here. You showed me the photo of Clara taken a few months ago on a night out with her girlfriends. Last Christmas. And in the photo she is obviously not pregnant."

He nodded.

"So, just consider the possibility that the baby isn't hers."

He looked at her sharply, shaking his head.

"Face facts, Nyah. How do you explain that her stomach is flat just before the time of the birth? Unless, as we've said, she had already given birth and lied about the birth date – but why on earth would she do that?

Nor would she be out living it up with her friends if she had just given birth. Look, my job is to think about the story I'm given and then look at that story from different angles. And one angle here is the possibility that Clara was never pregnant in the first place."

"Well, then, who does the baby belong to? And if it is not hers, then why did she let my mother take the child home? And she went to see Nana with the baby, remember?"

"True." She shook her head in exasperation.

She saw the sign for Pimlico and took the exit under the flyover. Not long after, she slowed as traffic thickened on both sides. Trees lined the busy footpaths as people made their way home from work, out for a drink, or a bite to eat in one of the chic restaurants. It was beginning to get dark and Lana was glad she had most of her driving done for the day.

"Can you check hotels in the area, Nyah? With vacancies? I had provisionally booked one closer to the airport." She glanced over at him. "I wasn't expecting company, and I really don't feel like driving back there tonight."

He pulled out his phone. "I haven't a clue where to look, Lana." He scrolled through his phone. "Why don't you ask Carly?"

Lana laughed. "How would she know?"

"Try her. These gadgets have many different functions. Hold on." He pressed a button and the screen lit up.

"*Carly is back! How can I help you?*" The silky voice filled the car.

Nyah leaned forward. "Where is the nearest hotel?"

"*The nearest hotel is the Dormund Hotel. It is 700 metres from your current location. The hotel has vacancies for the 26th of March. The number is…*" The voice rattled off the hotel number.

Nyah grinned as he typed it into his phone.

"Don't forget the area code."

"I'm not stupid, Lana."

"I never said you were stupid. Jesus, super-sensitive or what?"

Lana's phone rang. It was face down on the panel between them.

Nyah nodded at the device. "Want me to get that for you?"

Lana scanned the busy streets for a sign for the Dormund Hotel. "Maybe just check and see who's ringing me? Might be something to do with a case."

Nyah turned the phone over. "Oh, it's Peter. Want me to answer for you? Here, I'll tell him you're driving."

"*No! Don't answer it.*" Her tone was harsher than she had intended.

Nyah looked at her, a confused expression on his face. "OK."

"I don't want to talk to him, not now. I'm driving, Nyah. I'll call him later. Just put the phone back." *Just shut up, Lana* – he gets the message.

In fairness to Nyah, he did not comment. He just put the phone back on the panel as he waited for the Dormund to answer his call.

Lana wondered what was wrong with Peter. Why he was ringing her again – this was the third or fourth time in as many days.

Nyah cleared his throat beside her. "Ah yes, I'm just checking if you have any availability, for tonight?" He waited. "Two single rooms, yeah. Just the one night." He looked over at Lana. "Great, thank you. We should be with you in a few minutes."

Carly advised them to drive straight on for 300 metres and take a left. The Dormund was on the right-hand side.

Ten minutes later, they had parked the rental in the underground carpark and were checking in.

Suddenly, Lana felt very tired. She had been travelling all day, and the wine at the airport, the pent-up nervousness, the stress of the flight and the car rental mix-up had taken their toll. Her headache was gone, but she was tired and hungry and desperately wanted to take a shower.

But when she turned to tell Nyah, he was staring at his phone.

"What is it, Nyah?"

"Snap Map. It's this feature that people use on Snapchat ..."

"I know what it is. What about it?" She accepted a key card from the receptionist.

"Clara had it switched off. It was the first thing I checked when Mam called me from the train station, but she had it turned off so I couldn't see her location. I didn't think it was that unusual to be honest. Mam downloaded Snapchat to her own phone when Clara left for college in Belfast, just so she could keep an eye on her, she said. But she started giving Clara grief about not attending when she had a lecture. She could see her location and she knew where the building was ..."

"I know how it works, Nyah."

"Anyway, Clara would set it to Ghost Mode to hide her location, just to get Mam off her back. I've been watching it since she went missing yesterday because sometimes she turns it back on."

"Staring at it isn't going to make that happen, Nyah."

"She's here, Lana." Nyah fixed her with a stare. "I just know that she's here. My sister is in Pimlico."

CHAPTER 13

Lucy would not settle. Jenny had fed her. She had given her a wash in warm water in the bathtub. She had changed her into a fresh babygro, cuddled her, tried to get her to take the soother, rocked her back and forth in the buggy. But nothing would placate the child. She just would not stop grizzling and fidgeting. Jenny didn't know what to do – she was running out of patience. The baby was overtired and so was she.

After Nyah's earlier text about the photo of Clara and the girl with the tattoo on her arm, Jenny was utterly unnerved. She had drawn all the curtains in the house and locked all the doors. But it didn't make her feel any safer. A hot flush crept up her body and she pulled at the neck of her T-shirt to let in some cool air. She was on edge and the baby was adding to her distress.

She picked the baby up and cuddled her. "*Shush, little girl, shush …*" She gently teased the baby's mouth with a soother, hoping it would work this time. The little girl pushed against the rubbery teat with her tongue, but Jenny gently persevered and a moment later Lucy started to suck enthusiastically. Jenny wondered why Clara had decided not to breastfeed the child, at least for those first few months when she had to stay home and was unable to attend lectures. She remembered how well it had gone for her when she breastfed and later weaned Clara. But then remembered how difficult it had been to wean Nyah. He had refused to take the bottle and screamed, pushing it away with his little fingers, causing her breasts to fill with milk. She had given in quite a few times. Until she had to go back to work and had no choice but to get stricter with him. The child had been distressed though.

Jenny held the infant against her chest as she shifted her weight from one foot to the other, willing her to relax. She needed something to help *her* relax. Walking into the kitchen, she pulled open the fridge door with her free hand and reached inside for a half-empty bottle of white wine. Retrieving a glass from the cabinet over the sink, she poured herself a generous amount. She sipped as she resumed her rocking, back and forth, back and forth. The house was eerily silent except for the baby's sucking sounds. Finally, the child was beginning to calm down. They both were.

What did all this mean? Up to a few months ago she had thought all was well with Clara. She was pleased that she was all grown-up, making friends and a new life for herself. She had seemed happy whenever they talked on the phone, hadn't she? She appeared content and relaxed – attending university and living away from home was suiting her. Clara had kept in regular contact, calling or sending messages at least once a day. There was never a time when she didn't check in, even if she was only sending a love heart or a kiss emoji. Jenny began to worry about her less and less. Until after Christmas when the messages became less frequent. Jenny would ask if everything was OK and Clara would reply, sometimes hours later, that she was swamped with college assignments. Which fit with the time of year. The second term of college was always busier, Jenny knew that. And, of course, there was also the part-time job in the bar. She had promised to come home for her birthday in February, but that hadn't happened. She had made some excuse about being called in to work and that she would celebrate it up in Belfast. So Jenny had sent off another parcel with Clara's birthday gift.

Lucy was finally sleeping, her short little breaths wafting into her tiny lungs. Jenny smiled at how perfect she looked, the tiny nose and long dark lashes resting on her skin. She was like a beautiful little doll, and completely unaware of the distressing events happening around her. Jenny placed her glass on the kitchen counter and quietly made her way to the bedroom where the small baby cradle Nyah had picked up in the charity shop stood beside her bed. She gently laid Lucy on her side and layered the soft blanket over her little body. She had such a lovely temperament. All babies are cute, she thought, but some more than others. Her soft round face, plump lips, big dark eyes and tufts of blonde hair screamed adorable. Her little legs curled up to her tummy as she lay in her cot, the blanket gently rising and falling as she slept.

She used to watch Nyah and Clara sleeping in their cots when they were babies, checking they were still breathing, terrified they would come to some harm, even in their sleep. But nothing ever did happen. They grew up healthy and strong, suffering no more than a head cold every so often. She looked around her bedroom, styled for a middle-aged woman, not a baby. She would have to change that if Lucy were to stay here long-term. Jenny gave a small smile – she was jumping ahead of herself, wasn't she? Clara would turn up and take responsibility for her child. Anyway, Jenny was too old to be looking after a baby again. She felt exhausted after a couple of days. There was no way that she could do this full-time ... could she?

Retracing her steps back to the kitchen, she refilled her wine glass and brought it through to the living room. She sipped as she looked at the picture on the sideboard, her one and only photo of her husband, Danny Doyle. The easy smile, the dark eyes, his arm loosely draped around her shoulder. They looked like any other couple, happy and in love. Except they were not happy and in love. Well, not Jenny. She was at the beginning – she would never deny that. But after they were married Danny had changed, his controlling and jealous nature emerging. Not long after Clara was born he started drinking again. In the photo he looked like he was comforting her, but in reality he was holding on to her. Like she was his possession. She kept the photo in her sightline as a reminder that she had done the right thing all those years ago. Dare she ever try to forget, her memory wouldn't let her. She was extremely worried about the photo of the girl with the tattoo on her arm. The same design as Danny's. Why was she with Clara? What was their connection? She remembered the day Danny had come home to show her his new inking. One he had designed himself. Not one you pick out on websites with tattoo suggestions. The skin around the drawing was red and puffy and he had cling film wrapped around his arm. But she could see it clearly, the rigid fingers clutching the creature's throat. "*This tattoo is a reflection of my love for you, Jen.*" She hadn't thought it a gesture of love. It had looked more like a violent threat.

Her phone rang on the coffee table and she grabbed it quickly so as not to wake Lucy. Her heart thumped. She hoped it was Clara.

But it wasn't Clara. It was Nyah. She tapped the answer button.

"Nyah?"

"Mam, how are you? How is the baby?"

Nyah still hadn't called her by her name, *Lucy*. It was almost like if he did acknowledge her by name then she would actually exist.

"She's fine, finally asleep. I just put her down in her cot there, but she was pretty fidgety all evening. I guess she's missing her mother." She took a sip of her wine. "She's much too young to be separated from a parent."

Nyah sighed. "Yeah, I guess. Well, hopefully not for too much longer."

Her heart leapt. "Did you find Clara?" She put her glass down on the coffee table.

"No. Not yet."

"For God's sake, Nyah. She can't have just disappeared into thin air. She must have left some kind of a trace. What about that Snapchat thing?"

"*Em*, the app you downloaded on your phone when Clara moved to Belfast so that you could keep an eye on her movements?"

Jenny was indignant. "I did not download it for that reason, Nyah!"

Nyah laughed. "Mam, don't deny it. We both know why you got the app. Clara and I had a good laugh about it when she told me that you sent her a friend request. You are probably the only fifty-three-year-old in the world with Snapchat on their phone."

"I doubt very much if that's true, Nyah."

"Come on, Mam? You wanted to use the map feature. It was so that you could check up on her at college. Look, I get it, mothers don't want to let their kids grow up. And, besides, you have always been a helicopter parent, always."

A helicopter parent? What the hell was that? She decided she probably didn't need to know. "Anyway, what about Snap Map, Nyah? Have you checked it?"

"Of course I have! But it only works if the user has their location actually switched on."

"I know how it works, Nyah. And I also know that sometimes your sister turns it on."

"That's true. But it's off now and has been since she went missing. She must have it set on Ghost Mode. Clara doesn't want to be found, Mam."

"Oh, God! Where are you, Nyah?"

"Pimlico."

Jenny's heart started to beat a little faster. "What took you to Pimlico, Nyah?"

"It was just a hunch, Mam. We know Clara flew into London last night. And we know Dad was from Pimlico, so Lana hired a car at the airport and we came straight here."

"But why on earth would your sister go there?"

"To see Dad?"

Jenny was shocked. She had thought that by this time her son had assumed that the man was dead.

"You there, Mam?"

"I'm here."

"The photo ... I sent it to you – there is a girl with her."

"Yes. I saw it."

"Well, then you must have noticed that tattoo, Mam. There is only one other person I know with a tattoo like that. My father. He designed it himself, right?"

"Yes, he did."

"So the most likely explanation for the girl with Clara having that tattoo is that she knows my father. Right?"

"I suppose so."

"And that means that Clara may have met him too."

Tears sprang to Jenny eyes. She began to cry but tried to stifle the sound.

"Mam?"

"Yes?"

"What happened, Mam? What happened when you went back to the house that day? After you dropped us at Nana's."

Jenny hesitated. "Nothing. He wasn't here. He knew he had gone too far. There was no going back once he had attacked you, he would have known that. And after I found the courage to fight back. And so he left. I cleaned up the mess in your room, packed some more clothes so we could stay at Nana's for a while in case he changed his mind. I really had no way of knowing whether he would stay away or not, so I decided to keep you both at Nana's, to keep you safe."

Nyah was silent.

"Nyah?"

"I'm here. Look, we can talk about this when I get home. If Clara is in Pimlico, I'd better get out there and find her. Do you have any idea where he lived when he was here? Any address? For his mother or some other family he might have had here?"

Jenny tried to think. "I remember an uncle. He used to be in the merchant navy. David something or other, I can't remember his second name – it wasn't Doyle. He was at sea for several months at a time, so when he was on leave he would go out drinking with your dad. He was pretty wild, Nyah. They would go out and get really drunk and get themselves into all sorts of trouble. Harmless, but it got messy sometimes. When I was going out with your dad, he mentioned something about the uncle doing time. He wouldn't tell me what for."

"Where did he live?"

"He lived close to Pimlico, I'm pretty sure, but ... what was the name of the street again? He said it was a quiet residential area. What was it now?" She paused. "Medway Street! The uncle lived on Medway Street – I think it was number seven, or seventeen maybe. Either one or the other – I remember sending him a Christmas card one time." She hesitated. "Do you think she's there, Nyah?"

"I don't know, Mam, but I'm going to find out. I sure hope so anyway."

"She made some calls while we travelled down on the train from Belfast. We had to change at Connolly Station in Dublin and Limerick Junction. I remember she made a phone call each time while outside on the platform. She was pacing a bit."

"Did you ask her who she was talking to?"

"Not directly. I asked her if everything was alright and she said it was nothing that I could fix."

"What does that mean?"

"I don't know. I didn't press her about it. She seemed happy enough to leave Belfast when I woke her that morning but later she was in a mood – you know what Clara is like when she's in a mood. You can't get through to her."

"I know only too well."

"Look, call me the minute you hear. And, Nyah ..."

"Yeah, Mam?"

"Take Lana with you. The uncle, he's trouble. Like your father. I don't want you turning up at his house on your own. If Clara is with him, for whatever reason ... just, please be careful?"

"I will. I promise. Lana is coming with me."

"Call me the minute –"

"I will. Gotta go." He hung up.

Jenny held the device in her hand for a few moments longer, willing the call to reactivate. She was scared. Scared for Nyah, scared for Clara, scared for herself and the baby. Taking another sip of her wine, she opened the picture Nyah had sent her earlier. What was going on? What was Clara doing? She glanced over at the photo of her husband again, his arm around her shoulder, the hand dangling loosely over her chest, the tattoo clearly visible.

She had been hopeless with love for him to begin with. The way he looked at her, an intense look, his eyes mesmerising. Whatever he wanted, she would do it. And she'd thought she was lucky. All the girls were mad about him, and yet he had chosen her. By the time she realised that he was both controlling and dangerous, she was already hooked, and there was no way out. Until that day when she had finally stood up to him. The final straw being when he had hit their child. He'd lashed out at her many times. She'd suffered black eyes, a broken nose, and endless bruising. She'd hid the pain and injuries as best she could from the children. He even broke her rib once. The pain had been excruciating and it had taken weeks to heal. But she had never thought that he would hit Nyah.

After that day she had stayed with her mother. For much longer than she had initially planned. She needed to rebuild her life, but as time went on she knew she would have to eventually go home. And she did – and they got on with their lives. And, in time, Danny Doyle became a distant memory, and perhaps she had become complacent. She should have known that one of them would want to meet him at some point. Clara had been the apple of Danny's eye when she was first born. Then, in time, he had begun to get impatient with her too. She had been only three when Danny attacked Nyah – she couldn't possibly remember him too well.

Jenny finished her wine and got up to enter the kitchen to refill her glass. Closing the fridge door, she heard a sound. A sort of a clicking sound. It was coming from behind her. Her heart leapt into her chest. Turning slowly, she could see the backdoor handle moving up and down. *Jesus Christ*. Her heart was pounding now – there was no way she could control it. *Get a grip, Jenny*, she told herself. *You have been in the shit before, many times. You can deal with this. Whoever it is*. She carefully drew a carving knife from the stand on the counter, never taking her eyes off the door handle. She pulled the kitchen door back towards the fridge, allowing her a hiding place in case the intruder gained entrance, while still managing to see through the gap.

The handle had stopped moving. *Don't make a sound,* she warned herself, *keep still.* She heard footsteps retreating, followed by the sound of a car door opening and closing, an engine starting and the crunch of tyres on gravel as a car drove away from the back of the house.

Relief flooded through her. She moved to the kitchen window and carefully lifted the blind from the bottom. The car was black with a yellow registration plate. She could barely make out the letters as it disappeared around the corner of the house ... 89 ... N? And then it was gone, the tail-lights fading before disappearing into the night. Why had she not heard the car pull up? It must have arrived while she was in the living room talking on the phone to Nyah.

Whoever it was had tried to come in her back door. Jenny almost always used the back door. The drive led up to the side of her house and then around the back where there was a gravelled space for parking. Frequent callers then just knocked on the back door or even the kitchen window, knowing she would have heard their car approach. Friends sometimes opened the back door if it wasn't locked and called out to her. Only strangers walked around the front to ring the front door bell. So, whoever was here knew that, knew her routine. She bit into her fingernail as she thought about what had just happened. A yellow licence plate. Yellow meant the plate was English.

She pulled the blind lower over the window once again, and, even though she knew the back door was locked, she checked it again, sliding over the double lock.

She decided to forget about the wine, she needed to keep a clear head. Heading back into the living room she sat on the edge of the sofa. The house was unnervingly quiet now, and the silence enveloped her. She wished she had her mother still living with her. She needed her. Tears stung the backs of her eyes and she pressed her fingers against them, willing the tears to stop. She couldn't afford to break now. She had to stay strong.

She settled back into the sofa, clutching her phone, willing Nyah to call and tell her that this nightmare was over. There was no way she would be able to sleep now. No hope at all.

CHAPTER 14

Lana decided to leave the rental parked in the basement of the hotel carpark and take a taxi to Medway Street. She was done with driving for one day. She was exhausted but Nyah was pumped and full of nervous energy since talking to his mother. He was eager to check out Medway Street.

In her room she dropped her overnight bag on the bed and quickly freshened up in the bathroom. Teeth, face-wash, deodorant – that was all she had time for. She took off her blazer, pulled on the dark-green puffer jacket she had stuffed into her bag, and pushed her feet into socks and back into her trainers.

She met an anxious Nyah in reception.

"Taxi is outside. He knows the street."

She nodded and followed him out of the hotel. The night had turned cool and she zipped up her jacket against the chill. They got into the taxi and the driver merged into traffic.

She glanced over at Nyah who was sitting forward, anxiously watching every face on the street that passed them by, no doubt searching for his sister. He held his phone in his hand and every now and then he checked his apps, Instagram, Facebook, Snapchat, as if she was virtually there, within reach.

He turned towards Lana.

"I'll go in, OK? You stay in the car."

She noticed the hand that was holding his phone was trembling.

She looked at him incredulously. "Nyah, are you serious?"

"What?"

"Do you hear yourself? Honestly?"

"I don't want to put you in any danger in case there's any trouble. Mam said dad's Uncle David is bad news and I don't want you getting wrapped up in all that."

"Oh, for God's sake, Nyah! This is my job as I keep telling you!"

He didn't respond to that. How could he?

A few minutes later the driver took a left onto a quieter street. Lana could see from the sign mounted on the wall that they were on Medway Street. A few doors up, they pulled to a stop outside Number 7. Nyah leaned forward to talk to the driver.

"Can you just wait for a moment, please? We need to know if this is the right house."

The driver nodded. He didn't care either way. His meter was running.

Nyah and Lana got out of the car and Nyah knocked on the door. The blinds in the front room were drawn so it was impossible to see whether there was anybody inside. Nyah knocked again and they waited. They stood there for a good minute but nobody came to the door.

Lana noticed a bunch of kids playing football a few doors up. They were using their jumpers on the footpaths on either side of the street as goalposts. The kid in the makeshift goals closest to Number 7 was watching Nyah and Lana. Nyah signalled to him with his finger. The kid strolled over, hands in his pockets, all tough like. He glanced over his shoulder at his buddies to see if they were watching. They continued to play.

Nyah crouched down to his level. “Hey, mate, do you know who lives here? In number seven?”

The kid shrugged. Either he didn’t know or he wasn’t going to answer.

“I’m looking for my sister. She is nineteen years old. She has blonde hair down to her waist.” He pointed at the redbrick terraced house behind him. “Have you seen her going into that house?”

The kid smiled and then he laughed. “My granny lives there. She’s eighty-two years old and she don’t have no long blonde hair, mate.” He laughed again.

Nyah stood. The kid continued to laugh as he ran back to his place between the two mounds of jumpers.

Nyah turned to Lana, trying to hide his disappointment. “Right, let’s try Number 17. He turned and eased himself back into the car. Lana followed.

Nyah gave the driver instructions and they took off again.

The further up the street they drove, the quieter it got. The houses were terraced in blocks with a narrow gap before the next set. The driver pulled up outside Number 17 and, once again Nyah asked him to wait. They got out of the cab and Nyah knocked on the door. Almost immediately, a light went on in the hall and the door opened. A woman in her mid-to-late forties maybe, it was hard to tell her age, stood inside the door. She was dressed in a well-worn navy dressing gown frayed at the edges. Her bleached-blonde hair was piled high and messily on the top of her head. She had a glass of something in her hand. The liquid was clear but Lana was pretty sure it wasn't water. The pupils in her eyes were dark and glassy, and fully dilated.

"Can I help ya?" Her speech was a little slurred.

Before Lana could say anything, Nyah stepped forward. "Yes, *em*, does a David live here?"

The woman narrowed her eyes. She glanced from Nyah to Lana. "David who, love?"

"David Doyle?" Nyah said, though his mother had said he wasn't a Doyle.

The woman shook her head. "Never heard of a David Doyle."

Lana smiled at the woman. "Are you sure there isn't a David living here?"

The woman's mouth turned down at the edges. She pressed her hip into the doorframe. "Well, there was." She spat. "He's gone. Not David Doyle though, David Miller. And if you see the bastard, tell him I want my money back." She went to close the door.

Lana took a quick step forward.

"Hold on. Are you talking about David from the navy?"

At that, the woman looked Lana up and down. "Yeah, do you know him?"

Lana looked the woman in the eye. "Yes." One simple word. Lana didn't need to expand. She maintained eye contact. "He told me his name was David Doyle, but I knew he was lying.

The woman's expression changed and Lana knew she had her attention.

"Is that so?" She kept her eyes on Lana, as if considering what to do next. "Well, I wudda thought you'd be a bit young for him, even though nothing surprises me when it comes to that fucker."

Lana folded her arms across her chest and looked down at the ground. "I know what you mean. He ripped me off too." She looked over at Nyah and then back at the woman. "Look, can I talk to you? I really need to find him." The woman was watching Nyah. "Don't worry about him –he's my brother. He came with me as a sort of protection, you know? David can be ..." She let the sentence linger, but it was enough to get the woman on her side.

"I hear ya. Pretty handy with his fists, isn't he?" She held the door back. "Come on in, love." She staggered off down the dark narrow hallway. "Ignore the mess."

Lana turned towards Nyah and whispered. "Pay the driver. When you get inside find an excuse to leave us on our own. To use the loo or something."

She followed the woman into the house.

Nyah ran back to the taxi and threw the driver some notes. The car took off and he followed Lana into the house. The kitchen was in darkness except for a few candles lighting on the windowsill. There was a smell of stale cigarettes hanging in the air and a half-full ashtray sat on the kitchen table. The sink appeared to be full of dirty dishes and mugs, a few half-eaten takeout containers scattered along the kitchen counter beside an open bottle of cheap vodka. The woman picked up the vodka and poured herself a generous glass. She then pushed the bottle across the table towards Lana. "There're glasses in the cupboard – hopefully you can find a clean one." She sat back on her chair and crossed her legs. "Help yourself, love."

Lana found a glass and poured a small measure. She sat opposite the woman and took a sip. The liquid burned her throat.

Nyah coughed behind her.

"*Em*, can I use your bathroom, please?"

The woman laughed. "You're very polite, love. Not used to manners in this house." She pointed up the stairs. "First door on the right."

Nyah left the kitchen.

The woman reached inside the pocket of her dressing gown and pulled out a packet of cigarettes. "Mind if I have one?"

Lana shook her head. The woman lit her cigarette and inhaled deeply.

"Right, tell me everything. It's not often I share my vodka."

Lana took a breath, wondering what the hell she was going to say to this woman. She had to stall her. She took a gulp of the vodka, enough to make her eyes water. She pretended to get upset. "Please, my brother will be back in a minute. I need to know where David is. My brother is so angry."

The woman raised her eyebrows and glanced towards the stairs, clearly not believing her.

"I know he looks harmless but looks can be deceiving. Trust me. I need to find David before he does. The money he took from me, it belongs to my brother."

The woman shook her head – a look of understanding.

Lana glanced towards the stairs. "Please?"

"Look, I don't know where the geezer is now. Bastard left last month but not before giving me a black eye and running off with all me savings. I don't know how he figured out my hiding place. He must have been watching me, the prick. Anyways, he took off with over five hundred quid, the fucker!" She spat, a dribble of saliva landing on Lana's hand. "I don't know why – it's not like he needed the money. It's all about control with him, you see."

Lana shook her head in sympathy. "Where did he go?"

The woman shrugged. "I don't know, I told you." She bit her lip.

Lana could see she was debating whether to tell her something. Lana sniffed loudly, glancing towards the stairs again.

The woman drained her glass. "Look, he comes and goes, sometimes straight from prison, sometimes from somewhere else. I don't know for sure, and I don't really give a shit, but I guess there's another woman. Probably more than one. He is an ex-sailor after all." She shrugged. "I don't care much, to be honest. When he stays here, he helps pay towards the rent so it suits me in a way. And I'm hardly Mother Teresa myself." She laughed a coarse laugh. "But this last time he stole my money. He hasn't done that before. He crossed a line when he stole from me, you know?" She inhaled her cigarette.

Lana nodded her understanding, though she thought it ironic that a man could give the woman a black eye and that was acceptable, but stealing her money wasn't.

"There's a bar he hangs out in. The Old Rose. It's over in Greencoat Place. Not far from here. About a ten maybe fifteen-minute walk. Go back down Medway Street and head towards Victoria."

Lana could hear a toilet flush upstairs. She thought of something Nyah had said earlier. "Have you always lived here?"

"*Nah*. This is a council house." She smiled, showing a row of yellow teeth. "The funny thing is that David was a renter here before me. Then I became a legal tenant because a few years back he signed over the tenancy. It was during one of his stints in prison. He had to or he would have lost the agreement with the council. Because I had been living here a few years at the time I fit the criteria to take over the lease. They have all these rules in the council when it comes to housing, but sometimes there are loopholes that work in the tenant's favour. I got lucky."

A door opened upstairs. They could hear Nyah coming down the stairs.

"Have you ever met any of his family?"

The woman thought about that. "There is this one guy, a nephew. He's a bit weird. Has this funny-looking tattoo on his arm. Think he moved to Ireland. Got married over there and had some kids according to David. He visited a few times but I haven't seen him in years. And I mean years. What was his name again? Danny or something like that, I think. Oh, and there's a grandniece but I haven't seen her in a while either. Other than that, there is nobody else." She pressed her thin lips together.

Lana gave a small smile. "I don't think I have met Danny."

"Count your blessings. As I said, he's a weird one."

Lana smiled at the woman. "Thank you."

The woman reached for the vodka and poured. "S'alright, love." She took a drink, watching Lana over the rim of her glass. "What part of Ireland are you from, love?"

"The south. Moved over here a couple of years ago."

Lana wiped her nose with the back of her hand. She pushed back her chair as Nyah entered the kitchen.

"I know where to find him! This woman ..." She gestured towards the woman.

"Audrey," she provided.

"Audrey has told me." Lana smiled at her. "Thank you. And thanks for the drink."

"Be careful – he has friends there, in the pub. Everyone's a regular, you know?"

Lana nodded and took Nyah by the arm. They walked down the hall and out onto the street. Nyah closed the door behind them.

"I didn't have you down as a vodka-drinker?"

The taste of the cheap liquor made her want to gag. She found a pack of gum in her pocket and, wiping her mouth, she popped one in.

"Let's walk back to the main street and flag a cab. I wouldn't say we have much of a chance of getting one here." She checked her watch. "And don't they close pubs early in England?" She took off in the direction they had come from.

He caught up with her. "Where is he? Where did that woman say he is? This David Miller?"

"The Old Rose pub on Greencoat Place."

CHAPTER 15

Jenny's phone stirred in her hand. The shrill sound woke her from a fretful sleep. She was lying sideways on the couch, her legs tucked up close to her chest. She had fallen asleep while trying to stay awake. She was freezing cold, not having bothered with a cover. The room was in darkness except for the small shaft of light shining through the doorway from the kitchen, creating shadows in the hall. She was wondering what had woken her when the phone rang again. Rubbing the sleep from her eyes, she checked the caller ID. It was Nyah. *Oh please, let him have some news about Clara!* She pressed answer.

"Nyah?"

"Mam? Are you OK?"

She frowned, confused by his question. Why was he asking if she was OK? "Yes. Why?"

"I have a missed call from you. And you took ages to answer."

Did she ring him? She couldn't remember. Maybe she had when someone had tried to break in through her back door. She debated whether to tell him about the person who had been driving the black car. She decided against it. He had enough to think about. He had to find his sister and she needed him to concentrate on that.

"I was just ringing to see if you had any information on Clara?" she lied.

He sighed. "Mam, I told you I'd call the minute I had news." He sounded irritated, but she'd had to think of a reason for ringing him. "The answer to your question is yes and no. She wasn't at the house on Medway Street. There is a woman, Audrey Something-or-other, we didn't get her last name. She lives there now but on her own. It turns out she had an on-off relationship with Dad's Uncle David. David Miller. He sounds like a nasty piece of work by all accounts. In and out of prison, busted her up a few times and stole from her. I went upstairs while Lana had a chat with her in the kitchen – you know, pretended I was using the loo."

He sounded proud of his investigative skills. She didn't interrupt.

"I checked the bedrooms but there was no sign of Clara ever having been there, like, no trace. The main bedroom, the one I would say the woman Audrey uses, had clothes thrown all over the floor and on the bed. There were half-empty mugs and glasses lying around – it was just a mess. It was hard to tell what was going on with the other rooms. One had some clothes alright, a girl's clothes, hoodies and leggings, that sort of thing, but they definitely didn't belong to Clara. She is really slim, isn't she? You know the way she always gave out about buying kids' clothes when she was a teenager. Well, these hoodies were too big. Not the woman's either, the style was too young. The woman, Audrey, didn't mention anything about anyone living with her. Maybe she lets the room out. The third bedroom was completely empty. I had a quick look in the wardrobes, there was nothing in them. I'm pretty sure Clara was never there."

"So, another dead end?"

"Well, Audrey did give us some info about where we might find David. A pub called the Old Rose. Weird name if you ask me. We just pulled up outside now."

"Be careful, Nyah. If the uncle is somehow linked to Clara, it might not be a good idea to approach him on your own. Maybe you should involve the English police? They could contact the Gardaí here about my interview. That shows evidence that Clara is missing for more than twenty-four hours."

"I don't think they would help, Mam. What do I tell them? Ah, my sister flew in to London last night and we think she is with our dad, but I don't know where he is because I haven't seen him for decades so I'm trying to track him down through his uncle who is an ex-con by the way?" He paused. "I just don't see them taking us seriously. Besides," he lowered his voice, "Lana is fierce good at her job. You should have seen the way she handled Audrey – the woman hadn't a clue she's a private investigator."

"Good, that's good, Nyah." Jenny detected something different in the way Nyah spoke about Lana – admiration. She remembered when he had brought her down for the weekend – there had only been the one, but Jenny had noticed the way he looked at her, like a love-sick puppy, and Lana was completely oblivious. Or pretended to be. Jenny assumed he had grown out of it, whatever it was, just a crush maybe. And over the years he seemed to have. Nyah had never been short of girlfriends.

"Just be careful, watch your back. Don't do anything that doesn't feel safe, and stay together, OK?"

"Yes, Mam. Listen, I gotta go. Are you sure you're OK?"

Again, she hesitated. Should she tell him? "I'm fine, honestly, heading to bed now, but I'll keep the phone on my locker, so ring me the minute you find her, OK?"

"I promise."

He rang off and she placed the phone on the coffee table. The house was completely quiet, except for the clock ticking on the wall in the kitchen. She debated what to do. If she stayed on the couch all night she would be completely exhausted in the morning. If she went to bed, she probably wouldn't be able to sleep. She checked the time on her watch – it was just after ten thirty. She had put Lucy down around seven, hadn't she? So she would be due to wake for a feed soon. Miraculously, she had only woken once the previous night. She'd have to get some sleep or she wouldn't be any good to Lucy. Her head ached and she had a terrible taste in her mouth. She decided she would take some painkillers with a glass of milk and call it a night. That way, she might get a few hours at the very least, feed Lucy and then catch another few. Anything was better than staying up all night watching the shadows dancing across the walls, listening for sounds that shouldn't be there. She went into the kitchen, found the tablets, and poured her milk.

Her phone rang again as she was finishing her drink. It must be Nyah – he must have found her at the pub. God, she hoped he had! She desperately wanted to hear her daughter's voice. She answered without checking the number.

"Nyah?"

"Hello, Jenny, it's Megan."

Her heart sank. Oh, for Christ's sake, what was the woman doing ringing her so late? They had spoken earlier in the day when Jenny had bumped into her on the street. What reason would she have for calling her now, especially at this late hour?

"Megan, hi. This is a surprise. It's late. I was just about to go to bed. Is everything OK?"

"Everything is fine, Jenny, just fine."

But Jenny knew something was coming.

"I was wondering if I can come around in the morning? Do you have work?"

What? Why would Megan want to visit her? They had the odd chat when they bumped into each other, but their relationship wasn't really anything above acquaintance level. What was she up to?

"I need to talk to you about something. What time do you leave for the garden centre?"

Jenny didn't know what to say. If she lied, Megan would only try to find another way to see her. If Megan Carmichael was anything, she was pushy. The woman was like a dog with a bone when she wanted something. If Jenny suggested Megan call over, she risked her meeting Lucy again. It was one thing to fib about minding her boss's baby niece while out shopping, it was another to try to explain her being in her house. *Think, Jenny, think*. Maybe she could feed Lucy early and put her down for a nap – she did sleep a lot. She could judge the situation in the morning and ring Megan when the baby was sleepy.

"You there, Jenny?"

"Yeah. I am on a half day tomorrow. I don't have to go in until after lunch, but I have some errands to run in the morning. *Em*, can I ring you? I should be free about ten, maybe earlier, but let me ring you to confirm a time, just in case?"

Megan didn't reply straight away.

The silence on the phone was unsettling. What was the matter with the woman?

"That should be fine, Jenny. I'll be ready to pop over first thing. But I'll wait for your call first, so I will leave it up to you. Just make sure you call, OK?" She hung up without saying goodbye.

What the hell was that about? Megan was an unusual character, but that conversation had to be the most bizarre she ever had with her. She turned towards her back door, wondering if she had imagined the handle moving up and down earlier. But she knew she hadn't imagined it – she had witnessed a car driving off, hadn't she? She'd seen the registration plate.

She made up a few bottles of formula for Lucy's night-time feeds. Switching off the lights she passed the living room, stopping to look at the photo on the side table of her husband smiling out at her, his arm around her shoulder. She could almost feel his strong fingers kneading into her skin. She felt his eyes on her even after all these years – she was still under his control. She strode across the room and turned the photo face down with more force than she intended. "*Fuck you*," she muttered.

As she walked down the hallway, she passed Clara's bedroom. The door was firmly closed with a sign reading **Clara's Room. Do Not**

Enter! hanging from a hook. Clara had bought the sign on Etsy or Shein or some other online website and had it personalized in pretty colours. But the message was clear. Jenny placed her hand on the doorknob and turned. She tried to remember the last time she had been in here. It might have been Christmas. Clara had called asking that she send some of her things to Belfast by post. She kept meaning to come back and wash the bed linen, let some fresh air into the room but she hadn't got around to it. She scanned the room now. The black-and-white duvet cover printed with images of iconic New York landmarks, the white dresser that used to be covered with make-up bottles and brushes. There was a locker beside her bed with a lamp and a stack of books resting on top. She crossed the room and sat on the edge of the bed, picking up one of the books. She smiled as she read the title, *Hetty Feather*. Clara had never been interested in reading books when she was a child, despite her teacher's encouragement. Jenny had heard a book review for *Hetty Feather* on the radio. The reviewer had said that the series was very popular with eight to twelve-year-old girls so Jenny had bought a few and encouraged Clara to read at night. It didn't work. So Jenny would lie with her daughter on the bed and they would share the reading. Jenny would read two pages and Clara would read one. They spent a year doing that together, just reading Jackie Wilson books until Clara decided that she was ready to read on her own. She had particularly liked Hetty Feather's character. She had huge empathy for the girl who had no family.

Jenny opened the book and flicked through the pages. Something came loose and floated onto the floor. She bent down and picked up a piece of paper. It was blank on one side but there was something written on the other. The writing was small, cursive and hard to make out. But Jenny was sure it was Clara's. She placed the book on Clara's bed and brought the paper out to the hall so that she could see it more clearly under the light. There was a phone number written on the back and four words beside it – *The Old Rose Pub.*

Jenny's heart turned cold.

CHAPTER 16

Nyah tucked his phone into the back pocket of his jeans and followed Lana to the pub's entrance. Even from his position outside on the street, the music was loud. There was a lane at the side of the pub roofed with a canopy, sheltering the smokers and vapers braving the cool night air.

"You ready?" He made to open the door when Lana stopped him.

"Wait, Nyah. We have to plan this."

"What do you mean?"

"We don't know anything about this man. We don't even know what he looks like. What do you want to do? Go in there and ask the bartender if David Miller is around and could he point him out? It's not a line-up, Nyah – we need to tread carefully." She looked worriedly at the door, her shoulder-length brown hair framing her face, her forehead creased in a frown.

Her cheeks were pale, her full pink lips quivered from the cold – she looked beautiful just standing there. Nyah wanted to reach out and touch her, keep her warm, protect her from whatever was inside. Focus, Nyah, he told himself, keep your eye on what you have to do. Find your sister and get her back home to Ireland, and then ... and then what?

"You're right. I'm not sure how to approach the situation." He held up his hands. "Admittedly, I am out of my depth."

"We go inside, order a drink, and we watch. This place looks like a local hang-out. Audrey as much as said so, and that means people who know each other. Just follow my lead on this, Nyah. I know you are desperate to find your sister but the last thing you want to do is sabotage our only tip."

He nodded. "OK, but ..." He stopped. He didn't know how to communicate what he was thinking.

She read his mind. "But what if your dad is in there?" She rested her hand on his arm. "When was the last time you saw him?"

"The day of the beating. I was fourteen."

"So, chances are, he won't remember what you look like."

He glanced away. "I remember what *he* looked like."

"I'm with you, Nyah. We go in, we order, we sit and we watch, OK?"

He nodded. Lana pushed open the bar door. As the music pulsed around the crowded bar, the revellers barely noticed the couple as they made their way to the counter.

Nyah turned to Lana who was discreetly scanning the crowd.

"What do you want to drink?"

"I'm kind of thirsty actually, so a dry cider? Draft is fine."

He smiled back at her, shaking his head.

"What?"

"Wine, vodka and now cider? You really like to mix it up."

Her eyes grew wide. "The wine was because of my fear of flying, the vodka was work-related and now I'm a little bit thirsty, alright? It's been a long day." She nudged him. "Since when did you get so judgey?"

He laughed. "I'm kidding. It's just a new side to you that I haven't seen before."

"What do you mean?"

He shrugged. "In college, you were just a bit ... I don't know, cautious."

"I'm still cautious, Nyah. I'm just thirsty as well."

He laughed. "Fair enough." He looked around the bar. "Do you want to find a table?"

She nodded and he turned towards the counter to try catch the bartender's attention. A minute later he got lucky when a young lad pointed his finger at him. He couldn't be much more than twenty, Nyah thought. He was dressed in a black T-shirt and skinny jeans, his head was completely shaved and a dragon tattoo wrapped its way around the side of his neck.

"*Two halves of dry ciders, please, draft if you have it!*" he shouted over the music.

Keeping his head down, he cast his gaze around the bar. The counter was half-moon in shape, with customers sitting on stools on either side. He noticed a large area to the right side of the bar where several punters were playing pool, cues in hand, as they watched the game unfold. A cheer went up as someone potted the black ball followed by loud laughter as cues were chalked and someone inserted money into the metal slot to begin another game.

He felt his phone vibrate in his pocket. He hoped it wasn't his mother again. He adored his mother, but she was nothing if she wasn't persistent. However, when he saw whose number flashed across the screen, he wished it were his mother. His boss, Brad Fulham, was calling him. Nyah closed his eyes as if he could erase the number. There was no way he could answer the man's call. He would scream down the phone and, when Nyah explained where he was, he would scream some more. He rejected the call.

The song changed to a more up-tempo track and some of the crowd started dancing. The bartender put his drinks on the counter and Nyah handed over his card. He glanced over his shoulder – Lana had found a table near the door. Her chin was resting on the palms of her hands as her shoulders swayed in time to the music. She appeared casual, enjoying the atmosphere, but Nyah knew she was watching everyone around her, searching the crowd.

The barman came back with his card and receipt.

"Thanks, mate."

"Welcome." He turned his head to the guy beside Nyah, already moving on to the next customer.

Nyah hesitated. "Ah, excuse me?" Maybe it was the adrenaline, or the search he had carried out earlier upstairs in Audrey's house. He didn't know what made him do what he did next, but he felt confident. Confident enough to ask his next question.

The barman turned back, trying and failing to hide his annoyance.

Nyah didn't blame him – it was a busy night.

"Yeah, mate?"

"I'm looking for someone."

"Oh aye?" He cocked his head to the side and raised an eyebrow.

"Do you know where I can find David Miller? I believe he drinks here regularly." Something flickered across the barman's face. A moment later he pushed up his bottom lip and shook his head. "Never heard of him, mate." He quickly moved on to the next customer.

A girl bumped into Nyah, spilling some of his drinks on his puffer jacket.

"*Whoops, sorry!*" She continued to dance with her arms in the air.

Fuck sake.

He found Lana and set down their glasses.

"I just need to use the bathroom, find a towel to dry this jacket. Cider stinks if it dries in and it's the only jacket I brought with me."

"Go ahead."

He navigated his way through the crowds towards the back of the bar. Some guy was getting ready to rack up the pool balls with a triangle. He leaned forward and prepared to break. There were several stacks of coins on the table. Nyah imagined the games went on for hours each night.

Finding the loo, he grabbed several sheets of paper towel and wiped the wet cider from his jacket. Discarding the paper towels in the bin, he decided to use the urinals while he was there. He sighed as he thought about the last twenty-eight or so hours, and what they had learned about his little sister in that time. She had given birth to a baby, although there was a question mark over that because of her flat stomach in the photo. She had travelled to Limerick with the baby and their mother – abandoned them both at the train station and willingly got into a car outside. She had then caught a flight to London, and his gut told him that she was here, in Pimlico. The Old Rose pub might be a wrong move, but for now it was all they had. Oh, and when he did find her, he was going to murder her.

The door opened behind him and a guy came to stand beside him at the urinals. In his peripheral vision he could see six more urinals to his left. He wondered why the hell the man had chosen to stand beside his. Give a guy some space already. Maybe that is how lads took a leak in England. Back in Ireland, they would pick the furthest urinal available.

"Enjoying the night, mate?"

Jesus, conversation was expected too? Embarrassed, Nyah finished up, muttering. "Yeah, it's grand."

"Every night is like a weekend night in the Old Rose. It's just that kind of pub."

Again, Nyah nodded.

"Haven't seen you around here before?"

Nyah turned to wash his hands in the sink. "No, I'm not from around here."

The guy laughed. "I can tell by the accent, mate. Irish, right? We get a lot of Irish around here."

Nyah pulled on the paper towels and dried his hands.

"You on your own?"

Was he coming on to him? "Ah, no. I'm with someone."

The guy smiled, baring very white teeth. He was smaller than Nyah, by at least a foot, but he made up for it in width – the man was built like a tank. He obviously worked out in a gym, his taut muscles clearly visible through his red T-shirt. Nyah guessed the man was about his own age.

"Ah, you have a bird with ya? Well, I won't be keeping ya. In my experience, chicks don't like to be kept waiting."

Chicks? People still called women *chicks*? "No, it's not like that. We are not together. Just friends." Why was he telling this stranger about his relationship status with Lana? Now he would really think he was gay.

The guy nodded, a strange look appearing on his face.

Time to get out of here, Nyah.

"Say, you look familiar? Have we met somewhere before?"

Nyah shook his head. "No, I don't think so. Actually, I've never been to London before."

The man narrowed his eyes. "What brings you here now?"

"Just visiting."

"People don't just visit Pimlico, mate, it's not that kind of place. Not the tourist spot, Pimlico." He zipped up his jeans and came to stand beside Nyah at the sink, again a little too close." Only thing worth knowing about Pimlico is that Winston Churchill lived here once." He turned on the tap as he watched Nyah in the mirror.

Nyah was feeling very uncomfortable – the guy was totally invading his space.

"Unless you're visiting someone in particular?"

There was a change in the guy's tone now. Nyah could not be sure what had shifted, but something was off.

The guy stepped a little closer still. "Or maybe you're looking for someone?"

"Not really, I just dropped in for a drink with–"

It was a moment before Nyah realised he had been punched in his side. He bent over as pain shot up through his body, and then he felt a kick in the back of his knee. He gasped for breath as he doubled over in agony, winded. He crouched over to protect his body from the blows, covering his face with his hands as another kick struck his other knee. He grabbed hold of the sink basin as he fell forward, but not before the guy slammed his head against the basin. He could taste blood in his mouth as the bile rose up in his chest. He felt hot breath close to his ear and the smell of stale beer and tobacco. The guy pulled roughly at his jacket, lifting his head off the ground.

"My advice to you, mate, is to take your little girlfriend and get the fuck out of Pimlico, do you hear me?"

Nyah held on to the sink and again tried to pull himself up. The guy pushed his head full force against the damp wall. His head was spinning, his breath became shallow, he thought he might throw up.

"Let this be a warning. Make an excuse to your friend out there and get the fuck out of here." He let go of Nyah and took a step back.

Nyah heard the door open and close behind him.

His breath was coming in short sharp gasps and his head felt like it was going to explode. He used all of his strength to pull himself to standing. Leaning against the basin, he caught his reflection in the mirror. There was a trickle of blood running down his chin, a swelling beginning on his lower lip. He touched the back of his head. More blood. He grabbed a fistful of paper towels and held them against his head. What the hell had just happened? He was pretty sure that what he had just experienced wasn't just a random assault. He was threatening him, wasn't he? Did it have something to do with what he had asked the barman? He was pretty sure by the look on the barman's face earlier that he knew David Miller. *Shit*. Was the guy who had just assaulted him David Miller? That would make him, what? His granduncle or something? Oh for god's sake, what was he thinking? The guy was as young as himself. He leaned forward and threw up in the sink. He turned on the tap and splashed cold water onto his face and rinsed his mouth.

Lana was going to kill him. He had been impulsive and now he had ruined their chances of finding his dad's uncle. He switched on the cold tap and cupped some water into his mouth to ease the throbbing. Drinking several gulps, he felt his breath slowly return to normal. He splashed some more water on his face and grabbed some more paper towels, pressing the damp tissue onto his skin. There was a fresh cut on his lip, but other than that, he didn't look too bad. The guy knew what he was doing. Just enough damage to frighten Nyah off. Just enough to make sure he wouldn't come back.

Checking his appearance one last time, he left the toilets. The pain in one knee was much worse than he initially thought, but he tried to disguise it as he walked the narrow corridor out to the bar, the music becoming louder. He scanned the pool area, searching for the guy that had attacked him, but there was no sign of the man. Some guy was accusing his opponent of moving the white ball, holding up his cue in a threatening manner. Nobody appeared to pay him any attention as he pushed his way through the crowds. He glanced over at the counter – the bartender who had served him earlier was busy dealing with customers, paying no heed to him.

He reached Lana. Her head was stuck in her phone.

He lifted his glass and drank half his drink in one gulp. She looked up, a smile on her face. "Jesus, you're thirsty ... Nyah?" Her smile turned to concern when she saw his face. "What the hell happened to you?"

He leaned in close to her ear. "Keep your expression normal, Lana, we need to leave. Finish your drink, I'll explain outside."

If she was annoyed, she hid it well. She nodded and finished what was left in her glass. She slung her bag over her shoulder and they exited the bar. The door closed behind them and the music became a distant thud.

"Nyah?" Lana turned towards him, her expression full of concern.

There was a cab pulling in across the street. A group of lads climbed out as one leaned in the driver's window, offering cash.

"Come on." He grabbed her by the hand and walked as fast as his injured knee allowed him to, half dragging her behind him. He leaned into the open window of the cab and gave the address of their hotel. The driver nodded and pressed the meter button as they climbed in the back. Neither of them spoke. They were a few blocks away from the pub when, finally, Nyah turned to look at Lana.

She reached up and touched the cut on his lip. "What happened?"

"I'm sorry, Lana. I fucked up."

CHAPTER 17

It was hard to stay mad with Nyah. He had made a mistake and it may have cost them time, but she understood why he had done what he did. His mother was putting pressure on him, his boss was calling him incessantly and he was desperate to find his sister. What they did know for certain though is that he had ruffled some feathers when he asked the barman if he knew David Miller. Whether David Miller was in the pub or not they didn't know, but if he wasn't someone in there was protecting him. The question was why, and the bigger question was whether it had something to do with one of his stints in prison. Or Nyah's little sister Clara. If the attack was connected to Clara in some way, what did that mean? Was she gone now? Had she already left Pimlico?

Nyah winced.

"Sorry, I'm nearly done," Lana said.

Nyah was sitting on the edge of the bath, his chest bare, his jeans open at the top button to take pressure off the bruising on his side. She gently dabbed some cotton wool around the cut on his lip.

By the time they got back to the hotel, the blood had crusted around his chin. He had bruising at the side of his ribs, and his left leg had taken a battering. But other than soreness, she was pretty sure there was nothing broken. There was also a cut at the back of his head, but it didn't appear deep enough to require stitches. He would survive. This time. She guessed he was more annoyed with himself than anything else. He knew he had been reckless when he made the decision to quiz the barman.

"OK, you're all good." She turned and pressed her foot on the bin's pedal and disposed of the cotton wool. She then washed her hands in the sink and dried them on the towel.

Nyah didn't say anything, he just watched her movements in silence. In the cab he'd told her what had happened in the toilets, and he hadn't added much to his story since they arrived back at the hotel.

The lobby was quiet when they entered, with just a few stragglers checking in for the night. Lana had glanced, longingly, into the dining room where customers were enjoying their evening meal. The smell of cooked food reminded her that she hadn't eaten since that morning, and then she had only grabbed a bowl of cereal.

"Nyah?"

He had his right hand pressed against his side. Lana bet it hurt like hell. His disappointed gaze rested on the bathroom floor. She crouched down in front of him, forcing him to look at her. "Hey? It's OK." She tried to keep her voice gentle.

He shook his head. "I messed up, Lana. I've ruined any chance of finding my sister. You warned me to keep my mouth shut and I just couldn't stop myself. I mean," he threw his free hand in the air, "I don't know this world. My domain consists of data, algorithms and gathering people's personal information. Not shady characters who beat you up for asking a question. I thought I had a handle on it." He looked at her then. "I'm sorry, Lana, I really screwed up. I should have listened to you."

He looked so desolate she wanted to comfort him. "Nyah, what happened tonight is not your fault. You got a bit over-excited but I understand what you're going through. It's done now. So we learn from it and we move on, OK? Learn from the past, live in the present and move on. My dad taught me that when I was a young girl and, you know what, he was so right. We can't fix our mistakes, but we can learn from them. Your motive tonight was to find your sister. And, yes, you should have been more careful. What we have to do now is take in and absorb tonight's events. What you said to the barman, it somehow got back to David Miller, or someone who knows him, and that clearly has pissed him off."

"Yeah, but we don't know whether he has anything to do with Clara. His friend, the guy who followed me into the toilets, he could be protecting him for some other reason."

"I was thinking about that." She shifted her weight. "What did he ask you, exactly? Think about it. What exact words did he use?"

"He said something about visiting someone, was I visiting someone. I didn't get a chance to answer him ... he just started punching me and ..."

"What did he mean by visiting someone?" Lana sat back on the bathroom floor and rested her arms on her knees. Her hair fell forward and she tucked it behind her ears. She leaned her head against the bathroom wall. Suddenly, she felt very tired.

"I don't know exactly ... he said something like, was I visiting someone in Pimlico because it wasn't the type of place that people visit as a tourist and ..." He stopped.

"What, Nyah?"

"He said, 'Unless you are looking for someone'."

She leaned forward. "Are you sure he said those precise words?"

Nyah nodded. "Yes, just before he started punching me. Jesus, do you think he meant Clara?"

"I don't know – he could have meant David Miller, it's hard to know." She sighed. The long day was catching up on her. "I need a drink. Want one?" She grabbed the side of the bath to pull herself up and nearly pushed Nyah over the edge. He almost lost his balance. She laughed as she caught his shoulder to steady herself. "Sorry, I used to be able to do that in one easy go. Getting older, I guess. Did I hurt you?"

She smiled down at him, but he didn't smile back, the hand that was holding his side reached out to rest on her waist. He looked up into her eyes.

"Nyah?"

He pulled himself up so that he was standing over her. There was barely an inch between them. They stood like that for a moment, just looking at each other. Eventually, he moved his hand around to the back of her head and leaned in until his lips met hers. The kiss was soft, each exploring the other. Their bodies became closer and she could feel the heat of him as he pressed against her. He moved his hand down her back, pulling at the material of her top. She felt for the edge of his jeans and pushed at his zip, her free hand holding on to his waist. The kiss grew deeper, more urgent. He winced.

"Sorry! Did I hurt you? Sorry, I keep saying that." She smiled, caressing the side of his cheek with her thumb.

They both laughed, their foreheads touching.

"Are you OK?" she asked.

He gave a small smile. "I'm OK, are you?"

He looked a question at her. She took his hand and guided him into the bedroom. She sat on the bed, gently pulling him down beside her. He pressed his body into her as his lips found hers again. He lifted the bottom of her T-shirt and pushed the fabric over her head, her bra strap coming loose. He fumbled with the button of her jeans. She arched her body against his, her lips exploring, her leg sneaking under his thigh.

"Lana, I ..."

"*Shush* ..."

A phone rang. She wasn't sure if it was hers or Nyah's.

"Don't answer it," he whispered.

His breath was warm against her skin. She shook her head – her heart was pounding in her chest.

"I have to, Nyah, it could be important."

His mouth moved to her neck as she reached behind him for the jacket she had left lying on the bed when they had returned to the room. Finding it, she fumbled in her pocket until she found her phone. She brought the device around so they could both see the screen. He stopped what he was doing and turned to look at the device. He saw the name at the same time as Lana did.

Peter.

CHAPTER 18

Nyah found his T-shirt and carefully eased it over his head as he moved into the bathroom in search of his shoes. Where had he left his bloody shoes? He could hear Lana moving around inside the bedroom, quietly talking on the phone to Peter. He wondered why Peter was ringing her. *Again*. He knew that they had known each other while she was working on a case last year, but he thought it was just a casual acquaintance. That's more or less what she had said when they talked about him. They had met while she was solving a case and then they had both moved on. Lana had given the impression that the relationship was one of friendship and that Peter was just someone she once knew. So why did he keep ringing her? And what had made her expression change when she saw his name appear on the screen of her phone? She had overreacted in Ireland when he rang while they were on their way to the airport. But there was another question tugging at his conscience – why was it bothering him?

He found his shoes inside the bathroom door. He was exhausted, but he was also famished and he knew that he would have to eat something before he went to bed. And he definitely needed alcohol. He decided to get a drink at the bar and maybe a sandwich and he hoped Lana would join him once she finished her call. He thought about what had happened earlier, as he sat on the edge of the bath to tie his shoelaces.

Back in college, when they were in First Year, he had been crazy about Lana and he was pretty sure she had a good idea of how he felt, but she had never given him a hint that she had felt the same. There had been that one time when he had made a move on her, down by the river. But she had made it clear that she wasn't interested and so he had backed off. He spent the summer after First Year in Portugal, working in a surfer's bar, and there had been plenty of interest from girls during that time. Lana soon moved into the back of his mind, but he had never forgotten her. He was both disappointed and pleased that she changed courses the following September. Even though he would miss her, at least he wouldn't have to sit in a lecture hall with her every day. Absence makes the mind forget, right? However, miss her he did, and he had always kept an eye on her from a distance. There had been a few girlfriends over the years, but nobody that he was prepared to pursue a serious relationship with. He often wondered if his inability to commit came down to the fact that he still had feelings for Lana. His heart had skipped a beat when he met her in the café the other morning. And that had really surprised him.

She was still on the phone when he went back into the bedroom, so he signalled his intention to go downstairs and left the room. Once in the bar he would fire her off a quick text and ask her to join him. He took the stairs and less than a minute later he was striding across the lobby into the bar. It was late, and he knew it was unlikely that the kitchen would still be serving dinner, but he might be able to get them to make him something light.

He sat at the counter and ordered a glass of red wine. Red wine would help him sleep. The bartender said he would ring the kitchen to see what he could do about some food. Nyah took his drink and found a table over by the window. He sent a text to Lana to see if she wanted him to order her something. The message delivered straight away but she left him unread, meaning she was still on her call to Peter. And, again, the thought irritated him.

He settled back in his seat and turned his attention to the street outside. The rain had picked up again and the few people braving the elements were darting for shelter under raincoats and umbrellas. The hotel was built onto the street so that when you walked through the front swivel door, you stepped out onto the footpath. When commuters hurried past his window, he could just about reach out and touch them, they were that close. His little sister was out there somewhere and he wondered whether she was alone, or running from something, or being kept somewhere against her will. He knew she was strong, and well able to look after herself, but what he didn't understand was why she wasn't contacting him. Her lack of communication was causing him the most concern. If she was OK, why not call him and just tell him that? Then he would leave her alone to go through whatever it was she was dealing with. Her silence frightened him the most.

A couple hurried into the bar. They seemed to be roughly in their late 20's, maybe early 30's, or thereabouts. They appeared youthful anyhow. Their clothes were business-like, as though they had just come from the office – two work colleagues out for a drink. The woman pulled her long dark hair over her shoulders and pushed her fingers through the wet strands. The man gently held a hand on her lower back as they advanced towards the bar. He leaned in to say something as he helped her slip her arms out of her wet coat. She threw her head back and grinned up at him. He touched the side of her face with his thumb, his eyes twinkling, a suggestive smile playing at the corner of his mouth. Maybe not work colleagues after all – boyfriend and girlfriend, man and wife, or possibly an affair. They were close, whatever the relationship. Lana had done the same thing to Nyah not that long ago – caressed his skin with her thumb. He wondered now if he had imagined it, their closeness and their intimacy. Bloody Peter, why did he have to ring when he did?

Nyah's phone pinged on the table. He flipped it over and checked the screen.

One of Clara's flatmates had replied on Snapchat, finally. He unlocked his phone and clicked on the message.

Hey, Nyah. Sorry, but haven't heard from Clara, do u know where she is?

He could see she was online, so he quickly typed back.

Our mam paid her a surprise visit the other day, in Belfast. Found out she had the baby.

He held his breath, watching the three dots moving. How would she respond? And then she was typing again ...

Clara didn't know how to tell you. I'm glad you finally found out. Is she coming back to Belfast? It's just that we need to know if she wants to keep her room in the flat.

Is she coming back? He wished he knew the answer to that himself. So Clara *did* have a baby.

I don't know, Emily. Clara just disappeared, leaving her mam and the baby at the train station in Limerick. We know she took a flight to London last night, but we can't find her. She hasn't been in touch. Have you heard from her at all?

Now she was typing back straight away.

Are you serious? She hasn't texted me. I was in lectures all day and then I went to the library to study. Becky went home for a few days to visit her family so it's just myself here at the flat. I thought it quiet when I got home but, to be honest, the baby has changed Clara's routine so it's not weird that she wasn't up when I got in. The door to her bedroom is closed most of the time, so I assumed she went to bed, to catch up on sleep. London? What took her over there?

Nyah was frustrated. He wasn't learning anything from Emily about Clara, other than the fact that the girl knew about the baby.

We don't know. Look, if you hear from her let me know OK?

He was about to close out of Snapchat when he noticed the three dots dancing across the screen. And then she was typing.

How do you know she went to London?

He typed: **I have a friend who works as a private investigator. She got hold of the CCTV footage at the train station and then the airport. We know she took a flight to London last night. We followed her over here, but we haven't been able to find her yet.**

Again, the three dots.

You are in London now? Where are you staying?

What did it matter where they were staying?

The Dormund Hotel in Pimlico. We think she is in Pimlico. It's a long story. Anyway, gotta go. If you hear anything, Emily, get in touch OK?

He got a thumbs-up from his last message, signalling an end to their conversation. Emily hadn't told him anything he didn't already know. Still, he saved the messages so they wouldn't be deleted. He would show them to Lana whenever she decided to come down to the bar. His sandwich, plain ham on brown bread, arrived – nothing too special. But he was ravenous. He couldn't remember when he had last eaten, so he dived right in. He was on his last bite when his phone pinged again. It was Lana, announcing that she was calling it a night and that she would see him in the morning at breakfast. He pushed aside his disappointment. Though what did he expect from her at this time of night? They had been moving around all day, from pillar to post, and it was after midnight now. Turning in and getting a good night sleep was probably a smart idea. Still, he couldn't help but feel let down. One minute they were all over each other, and the next he was eating a bland sandwich alone at the bar. He finished his drink and ordered another.

CHAPTER 19

Jenny teased open Lucy's lips with the teat of the bottle, but the baby kept pushing against it with the bud of her tongue. She has had enough, Jenny thought, just over three ounces. She tried to remember what amount of milk babies Lucy's age should be drinking, but it had been so long ago that she couldn't recall.

She placed the half-empty bottle on the kitchen counter and rubbed her eyes with the palms of her hands. She was shattered – the night had been fretful. She had tried to sleep, but she had been woken several times drenched in sweat, the burning sensation of a hot flush on her skin as it crept up her body. The only release was to turn her pillow over and pull the duvet away from her body until she cooled down. After a while she would snuggle back down under the duvet, until a short time later it would start all over again. And every time she woke, for a second her life reverted back to two days earlier, when Clara was in college in Belfast, Nyah was at work and everything was right with her world. And then, she would remember. Lucy had only woken twice for a feed thankfully. She had slurped her milk for about twenty minutes and then pulled away from the bottle.

Of course, there was also the piece of paper with the phone number and the name of the pub niggling at her brain. The same pub Nyah was going to visit with Lana, but for the life of her she didn't know where Clara had got the information from. She groaned when she thought about her meeting with Megan later in the morning. She wondered what the woman wanted to talk to her about. She guessed it had something to do with her hugely successful daughter Alexis and, if so, she was going to get rid of her as fast as she could.

She checked her watch. It was just after seven in the morning. She wondered if Nyah was up yet. She needed to talk to him as soon as possible.

He answered after a few rings, his voice scratchy, full of sleep.

"I woke you? Sorry, Nyah, it's Mam. I thought you might be up."

"Hi, Mam, it's OK. I didn't sleep very well last night."

"That makes two of us. What did you learn from your visit to the pub?"

He sighed. "Nothing really – the Old Rose was a dead end."

Really? Jenny didn't think so.

She was about to tell him about her find – the piece of paper – when he continued: "I'm meeting Lana for breakfast shortly, to plan the day. I hope we find Clara soon. My boss is going to lose his rag if I don't get back to work." His tone sounded quite flat, much less enthusiastic than the day before. "Emily got in touch last night but she doesn't know anything about where Clara might have gone. The other flatmate, Becky, is gone home for a few days so that's why you didn't meet her. I don't think you met Emily either?"

"No, I wasn't there long enough. According to Clara she was away for the night." Lucy's head found its way into the crook of Jenny's neck and she felt her warm breath against her skin. The milk had done its job and the baby was fast asleep. "Hang on a minute, Nyah. I've something to tell you but I must lay the baby down."

"OK."

She put her phone down and carried Lucy into the bedroom. She gently laid her down in her cot and covered her with her blanket. Then she picked up the piece of paper with the phone number from her locker.

She went back to the living room and picked up her phone.

"You still there, Nyah?"

"Yeah."

"OK. I found a piece of paper with a phone number last night, with '*The Old Rose Pub*' written beside it."

"*What? Where?*"

She explained as she left the living room and moved into the bathroom.

"So how did she get that?" he asked, his voice full of trepidation.

"I dread to think." She could hear a tap running in the background and the sound of Nyah brushing his teeth.

"Sorry, Mam. Just brushing my teeth."

"I can hear."

She heard him spitting into the sink. She waited.

"Listen, Mam, I gotta get ready to meet Lana. I'll tell her about your find. I'll call you in a while. I promise to keep you updated." He sniffed. "Love you."

And he was gone.

She looked into the mirror above the sink and barely recognised the woman staring back at her – the skin under her eyes was puffy and red and her hair was matted around her head. She turned on the tap, splashed cold water onto her face, and set about applying creams to fill in the creases in her skin. It didn't make much of a difference and she knew she would be no match for Megan's perfection this morning. She ran a brush through her hair as she walked into the kitchen to make coffee.

She had the phone number of the pub in her pocket and she was tempted to dial, but fear gripped her. She didn't know who might answer the phone. And, anyway, what would she say? She checked the clock on the wall: it was just after eight. She wondered if Megan was free now. She would text her and say she had an hour if she wanted to pop over, that her boss had called her in to work early. If the woman couldn't make it, then that would suit her. She typed a quick text and pressed send. She had just filled the kettle when her phone beeped. It was a message from Megan announcing right now worked for her and that she was on her way. *Shit.* The woman must have been sitting beside her phone. So much for getting away with not talking to her, but at least Lucy wouldn't wake. There would be a good two hours before there was any sound from the bedroom. With any luck.

She carried her coffee to the bathroom and brushed her teeth. She applied a light tinted moisturiser and pencilled her lips with a pale-pink liner. She was relieved to see that the puffiness around her eyes had reduced somewhat. She rarely wore make-up during the day, but she was sure that Megan would arrive with a full face on, so she wanted to cover up any blemishes – the less Megan had to observe and comment on, the better.

She quickly dressed in jeans and a white T-shirt and eased her feet into a pair of pale-blue sliders. No doubt, Megan would be dressed for a lady's lunch, or an evening meal in a fancy restaurant, but Jenny had to draw the line with her outfit. She was comfortable in jeans and T-shirts, and comfort gave her confidence.

Her mind was drawn back to a time when she was first dating Danny. There had been a gig in one of the student bars in Galway and everyone in her year was going. She had only been seeing Danny for a short time, just a few dates here and there really. They weren't officially going out or anything, but at the same time everyone who knew her was aware they were together. Jenny had arrived to the gig with her two friends, having got dressed in one of the girl's houses. They had knocked back a few shots while they were getting ready and everyone was in flying form. Nobody could afford to buy alcohol in the bars back then – student grants didn't go too far. So, if you fancied something stronger than a soft drink, you had to bring your own. This had been the norm at the time. Nobody was bothered by it and in fact it was expected that students would carry bottles of liquor in their bags. Jenny was well on her way to getting drunk, dancing with her friends, when Danny arrived in with his arm around another girl. They had their backs to the dance floor so Jenny couldn't see who it was until the girl turned around and flashed a smile. It was Megan, dressed in a short black leather miniskirt, knee-high boots, and a low-cut lacy red top, her blonde hair backcombed high up on her head. Jenny had heard something about Megan attending some third-level institution in Galway, but she had never met her on her own campus.

Megan grinned at Jenny and strutted onto the dancefloor, air-kissing her on both cheeks, before holding her back at arm's length.

"Jenny, honey, I've been looking for you! Where have you been hiding this gorgeous creature?" She gestured towards Danny who had joined them on the dance floor. He put his arm around Jenny's shoulders as Megan watched. "You two make a lovely couple. Next time you get home to see the family, bring him with you! Gotta go!"

She kissed them both and left the gig, but not before Jenny caught the look she gave Danny. Jenny had asked him how he knew Megan and where they had met but, typical Danny, he had just shrugged and said something about bumping into her in the bar. They knew a mutual friend and got talking and then realised that they both knew another person: Jenny. He told Megan he was going to meet Jenny and she asked if she could tag along. He had then teased Jenny, said that she was jealous, and a few minutes later she was in his arms and forgetting all about Megan.

Jenny heard a car pull up at the back of the house. She pushed the memory aside as she moved quickly to open the back door in case a loud knock woke Lucy. She would have some explaining to do if the baby started crying.

Megan was climbing out of her silver car and, true to form, she was dressed up for an event – a camel flared trouser suit with a crisp white shirt peeking out from under the collar and cream stilettos. Her make-up and hair looked like she had just stepped out of a salon. *How did the woman do that? At eight in the morning?*

As she approached Jenny, the scent of an expensive perfume filled the air. She leaned in for a kiss, though she barely touched Jenny's cheek. The fragrance nearly suffocated her.

"Jenny, darling, thank you for agreeing to see me."

"No problem, Megan. Listen, I have to leave for work soon so what's this about?"

"Let's go inside."

Megan made for the back door kitchen, her heels crunching on the gravel drive.

Jenny scowled. The woman could be so dramatic. This was going to be painful – she just knew it.

CHAPTER 20

Lana poured from the coffeepot into a cup and stirred. She blew on the hot drink before taking a sip. She needed this – her head was heavy and she felt a little jittery, as if she wasn't fully in control of her own body. She had woken during the night with a pounding headache, her throat dry and, what's worse, she didn't have anything to drink in her room and not even a painkiller in her bag. She had gone into the bathroom and splashed cold water on her face, cupping some into her hand to fill her mouth, and it had helped a bit, but she had not slept when she climbed back into bed – the events from the previous day whirring around in her head. Peter's phone call, what had happened with Nyah before he rang ... and now she would have to face Nyah across the breakfast table. Christ, she had made a mess of things! Why couldn't she have resisted temptation with Nyah, like she had done all those years ago? It hadn't been easy then, but she had managed. Now, she had blurred the lines between them.

She took another sip of her coffee as she glanced around the breakfast room. It was still quite early and only a handful of guests were seated at the tables, drinking their juices, waiting to be fed, bleary-eyed from sleeping in a hotel bed.

She wondered whether they would find Clara today. Hopefully, they would, and then she could head home. Home to where though?

When Peter had called the night before, he asked her to come down to Castle Cove at the weekend. So they could *talk*. He wanted to "explain everything". He said, once he told her the truth, she would understand.

She couldn't see how she would ever understand. She couldn't see what there was to explain. She had trusted him and he had betrayed her.

She sensed movement at the door of the breakfast room and when she looked up, she saw Nyah standing there. Her heart skipped a beat, and she pressed her hands into her lap to stop them from shaking. *Calm the fuck down, Lana,* she told herself, it was just a moment between two adults, happens all the time. She straightened up her shoulders and planted a smile on her face as he approached. He looked unsure of himself too. She decided to take the lead.

"Coffee? It's still hot."

He looked relieved. He sat and she poured. She glanced at his demeanour as he added milk to his cup and stirred. His face was drawn and he had dark circles under his eyes. She guessed he hadn't slept any better than she had.

"Nyah, I just want to explain ..."

He held up his hand for her to stop. He gave a small smile and shook his head. "We just got carried away in the moment, Lana. There's nothing to explain, honestly. I'm good, we are good."

She relaxed a bit. She was relieved by what he said. Although somehow she didn't feel any better. She observed him over the rim of her cup as she took a sip of her coffee.

"Did you stay long in the bar?"

He shook his head. "Just a couple of drinks and a sandwich – it was pretty basic." He took his phone from his pocket. "I heard back from Clara's flatmate in Belfast – Emily. These are the messages she sent last night."

He handed his phone to Lana and she scrolled through the messages.

"She doesn't seem to know anything," he said. "Though she is confirming that Clara had a baby."

She looked up at him. "Didn't you ask her about the photo? About the girl with the tattoo on her arm?"

"No, didn't think, sorry."

"And the one taken at Christmas where her stomach is completely flat?"

"No, I didn't."

"How could you forget?"

"I guess I was a bit ... distracted." He flushed a little as he held out his hand for the phone. "I'll send her off a quick message now."

She handed him the phone, embarrassed. She had forgotten that he had dealt with Emily directly after the bedroom incident.

He sent the message and put down the phone. "There's something else. Mam just called. She found a piece of paper inside Clara's favourite childhood book. The Old Rose pub is written on the paper along with a phone number."

"*What?*" Lana leaned forward.

"She said it fell out when she was flicking through the book. Clara hasn't been home since last summer, Lana."

"So she knew about the pub way back then!"

“She did.”

”No indication how?”

“None.”

“This is a definite lead. I’d already decided we should go back to the pub today – maybe just to sit in the car and watch. Clearly, something is going on there. If we get lucky, we might see Clara going in or out.”

“Right. That’s a plan.” He hesitated, then said, “Look, Lana, my boss – he’s calling me every five minutes. I can’t stay here in London indefinitely. I have to go home.”

“Don’t worry, Nyah. I’ll stay on.”

“But ...” He shifted in his seat. “Money, your fee, Mam and I ...” He looked away, embarrassed. “We are not exactly loaded. I mean, we can pay you for your time these past few days, but if this goes on any longer I don’t know what we’re going to do.” He sighed. “I thought we would have found Clara by now ...”

Lana reached across the table and touched his hand, “Nyah, you’re an old friend – don’t worry about money, please.”

He glanced down at her hand on his. “You’re a professional – you have to be paid for your time.”

There was something odd about his tone. Cold almost. *You’re a professional.*

“Clara is your sister. I want to help you find her. So, don’t worry about money, OK? Besides, I just finished a case, so the timing is good.” She withdrew her hand just as a waitress approached. She was glad of the distraction – things were definitely awkward between them this morning.

"Excuse me? Are you Nyah Doyle?"

Nyah looked up, surprised.

The waitress had an envelope in her hand. Lana caught the admiration in her eyes as she looked at Nyah. He didn't seem to notice.

"The receptionist asked me to give you this, sir."

Nyah regarded the small white envelope with Nyah Doyle printed on the front in block capitals.

"Did someone hand it in?" he asked.

The waitress shook her head. "I don't know, sir. The receptionist came to the door and just asked me to give this to you." She handed the envelope to Nyah and left.

Nyah frowned at Lana. "What could this be?"

Lana shrugged. "Open it." She felt dread creep up her body. This was alarming. Nobody knew they were here in Pimlico except for Nyah's mam and the people they met last night – Audrey and the guy who had beaten the crap out of Nyah. But none of them knew the name of the hotel they were staying in. Had they been followed? She glanced nervously around the room.

Nyah opened the envelope and pulled out a piece of folded paper. Turning it over, his face paled.

"What is it, Nyah?"

He passed the paper across the table.

Two words were written in capital letters.

GO HOME

CHAPTER 21

Jenny closed the door leading into the kitchen as soon as she entered the house. Megan was standing by the sink, a framed drawing in her hand. She turned as Jenny entered the kitchen.

"I remember this."

Clara had been quite creative when she was small and she loved animals. She was always drawing creatures – squirrels, robins, horses, insects, her face set in concentration. When she was in sixth class there had been a competition at the school where each child had to draw or paint a picture. The theme: **Our World**. Clara had been studying the book *Animal Farm* at the time and she drew her inspiration from that. She had drawn a farm with her favourite animals on the right-hand side of the page. She had pigs and sheep and horses and dogs and cats. All creatures great and small living together happily grazing, drinking water and playing together. On the left-hand side, she had painted what could only be described as a portrayal of the opposite of a happy farm – the same animals, but this time with grotesque features in agonising pain, tongues hanging out, eyes red. Some were lying flat on the ground, with blood streaked around their corpses. It was a masterpiece of imagery and Clara had won first prize for her originality. There had been a presentation by the principal after the end-of-term musical and all the parents were there. Clara won a top-of-the-range painting set, brushes, easel and a selection of colours, along with two plain canvases. The school had framed the picture and Jenny had placed it on the windowsill in the kitchen. It had been there ever since.

"Oh yes, *Animal Farm* through Clara's eyes," Jenny said.

When Jenny first saw the painting, she had gently tried to get Clara to talk about what had inspired the dark images. Clara had just shrugged and replied, "*They – they just came into my head*." She was going through a young adolescent phase at the time. Jenny had hoped the disturbing images had just sprung from hormones swimming around inside Clara's young body, preparing for change, It wasn't long after Megan's son Luke had died and Jenny had been worried about how Clara had been affected by that.

Sometimes Jenny felt bad that she found Megan so annoying. The woman really had been through a terrible time.

"Not all of them are living in harmony," said Megan. "I wonder what she meant by the divided images? What was she – eleven or twelve at the time? She really is very good, you know. Actually, it's surprising that she didn't pursue Art in college. What did she do again? A degree in something to do with marketing, wasn't it?" She placed the drawing back on the windowsill and folded her arms across her chest as she pressed her hip into the kitchen counter. "Maybe if she had taken Art, she wouldn't have dropped out." She smiled sweetly.

Jenny pushed down her annoyance. Megan had a knack for giving a compliment and taking it back at the same time. Megan, the proverbial mean girl. Jenny remembered her mother telling her one time – "*Jenny, there are mean girls everywhere – you just have to figure out a way to look through them. Stay true to yourself, love. The trash will eventually take itself out.*"

"Coffee? Or tea?"

"Tea, please, no milk, no sugar."

"Have a seat."

Megan pulled a chair out and sat at the kitchen table. She played with a coaster as she watched Jenny fill the teapot before placing it on a tablemat.

"I like what you've done with the kitchen, Jenny. It's very – retro or something. Isn't that what everyone is striving for nowadays? Out with the new, in with the old. I bet you drink your tea out of jam jars." She laughed at her joke.

Jenny ignored the jibe and fetched two mugs, placing one in front of Megan. "See? No jam jars." She sat and poured. "So, what brings you here, Megan?"

Megan hesitated as she moved the coaster around the table with her forefinger. Her nails were painted a bright red and had been shaped with a flat square edge. "It's kind of awkward, Jenny – give me a minute ..."

Jenny glanced at the clock on the wall: it was heading towards half past eight. She'd have to pretend to leave soon, having told Megan she'd been called in to work. She poured milk into her own mug and stirred. "Would you like a biscuit with that, Megan?"

Megan shook her head. "God no. I never eat in the mornings. In fact, I usually don't eat until lunchtime. I know that's probably not the way to do it. What is it they say, breakfast like a king, lunch like a –"

"Megan – I hate to rush you but I have to leave for work shortly. So say what you have to say. Look, if it's about Clara and college, I know she has taken some time out. So, even though I appreciate your concern, you're not telling me anything new, OK?"

"It's not that, Jenny. Well, Clara does have something to do with my visit, but it's not about her leaving college – that's not why I'm here."

What was it then, thought Jenny. *The baby?* "Go on."

Megan performed a little ceremony, playing with the coaster, her expression changing, inhaling before she spoke. "My Alexis will be doing her Co-op in Galway – remember I told you? She's home at the moment, waiting for her placement."

Jenny nodded, frowning.

"A few weeks ago, she got a call from Clara. She was asking her for help. She said she was desperate, and that she couldn't tell you."

She did know about the baby! Jenny's heart began to pound. "What kind of help?"

"She wanted a car."

A car! Jenny tapped the side of her mug. "That's ridiculous. Clara doesn't even drive – what would she want with a car? And, if she did, why would she ring Alexis?"

"Because my husband runs a car dealership, Jenny, and she wanted my daughter to take one from his garage. Most of those cars are off the road, untaxed and uninsured. And untraceable. Or, the owner is trying to move it on."

"But Clara was in Belfast. How could that work?"

Megan shrugged. "I don't know."

Jenny laughed incredulously. "That's ridiculous, Megan. And what would Clara want an 'untraceable' car for, in any case?"

Megan glanced over at Clara's drawing on the windowsill. She appeared to be about to say something else and then she lifted her cup and drank some tea.

"What? Tell me, Megan?"

"She said Clara was acting weird ..."

"What do you mean 'weird'?"

"Panicky weird. Clara told Ally that she might have to leave Ireland soon and she couldn't explain why, but it was important that she had transport and that Ally was the only person that could help her." She reached a hand across the table and placed it over Jenny's.

Jenny instinctively pulled her hand away.

"I'm sorry, Jenny, I know you don't want to hear any of this about your daughter, but I thought it only fair that I tell you. Yesterday, when I met you with the baby – your boss's niece?"

Jenny nodded.

"You looked worried, and I wanted you to have some idea about what's been going on with Clara. I mean, let's face it, even though they've left school, it doesn't stop us worrying about them, does it? We probably worry now more than ever."

Jenny gave a half smile at that. Megan knew all about worrying about her children. She had lost her own son when he was only a child himself, barely fifteen years of age. Alexis had been the only member of the family at home at the time of the accident. She was sitting beside him, holding his hand when her mother arrived back from work. Considering what Alexis had been through, it seemed she was quite well adjusted. According to her mother, she was the perfect daughter.

Jenny tried to process what Megan had just told her. Clara had been quite friendly with Alexis in primary school. But their friendship ended after Luke's death. The following year they moved on to secondary school and started to mix with different groups of friends. Jenny remembered that she had never really seen Alexis with pals at school events. The girl always seemed to skitter around the various activities on her own. So why would Clara go to Ally for help, of all people? Instead of her mother? Or even Nyah? If Clara didn't want to talk to her mother about her problems, why didn't she talk to her brother? They had always been so close. She could feel Megan watching her.

"What did Ally do?"

"What do you mean?"

"About the car? I assume she didn't steal a car for my daughter out of her father's garage?"

Megan half laughed. "Of course not. Ally would never do anything like that."

There it was again, the smugness. Ally the perfect child. This woman was looking for a slap. *Get a hold of yourself, Jenny. Keep your powder dry.* "How did you know about the car?"

"Ally told me, of course. She tells me everything."

Jenny stood and started clearing the kitchen table.

"Right, well, thanks for coming over, Megan. I appreciate it."

Megan stood and pushed her chair under the table. "Can I do anything for you?"

Jenny opened the back door, making it clear their conversation was over.

"How is Clara, by the way?" Megan asked. "I hope she's OK?" She looked towards the closed door that led to the rest of the house. "You said she'd come home? When she dropped out of college?" Her face was full of concern.

Jenny didn't believe one wrinkle of it. "Yes," she said. "But she's gone back to Belfast now. She has ... other choices." She could tell that Megan didn't believe her.

Megan nodded. A look of something strange crossed over her face. Disbelief? Pity?

Take control, Jenny, and get rid of the woman. "I appreciate you coming over, Megan. I will handle things from here."

Megan laid a hand on Jenny's arm as she exited the kitchen, a sympathetic smile on her face. "I'm here if you need me."

She walked across the gravel and sat into her car.

Jenny hated the woman even more than before, if that was possible. The bloody cheek! Though she feared that Megan might have been telling the truth or at least part of the truth. Someone had collected Clara from the train station and dropped her to the airport. Could it have been Alexis?

Jenny slowly let out a breath as she held on to the kitchen door, watching the silver car reverse and disappear around the corner of the house. What the hell was going on now? Just when she thought things could not get any more confusing. What was her daughter up to? Asking Alexis to steal a car from her dad's car dealership!

Her thoughts were interrupted by the sound of a baby crying. Good girl, Lucy, she thought. At least the baby hadn't let her down. Closing the kitchen door, she went to tend to her granddaughter.

CHAPTER 22

"Nyah, come and sit down. We can work this out – come on."

He had been pacing Lana's room ever since they had come upstairs after receiving Clara's note. Assuming it was Clara's.

He stopped and gestured with the piece of paper in his hand. "This is from my sister. I'm sure. She was here, in this hotel. Maybe last night. Maybe looking for me. *What the fuck?* Why didn't she just call me? It would have been much easier than coming to this hotel."

"If she called you she would have had to talk to you, Nyah. Would have had to explain. Clearly, she doesn't want to."

"If only I hadn't been so ..."

He didn't need to finish – she knew what he meant. If only he hadn't been in Lana's room, distracted and doing other things, he might have been downstairs in the dining room or bar.

"You have no proof that the note was left at reception last night, Nyah. Reception didn't give it to you then or bring it up to your room. It must have been dropped in early this morning."

They had asked the receptionist what time the note had been delivered and who by, but the young man had come on duty just before eight to take over from the night receptionist and, by that time, the envelope was already lying on his desk. Lana had asked if they could look at the CCTV footage of the reception area, and the receptionist had called the duty manager for permission. She was at a meeting offsite, so hopefully she would be back soon and they could see for themselves.

Nyah continued to pace.

"What does this *mean*?" He ran his hand through his hair.

"Let's go through what we know. Clara is in Pimlico. She knows you are here. She has gone to the trouble of calling to your hotel to tell you to go home. To *warn* you to go home, which means she must know about your confrontation at the Old Rose pub last night. In some way, David Miller must be connected to all of this." She looked at Nyah. "And your dad."

He waved the paper over his head. "So does she think I'm just going to accept this message now? *Oh, sure, Clara, I'll just head home! You mind yourself. Get in touch when you're back in Ireland.*" He shook his head. "This is driving me crazy." He started pacing again.

Lana stood and stopped him mid-stride. She held on to his wrist.

"Nyah? *Nyah, listen to me. Stop*. I know you are upset but this is not helping. You have to take control. And if you don't think that you can, then, maybe you should ..." She stopped.

He narrowed his eyes. "Maybe I should what?"

She held his gaze. "Maybe you should go home. As you were saying, you have to get back to work anyway. I can continue the investigation on my own."

He shook his head. "No way! Not now."

"You are too close to this, Nyah. I mean, it's understandable. Clara is your little sister, but ..."

"I'm not leaving here without her, Lana."

He held her stare, but she didn't reply. If Nyah wanted to help, he needed to calm down and take control of his emotions.

He pulled his hand free and sat on the edge of the bed. "Look, you're right, I'm sorry. I need to focus. It is just a shock seeing that note. I mean, I cannot believe she was here in this hotel while I was upstairs sleeping. Why didn't she come to my room? Nobody would have known she was here." He glanced around the room. "Or phone me. This is fucking surreal, Lana."

"Nyah, as I said, clearly she doesn't *want* to talk to you or have to explain herself. Whatever's going on. She wants you to keep out of it."

"Why? Because it's a dangerous situation, that's why!"

"Possibly – but not definitely."

Nyah stared at the carpet then looked up. She saw fear in his eyes.

"I'm afraid, Lana. I'm really afraid. Up until now, I thought that maybe Clara's disappearance was just – I don't know – I thought that she might be involved in something, yes, but I didn't think it was anything serious, you know? And that maybe, whatever it was, she was in control of it. That I would find her and there would be a perfectly reasonable explanation for everything. I even thought, coming here with you, that I was overreacting, but not now ... since that note arrived, I've changed my mind."

The phone rang on the locker beside the bed. Lana picked it up. "Hello?" She nodded. "OK, we'll be right down." She replaced the receiver. "That was the guy from reception – his manager is back." She quickly grabbed her jacket, phone and wallet. "We look at the footage and we go from there. Once we know for sure that it was Clara who delivered the note and what time she delivered it – we can make a plan. OK?"

"I know it was Clara."

"Yes, but let's confirm that, OK?"

He nodded, though she could see that he wasn't going to humour her.

She reached up, held his shoulders and looked in his eyes. "Nyah, stay with me? We will find out what is happening to Clara, OK?"

He nodded.

"Right, now, let's go."

She left the room and pressed the button for the lift, Nyah following close behind. When they arrived on the ground floor there was a small queue at reception – guests were waiting to check out. Lana thought it could take a while if they stood in line with the others. She spotted a woman of African origin in a blue trouser suit, a gold label on her collar. The woman held a clipboard in her hand and she appeared to be cross-checking some luggage on a trolley with a porter. The porter nodded at the woman and pushed the trolley towards the lifts.

Lana approached the woman.

"Excuse me, are you the hotel manager?"

"Duty Manager." She smiled. "How can I help you?"

Lana extended her hand. "My name is Lana Bowen and this is my colleague Nyah Doyle. I work as a private investigator in Ireland. We requested to see the hotel reception's video footage from last night and this morning?"

The woman shook hands. “Ah yes. Nice to meet you both. My name is Pam Yeboah. Can you tell me what this is about?”

Lana glanced at Nyah. “Nyah here – his sister left Ireland two nights ago without warning or explanation and nobody has seen her since. We are all beside ourselves with worry for her safety. We believe she left a note for Nyah in reception either late last night or this morning. We desperately need to check the cameras. Please – it has been so awful for Nyah and his mother.”

Pam looked from Lana to Nyah. “Do you have any ID with you?”

“Of course.” Lana pulled her passport from her jacket pocket and Nyah did the same.

Pam checked the passports, her expression blank. She looked at Nyah. “Shouldn’t you call the police? Ask for their advice?”

Lana shook her head. “That would take time, as you know. Clara is already missing nearly forty-eight hours. If she was here last night, we just need to know that she is OK. Please?”

“I really think that you should call the police.”

“Please help us, Ms. Yeboah? Time is so important.”

Pam sighed and handed the passports back. “I have everything set up in my office. If you’d like to follow me?”

She turned and walked around the reception desk and entered a small room behind. Lana and Nyah followed.

She talked over her shoulder as she tapped on a keyboard. “I had a brief look from about thirty minutes after midnight. I saw you walk through the lobby?” She nodded towards Nyah.

They leaned forward and saw Nyah stroll past the reception area, his hands in his pockets.

"For some time after that the lobby remained empty. Nobody entered or left until one in the morning when a delivery driver arrived." She turned to Lana. "Deliveries are not supposed to come in through the main entrance of the hotel but, sometimes, if the kitchen doors are closed, they have no choice. And our kitchens are generally closed at that time. They have to get their sleep too." She rolled her eyes. "It's a constant argument between management and delivery staff. We try to keep the lobby clear of service staff but they just want to make their delivery and get on with their day." She pressed fast-forward and the screen moved at speed. "See? Here, someone comes in through the swinging doors and approaches the desk." She pushed her chair back from the screen. "The time is 1.14 am."

They watched the black-and-white monitor as the revolving doors began to move, and then a shadow emerged and advanced towards the reception area. The figure was of slim build and dressed in black – a hoodie and leggings or jog bottoms that appeared loose, as if they were too big for their owner. The hoodie was pulled down low over the person's face. It could be anyone.

Pam glanced at them. "I know. You can't see who it is from this footage – but look at this." She clicked on the keyboard and the screen changed position. This time, the view looked out from behind the reception area. The figure approached the desk and handed over an envelope. The head was bent low, a strand of blonde hair escaping from under the hood. The receptionist appeared to ask a question and the person under the hood looked up. Lana heard Nyah's intake of breath from behind her. There was no mistaking who it was. Lana remembered the photo images and also the young girl she had met years earlier, and the secret she had told her: "*You can't tell Nyah – promise me, Lana – he can never know about Animal Farm.*" The white-blonde hair hadn't darkened all that much, though it was not as light as it was when she was a young girl. The piercing blue eyes were exactly the same. The person on the screen was Clara.

"Do you have any cameras outside the building?" Nyah asked.

Pam nodded. She stopped the video, clicked a few buttons and the view on the screen changed to the street outside the hotel. In real time. People were walking up and down the path, heading to work or school or the shops. Traffic appeared busy. Cars and heavy goods vehicles barely moved on the road outside. A taxi pulled up at the front entrance of the hotel and an elderly couple climbed out and stood to the side as they waited for the driver to take their luggage out of the boot. The porter they had seen earlier in the lobby walked out to greet them with his trolley. The couple were smiling and chatting as the porter said his hellos, delighted to be on their holidays for a few days no doubt. It was strange watching people living their lives on a screen, going through the motions when they were just a few yards away, oblivious to the fact that they had an audience.

"I'll go back, shall I? To say, midnight?" Pam asked.

"Midnight would be good, thank you," Nyah said.

Pam moved the icon back through the recording until a few minutes after twelve. The street was much quieter. The odd car passed by, but other than that the monitor was fairly lifeless. The minutes droned on and on and nobody spoke in the tiny office until a short while later a head popped around the office door.

"Sorry, Ms. Yeboah, I have a guest who wants to pay their bill with a voucher but the scanner is not accepting the code."

Pam nodded. "I'll come out now, thanks, Ralph." She turned to Lana. "OK if I leave you to it? Vouchers are the hotel's biggest enemy." She smiled. "I'll need the office back shortly to conduct some interviews." She glanced at her watch. "In about an hour. But you two are welcome to stay here and watch the recording until then." She made a grimace. "Interviews. I absolutely hate them."

Lana smiled and thanked her.

Nyah stood in front of the monitor with his arms folded across his chest, his face set. He hadn't taken his eyes off the screen, even though there still wasn't any activity, other than the odd set of car-lights passing up and down the street. He checked the time: it was about twenty minutes past midnight. He had still been in the bar at that time, paying his bill and getting ready to leave. He had been watching the couple who came in from the rain, their movement, their closeness. The two had left and he was alone in the bar so he had paid the barman for his sandwich and glass of wine and he ...

Suddenly there was movement on the screen. Someone, dressed in black, a hood pulled up over their head, entered the frame. The solitary figure walked a few steps along the path, stopped and leaned against the windowsill of the building across the road. Nyah swallowed, feeling a lump in his throat. He knew it was his sister and she had been just across the street from him a few short hours ago. And he had no clue. *Jesus*. Suddenly he was furious. He wanted to put his fist through the screen. What the hell was she playing at? He was right there. Why didn't she walk across the street and talk to him? Nobody would have seen them together, nobody! He was so angry with his sister for putting him through all of this, for putting his mother through all this uncertainty. Not to mention her baby daughter. That is, if it was really her daughter. What the hell was she trying to achieve by all this cloak-and-dagger carry-on? **GO HOME**. The words flashed in front of his eyes. As if that were possible now! Didn't she know him at all? Telling him to do something generally resulted in him doing the opposite. They used to joke about it. He was stubborn if he was anything. Clara had eventually copped on.

"Is that Clara?" Lana interrupted his thoughts, pointing at the screen.

He had almost forgotten she was there. Unexpectedly, he found that he was annoyed with her too. He was infuriated that they were here in this hotel, in a poky little office, watching videos of his little sister playing spy. And every so often, his phone vibrated in his pocket. He knew it was his boss trying to get through to him.

"Yes, it's Clara!" he snapped. "That's fairly obvious, Lana." He gestured towards the screen. "Are we not watching the same thing? I thought you were supposed to be a private investigator? My sister stood across the street and watched me through the window of a bar until I went up to bed. Then she waited another short while, probably to make sure I didn't come back down. And she delivered her note. And, where were you? Upstairs in your room on the phone to Peter in bloody Castle Cove, Peter who is *just an old friend!*"

He stopped when he noticed her expression change. What the hell was he doing? He could see by the look on her face that she was shocked by his outburst, and probably a little hurt, and he immediately regretted it. He waited for her to say something, but she didn't. Instead, she continued to watch the monitor without making a comment. He sighed.

"Lana, I'm sorry, I didn't mean ..."

She shook her head, her expression unreadable. "It's fine."

"No, really, I shouldn't have said that. I am just so angry with Clara. But that is no excuse to take it out on you. Whatever is going on with Peter, that's none of my business ..."

"Really, Nyah, it's fine. Let's just continue to watch until she leaves. If we get lucky, we might see if someone picked her up."

He hadn't thought of that. They watched in silence until, about forty minutes later, Clara pulled her hood closer around her face and crossed the street to enter the hotel. Nothing happened for the next few minutes. Then Clara came back out of the hotel and took a left. A moment later, she disappeared from the frame and that was the end of that. They couldn't see where she had gone.

Nyah sighed. He turned to Lana. "Now what do we do?"

"We go back to the pub." She turned and left the small office.

He followed her.

"Lana, I've been thinking about that. I'm not so sure it's a good idea. Remember what happened last night?"

"The bartender knows something. And your mother found a note in Clara's book with the pub's contact details."

"But we can't just go in there and ask him."

"No, but he has to finish his shift at some point, or start his shift, one or the other."

She walked around the reception desk and scanned the lobby before she spotted Pam talking to the elderly couple they had seen arriving in the taxi. The three were standing close to the lift. She turned to Nyah.

"We go back and this time I go inside and see if he is working. I didn't order drinks from him last night, so it is unlikely that he remembers me. If he is off, I come back out and we sit and wait for him to show up for work."

She crossed the lobby to Pam.

Her attitude was crisp, more formal with him, and he cursed himself for snapping at her. Lana had gone above and beyond the call of duty to help him find his sister and she didn't deserve his frustration. And what's more, he couldn't understand, entirely, why he had been short with her in the first place. He had no right. He caught up with her as she was thanking Pam for her help.

"My pleasure. I hope you find what you're looking for." Pam gave a small smile as the lift door opened and the elderly couple entered.

Lana went to follow them.

Nyah touched her shoulder and the lift door closed before she made it inside.

"Lana?"

She turned, a question in her eyes. To anyone who didn't know her, she appeared indifferent. A woman with a job to do, her expression one of focus. But he knew by the turn of her mouth, the look in her eyes, that she was hurt.

"I'm so sorry, OK? There are no buts, I shouldn't have spoken to you like that. I regret it and I am deeply sorry."

"Nyah, I told you – it's fine."

"No, it's not fine. I was wrong. I'm an idiot."

She held his gaze for a moment, and then she grinned. "Yeah, you are an idiot, Nyah. We all know that! Come on, we need to get moving."

He gave her a small smile, relieved. He'd omitted to say that he was also disappointed about last night, that their encounter had been cut short by Peter's phone call, but now was not the time.

"I don't have to go back to my room for anything," he said. "I'm good to go."

"OK. I'll go upstairs and grab my key card and meet you here in five minutes?"

He nodded at the seating area close to the hotel entrance. "I'll be right over there."

The lift doors opened again and Lana got in.

Nyah walked across the lobby, sat on the edge of one of the loungers and took out his phone. He tried his mother, but she didn't answer. He frowned. It wasn't like her – she usually sat by her phone. He fired her off a quick text, asking her to give him a ring. Then, he sent another one explaining that there was no real news to report, in case she got her hopes up. He didn't want to tell her about Clara visiting the hotel. Not yet. He let out a breath. *Jesus*, this was beyond maddening. Not for the first time he thought about what he would say to his little sister when she was standing in front of him, the words swirling around in his head. And not very kind words. He also couldn't shake off the feeling that he felt completely helpless because, not only was he not able to contact her, but there was nobody he could ask where she might be. He realised how removed from Clara's life he had become, and he blamed himself for that. He should have been checking in with her more often. Emily and Becky hadn't been any help. Emily still hadn't responded to his message about the girl with the swan tattoo and the Christmas photo.

He opened his Instagram account again and clicked on Clara's profile, scrolling down through her most recent photographs for probably the hundredth time. He didn't know what he might find that was different from before, but there was no harm in looking while he waited for Lana. He found the bunch of photos she had posted at Christmas, including the one where she was wearing the skimpy red dress with her two flatmates. As he scanned through the photos from that night, he found a picture of the three friends with another girl. This girl was not the one with the tattoo. He pinched the screen to look at her more closely. Narrowing his eyes, he felt like there was something familiar about her. He was sure he had seen her somewhere. But where? She didn't look particularly happy to have her photo taken, judging by the look on her face. The three girls, Clara, Emily and Becky were grinning for the camera, a stark contrast to girl number four who was looking away from the lens, her dark fringe hanging over her eyes, her expression moody and serious. Who was she and how had he missed her?

The lift doors opened and Lana came across the lobby towards him. She was dressed casually in her blue jeans and a black T-shirt and he thought she looked beautiful. She had tied her brown hair into a high ponytail with some loose tendrils falling around her face. She pulled her jacket on as she approached him, nodding towards the exit door.

"Ready?"

He put his phone back in his pocket and followed her down the stairs to the basement leading to the underground carpark.

CHAPTER 23

Jenny pulled in across the road from Skaters car dealership. The small unit was set in an industrial estate on the outskirts of town, with approximately fifty cars on display, all second hand. The kind of clients the dealership attracted were generally low-income earners, punters not too pushed on a car's aesthetics, the majority merely looking for a set of wheels to get around. Car dealerships like this one always did business – there were plenty of people who couldn't afford the fancier, more sophisticated models, but didn't have the knowledge to go about buying second-hand cars without some expert advice. That's where people like Megan's husband, Ned Carmichael, came in. He offered guidance and gave a guarantee – so, if the car fell apart, there was some form of comeback. For a few months at least. Jenny could see Ned, standing outside the entrance, his cheap navy suit hanging loosely over his skinny frame, his thinning grey hair combed across his forehead. His appearance was a stark contrast to that of his wife – the man had aged considerably since Jenny had seen him last. The years hadn't been kind. He pulled on his cigarette as he scanned the used cars, as if willing them to disappear from the yard. Megan's '*business development manager*' looked more like a worn-out salesman. He appeared nervous, his eyes darting around the lot. Jenny wondered why. But, then again, the man was married to

Megan – that surely came with a lot of pressure. It couldn't be easy if he was constantly trying to measure up. The woman must be a nightmare to live with.

Jenny tried to remember what Ned looked like when he first started dating Megan. Indeed, everyone in their wider friend group had been surprised by her choice of boyfriend. Up until that point, she had gone for lads with a real bad-boy image, the kind that would bring all the fun but were sure to break your heart. The likes of Danny Doyle would have been right up her street. But Ned was different. Ned was safe. And, dare she say it, Ned was boring. Megan probably thought Ned was the man that would bring her what she wanted – the house, the kids and the great job. So she could host her dinner parties and discuss the amazing people they knew, and the trips they had taken, recounting their remarkable lives. There was one tiny problem with Megan's plan. Ned looked like he was smart, but he wasn't actually that smart. His uncle owned Skaters car dealership and Ned had left school early and started working under the man's wing, learning the trade of selling cars. But the job was going nowhere, and it never would. When the uncle retired, Ned was sure that he would inherit the business, but he was wrong. Megan no doubt had thought that Ned would eventually inherit the lot. The uncle put Skaters Car Dealership up for auction. The winning bidder remained anonymous. The locals suspected a vulture fund, and there were other rumours too – that maybe a private buyer from overseas had invested. But nobody really knew. The new owner wanted Ned to continue his day-to-day routine, buying and selling used cars. So nothing changed. The whole operation appeared odd. A new investor generally made clever, lucrative changes, but not here. Time was standing still at Skaters.

Jenny considered how to approach Ned. She had Lucy in her chair, strapped into the back seat of her car. She glanced over her shoulder and smiled at her comatose state. The baby was drunk on milk. Jenny scanned the carpark and noticed that there were a few spaces by the front door. She could just leave Lucy in the car, couldn't she? With the window slightly open. That way she could have a chat with Ned outside, while still keeping an eye and an ear out for Lucy.

Jenny watched as Ned threw his cigarette on the ground and squashed the butt with his foot. Jenny was just about to start the engine when she noticed a black car pull into the yard. She decided to wait a bit. She didn't want to start into a conversation with Ned when there was the possibility of another customer vying for his attention. The driver slowed at the showroom entrance before continuing around the parked cars in the lot, coming to a stop almost parallel to Jenny's car on the other side of the fence across the road.

Ned was watching the car. He seemed a little uncertain. He peered over his shoulder before scanning the carpark. Then he checked his phone. He seemed to call something in through the door of the showroom and then he strode across the yard. Jenny watched as he smiled, leaning into the driver's window. He must know the driver, Jenny thought. She squinted as she tried to get a better look. Lucy made a noise in the back seat. Jenny turned to check on her, but the little girl was just kicking in her little chair. Jenny felt her heart swell. A few days ago, she hadn't even known this baby existed, but now she couldn't imagine life without her. She was falling hard for this child.

She turned towards the black car and watched as Ned walked around the rear of the vehicle before climbing into the passenger's side. He closed the door and leaned across to ... wait, was he *kissing* the driver? She watched as Ned's hand reached across to the driver. He appeared to be holding her head, a blonde head, and yes, he was kissing her. *What the fuck?* Megan had blonde hair. Maybe it was his wife. Wow, thought Jenny, still in love after all these years! She had clearly read that one wrong. But Megan's car was silver, wasn't it?

The lovers parted and the driver started the car, slowly moving around the back of the lot and not passing the front door this time. It drove out through the main entrance. A moment later, they passed by Jenny's vehicle. The driver of the black car was not Megan Carmichael.

Jenny's jaw dropped open. She was in shock. Was Ned playing away on his wife? It was almost laughable if it wasn't so tragic. His wife was drop-dead gorgeous, if in a very made-up kind of way. She was certainly glamorous. What the hell was Ned doing with another woman? He had always been the one punching far above his weight, hadn't he? Megan was way out of his league. Jenny wondered if Megan knew, or guessed what was going on, and right under her nose by the look of things.

Shit.

Now what? With Ned gone, she didn't have any reason to visit the garage. She glanced across the road towards the entrance of the showroom and noticed that the door was wide open. So someone must be running the shop. She nibbled on her fingernail as she pondered what to do. She could always check in with whoever was working the desk, make a few enquiries about a second-hand car. Ask about mileage and road tax, that sort of thing. Her own car was in fairly good condition, but she could say she was buying for her daughter and wanted to see what she could afford for her budget. And, while she was there, she could maybe sneak in a question or two about Ned, and see what his colleague had to say about him. Maybe Ned was taking a late lunch break and would be back soon.

She started the engine, crossed the road and entered the dealership. There was a row of cars parked opposite the front of the showroom and she found a space directly opposite the door and reversed in so that the car would be facing the entrance. She opened the back windows just a little to let some air into the car, just in case the baby got too warm. She got out and closed the door quietly. Glancing into the back seat, she could see Lucy was still fast asleep. Do this quickly, she told herself, before she wakes up.

She advanced towards the entrance, climbed the steps and went in. She could see there was a head bent over a laptop in the reception area, thick black hair pulled back on one side with a comb. Jenny had been quiet on her approach, and whoever was behind the desk didn't look up. There was nobody else inside the showroom. Jenny cupped her hand around her mouth and coughed. The head behind the reception desk sprang up.

Jenny's eyes widened. The girl behind the desk was Alexis Carmichael.

"Alexis?"

The pale complexion, the jet-black hair, a pair of kohl-painted eyes that peered out at Jenny from under a thick heavy fringe – the girl was nothing like her mother. Jenny again wondered how Megan had chosen Ned as her husband and how, together, they had produced this daughter. The three family members couldn't have been more different from each other. She tried to remember what Luke looked like, but couldn't remember him clearly. He was four years older than Alexis and Clara at the time of his death, and six years younger than Nyah. Alexis had just turned eleven if she remembered correctly – she had a party a day or two before at the house to celebrate. Jenny remembered collecting Clara and having to park a few hundred metres from the house, there were that many cars. A typical Megan Carmichael event.

Initially, Alexis looked startled when she glanced up at Jenny. After a moment she seemed to pull herself together, appearing more confident. She gave a small smile. "How can I help you?"

"It's Jenny, Clara's Mam. How are you, Ally?"

The girl blinked, her confidence slipping again, her eyes darting from Jenny to the door like a trapped animal searching for an escape route. "Oh, sorry, Mrs. Doyle, I didn't recognise you."

"How are you, Ally?" Jenny repeated, more softly this time.

Alexis gave a small smile. "I'm fine." She moved some papers around on the desk.

"Your mum said you're waiting for your Co-op placement in Galway?"

"Yes – I'm helping my dad out here at the moment."

"That's nice. For you both. So, *em* ..."

"Is there something I can help you with, Mrs. Doyle? My dad isn't here, but he shouldn't be long. He just left to do a test drive with a client. Test drives usually take only about thirty minutes."

So that's what he told you, thought Jenny. If Alexis knew that her dad had just sat into a car and kissed a woman who wasn't her mother, then she hid it well.

"Are you after a car? I don't know much, to be honest, but you're welcome to have a look outside while you wait?" She straightened her back – her confidence had returned.

"No, I don't want to buy a car, Alexis."

Jenny looked over her shoulder, out to where the car was parked. She could just about see the top of the car-seat inside the vehicle and she hoped that Lucy hadn't woken. There were no sounds of a baby crying at least.

She looked back at Alexis. The girl looked confused and a little guarded.

"Oh, right. OK, what can I do for you then, Mrs. Doyle?"

"I'm here about Clara. You were good friends when you were younger, before ..." Jenny didn't finish.

Something changed in Alexis's expression then. She blinked a couple of times as she bit her lower lip. She swallowed. "Yeah?" The word was barely audible.

"Have you seen her lately?"

The girl shook her head.

"Are you sure?"

Again, Alexis shook her head.

"You know she went to Belfast University?"

Again, a nod and a shrug, but nothing more.

"I went to visit her a few days ago."

Alexis shifted in her seat, clearly nervous now, her eyes darting all around the showroom.

"Do you know what has been going on, Ally?"

"Going on? What do you mean, Mrs. Doyle? I haven't spoken to Clara since our graduation. And even then, it was just a '*Hello, what are you up to in September*' kind of conversation, that sort of thing."

"Really?" Jenny took a step closer. "Alexis – did Clara phone you a few weeks back?"

"What? No."

"Looking for a car?"

Alexis laughed. She seemed to relax a little, amused by the question. "What? Why would Clara want a car? She can't even drive. And she was in Belfast. "

So Alexis knew this fact about Clara – that she couldn't drive. "I don't know, Alexis. You tell me."

"Why would I know?"

"Clara called you."

"No, she didn't!"

They heard a car pull up outside. A door opened and closed, and then the baby cried. Something changed in the girl's expression. *She knew about the baby.*

Jenny grabbed a piece of paper from the pad on Alexis's desk. She scribbled down her number and passed it to Alexis. "Clara is missing,

Ally. And I think you know where she might be. Phone me if you want to talk." She turned and left the showroom.

Ned was pointing at one of the cars in the yard, no doubt pretending to deliver one of his sales pitches. The woman behind the wheel laughed before she sped off. Jenny ducked into her car before he could see her. She watched as Ned headed up the steps towards the showroom, a big grin splashed across his face.

CHAPTER 24

They drove to the Old Rose pub, thanks to Carly on the satnav. Nyah watched Lana's hands as she gripped the steering wheel, her knuckles curved gently around the rim as she stared straight ahead. There was something very attractive about the way she drove a car, he thought. She appeared confident and in control as she moved through the streets of Pimlico.

A short time later, they pulled up across from the pub.

Lana turned off the engine as they both observed the building. The front door was open, but there was no sign of punters outside the bar at this time of the day. A lorry was double-parked, half-blocking the lane, the name of what must be a brewery painted in giant letters on the side. There was a hatch door open down the side lane, the same lane that was filled with drinkers the night before. A guy was passing barrels down the hatch to whoever was catching them in the cellar beneath, and judging by the expression on the guy's face, there was a conversation going on.

Lana rolled down the window.

"*Another one coming to ya ... passing it down now ...*"

The guy hidden from view shouted something through the hatch. They were coordinating the passing of beer barrels.

A few minutes later, the last barrel was handed down the hatch. The guy above ground took off his gloves and wiped his forehead. He peered down the hatch and held out a hand to help the receiver emerge.

"Thanks, mate."

Bingo! It was the barman from the night before. He leaned against the hatch door and lit a cigarette. The handler waved, before climbing into his lorry and taking off. The barman pulled on his cigarette as he looked at his phone.

"Time to go have a chat with our barman." Lana opened the door and quickly advanced across the street.

Nyah kept the window down so he could hear the conversation.

"Hi?"

The barman looked up. "Alright, love?"

"Yeah."

Lana said something Nyah couldn't hear. She was gesturing with her hand and then she reached into her pocket and pulled out her phone. She held the screen out to the barman. Suddenly, the guy appeared nervous. Nyah watched as he dropped his cigarette and got up to close the hatch door. Lana continued to talk with him. The barman appeared even more nervous than before. He glanced back at the pub and then again at Lana. He leaned in and said something to her and she nodded. Then he disappeared through the side door of the pub.

Lana crossed the street and climbed into the driver's seat. She pulled on her seatbelt and started the engine. Checking her mirrors, she moved onto the road.

Nyah shrugged. "Well?

"I got an address."

Nyah typed the address Lana received from the barman into the satnav. Carly told them they were fifteen minutes away from their destination. Neither of them smiled this time as the silky tones resonated inside the vehicle. The atmosphere had changed, the journey was more urgent. Lana followed instructions as she drove, the silence only interrupted by the voice giving directions. It was mid-morning and traffic was light as they'd missed the early-morning rush, which was no harm because it appeared the satnav was bringing them closer to the city centre. The buildings were taller and the commuters seemed to be walking a little faster as they zipped past the streets lined with shops, fronted by busy market stalls selling fruit and vegetables, trinkets and spices.

What Nyah noticed most as they continued along their route was the noise – there was a lot of noise. People shouting to each other or at each other, horns honking, taxis, trucks and buses stopping and starting. He glanced up at the tall buildings. Some had washing hanging out on their balconies or draped over railings. Music blared and rhythms changed as they moved through the city traffic. He couldn't imagine he would ever sleep if he lived in a big metropolis like this one. Admittedly, it wasn't exactly peace and tranquillity in his own flat back in Ireland, but the sound level had nothing on this chaos. There was an air of urgency, a sense of survival – a jungle in a city came to mind. He sighed as he stared out the car window, taking it all in.

He was in the shit.

His boss had called him that morning, and again Nyah hadn't answered. Up until now the man would ring off and then a few hours later he would call again. But this time was different. This time his boss left a message, a nasty message. He threatened to fire Nyah if he didn't return his call by the evening and Nyah knew the man could and would follow through with his threat – the small company was his own after all, and there wasn't exactly a HR department to support employees. Nyah decided he would ring him in the afternoon and come clean, tell him everything. Then surely he would have a heart and allow him some leave. His sister was missing after all. It wasn't an everyday occurrence. And if he didn't show a bit of humanity, then to hell with him. He would tell him where to stick his job. Maybe it was time Nyah found something new anyway. Having been away from his computer screen the past two days had made him realise how uneventful his life had become. He was bored. That's why he was drinking and socialising every night. He seemed to be living to work. Where was the logic in that? It should be the other way around – he should be working to live.

Nyah's head was spinning. The barman, Jeff, had told Lana that Clara had just started working in the Old Rose as a kitchen porter. He said she was staying in his flat in South West London and that she was a friend of his workmate, Bella, who was from Pimlico. Bella had been away for a while and returned to London about a month earlier. She had needed a place to stay so Jeff said she could hang out in his flat until she got herself sorted. They had dated for a while, on and off, whenever she was back in London, and a few days ago Bella asked if her friend Clara could sleep on the sofa. Just for a couple of days.

"So, tell me again what the barman said?"

"I told you already, Nyah."

"I know, but I want to hear it again, to make it clear in my head."

"I asked him if he could help me find a friend. I said it was really important that I find her, that her life depended on it. He said he didn't know how he could help, but he would try. I explained that I thought she had visited the pub, the Old Rose. So, I showed him Clara's picture. I knew by his face that he recognised her immediately."

"Yeah, but why did he give up the information so easily? Last night, I got the shit kicked out of me for asking about David Miller."

"That's the thing, Nyah. I think you asked for the wrong person. When you asked for David Miller, the barman panicked and thought you were fishing for information about the man. I would say he operates his business in the pub, something illegal, and that Jeff and the rest of the staff know about it and turn a blind eye. Probably the regulars know too. You heard what Audrey said about him – the guy's a sleaze."

"I should have listened to you."

She gave him a withering glance.

"Don't say I told you so."

She shrugged. "I didn't open my mouth."

"What else?"

"Just that the chef was throwing a tantrum in the kitchen because Clara hadn't turned up for work that morning. Jeff said that they had all gone back to his flat together the previous night when their shift finished. He left early this morning to sort out the beer kegs – he knew there was a delivery due in. Nyah, I told you all of this."

"I know, I know ... just, please, Lana? I need to hear it again."

"Jeff said his on-again off-again girlfriend Bella hadn't come into work either. The chef rang Bella, but she didn't answer and they don't have a number for Clara."

"So, it sounds like Clara was there last night, in the Old Rose. While we were out in the bar having a drink, she was in the kitchen cleaning up."

Lana kept her eyes on the road.

He cursed himself. He was an idiot. His little sister was on the premises while he was playing detective.

He glanced at the satnav – the device read that they were seven minutes from their destination. The traffic was getting heavier now and the drivers less tolerant. An underground train must have just pulled in as crowds piled out of a nearby Tube station.

"Did he say anything about why she chose to work in the Old Rose? I mean, it is a coincidence, you have to admit. That my dad's uncle drinks in the same pub. London is full of boozers."

"No, he didn't. But you're forgetting that Clara knew about the Old Rose last year, before she came to London. Looks like Clara must know David Miller."

"How?"

"I don't know the answer to that, Nyah. But I do think they must have been in contact."

"*Turn left. Your destination is on your left.*"

Lana slowed as she approached the turn, only to realise that it wasn't a turn as such, well, not for cars. It was a lane with dumpsters and scattered brown boxes. A large sign hung loosely from the redbrick building: **No parking.**

Nyah put his hand on the door. "Let me out while you find parking."

"No way, Nyah. We go in together."

"Hang on." He raised his voice. "Where is the nearest car park?" Carly told them there was one three hundred metres ahead.

Lana proceeded and they found the high-rise car park easily enough. As she pressed the button on the parking meter and grabbed the ticket, the barrier went up. The carpark was full on the lower floors but they found a spot a few levels up.

Lana locked the car and they took the stairs down to the ground floor, Nyah practically running.

"Nyah, hold up! We'll get there, OK?"

"Sorry, but I'm not risking missing her again. If that Jeff guy calls his girlfriend Bella, or whatever she is to him, well, it might scare Clara off."

They emerged from the carpark and walked swiftly side by side before turning into the lane with the dumpsters. About halfway along, there were a couple of steps in front of a black metal door with a box attached to the side panel. The box was lined with names and numbers and buttons.

"What number again?"

"He said Floor seven, Flat fourteen. She's a long way up. Hope there's a lift." She pressed the button and waited. Nobody answered.

"Press it again."

She pressed again and still nothing.

Then they heard steps inside and the door opened slightly. A young woman juggled with a double buggy as she tried to push the door open from the inside.

"Here, let me help you!" Nyah pulled the door back and lifted the buggy down the steps.

"Thanks, love. Whoever designed this bloody building wasn't thinking about prams and wheelchairs, were they?" She took off down the lane.

Nyah looked at the open door. "Let's go in."

He pulled back the metal door and they entered.

The cement floor that greeted them was uneven and flanked by damp walls, moisture streaming into the crevices. The surfaces were covered in graffiti – Nyah reckoned they hadn't seen fresh paint in a while. There was a stairwell to the right opposite a set of steel doors. Great, he thought, a lift. But there was a handwritten note stuck on the lift door – *OUT OF ORDER*. Nyah started up the stairs, and he could hear Lana behind. He was out of breath by the time he reached the fourth floor but he kept going, Lana's steps following closely behind.

On the seventh floor, he set off down the corridor, turning his head from side to side as he counted the door numbers.

Number 14 was at the end of the hall. The door was slightly ajar. He stood and stared, listening for any sound of movement inside. There was nothing.

He knocked hard on the door.

Nothing.

Lana joined him, gasping for breath.

Nyah pulled his jacket sleeve down over his fist and carefully pushed open the door. They could see immediately that the place was in a mess. A wooden coatrack blocked the hallway, a silver picture frame lay smashed on the carpeted floor, the glass broken into tiny pieces.

"Nyah, I'm calling the police. Don't go inside."

He watched as she took her phone out of her pocket and dialled.

Nyah ignored her order and took a step forward.

"*Clara?*" he called out into the empty hallway. "*It's me, Nyah!*"

He could hear Lana talking on the phone, rattling off the address.

He entered the apartment, turning the corner at the end of the hall that opened out onto an open-plan living area, a kitchen-cum-dining room with a grey sofa and TV to the left. The space was tiny and would have been cosy if it wasn't for the overturned furniture – a broken cup and plate shattered on the tiled floor, the kitchen cabinet doors pulled wide open. He noticed a high stool tucked under the kitchen counter and a black jacket, with a gold tiger design, draped over it. Nyah's heart skipped a beat. The jacket was Clara's. She had been wearing it before she left for college last September. He had teased her about it, called it tacky. He felt his heart hammering in his chest. Lana was shouting for him to come back outside the apartment but there was no way he could do that. Not now. It was as if his body wanted to keep moving.

Then he noticed dark stains on the floor behind the couch, a trail of blotches that stopped at a door at the end of the room. He froze in horror. He was sure it was blood. He carefully avoided the marks as he advanced towards the door. Taking a deep breath, he pushed it open with his elbow.

Swallowing hard, he called, "*Clara!*"

"*Nyah, don't go in there!*"

Lana's voice was more distant now, and he could hear sirens on the street outside as he slowly moved further into the room. There was a double bed, the covers tangled in a knot, clothes lying on the floor. Shoes, make-up brushes and a broken lamp were scattered precariously around the room. He narrowed his eyes as he followed the bloodstains to the edge of the bed. He could see blonde hair on the carpet on the other side of the bed. *Oh, fuck no, fuck no* ... He could hear the alarm in his own voice, inside his head, mixed with Lana's pleading with him to turn back. He ignored the warning. He advanced around the bed and then he saw her lying on her side, her left arm extended above her head, her nails painted yellow, her blonde hair covering the side of her face. Her body lay at an odd angle. She was dressed in denim shorts and a bright pink T-shirt and there was a lot of blood on the carpet around her head and neck.

He sat on the bed and dropped his head into his hands. *Breathe, Nyah*, he told himself, *breathe*. He lifted his head and something caught his eye. *What the fuck?*

Sometime later he was aware there were other people moving around him, a voice telling him to leave. A hand landed on his shoulder, pulling him off the bed. He left the room in a daze, glancing at Clara's jacket as he passed.

He found Lana in the hallway outside the flat. She searched his eyes. Her own were full of sympathy.

He turned away from her and vomited on the floor. Someone was rubbing his back. Someone else handed him a bottle of water and tissue paper. When he looked up again Lana was watching him, her expression full of sadness.

“Come on, Nyah, come with me.” She took a hold of his hand.

He shook his head and wiped his mouth. “It’s not her, Lana.”

She frowned up at him, a question in her eyes.

“It’s not Clara.”

CHAPTER 25

Jenny pulled into the carpark of her mother's care home, turned off the ignition and released her grip on the wheel. She noticed her knuckles were white and they felt stiff. Nyah had just phoned to tell her what had happened. At first, it was difficult to understand what he was saying. He sounded incoherent, upset, and then Lana had taken the phone from him and explained the situation about the girl. Bella. That poor girl ... and to think Clara was with her. She might have been murdered too. Suddenly, everything had become a lot graver. Up until now, Clara had disappeared and nobody, bar her family, had taken that too seriously. But now everything had changed. After she got off the phone to Lana, the first thing she had done was call the detective she had met at the station. He said he would drop by to see her at the house in an hour – that he had something he wanted to talk to her about. He was unforthcoming about what that *something* was, though his tone sounded serious.

Jenny leaned her head against the steering wheel and let the tears fall. Clara had been in a flat with a girl that was murdered. What was going on? She wiped her eyes with the sleeve of her top and glanced around the stunning gardens, bewildered. She felt stuck, rooted to the spot. She had no idea what she should do now. Her beautiful daughter was missing and probably in grave danger. Her hands were trembling and she gripped the steering wheel to steady them. She wished she could go back in time, forty-eight little hours, when her whole world revolved around a greenhouse. She had been vaguely bored with her life lately and the humdrum day-to-day routine. But now she would give anything for that normality. She had called her boss and explained that she wouldn't be in for the rest of the week. She didn't tell him the reason why, and in fairness to him he hadn't asked. Maybe she wouldn't go back at all. Like, if Clara didn't return, who was going to look after Lucy? She pushed the thought away – she wasn't going to think like that. They would find her. She pulled herself together. She didn't have long – that detective was calling and she didn't want to miss him.

She draped Lucy's bag over her shoulder and stepped out of the car. She unlocked the baby's car seat and carried her into the care home. It was mid-morning, almost twenty-four hours since she had been here last and once again there were no visitors around. Cliona was chatting away on the phone when she walked past reception. She gave Jenny a quick wave.

Jenny scribbled her signature on the sign-in sheet and walked down the corridor towards her mother's room. She passed the living area where a young girl playing an accordion was entertaining several residents. There was no sign of her mother amongst them.

She continued and found her in her room, sitting on her usual chair facing the garden, her favourite fluffy purple blanket draped over her legs. She was dressed today in a cream frilly blouse and a red cardigan, her white-grey hair curled around her face. Someone had applied rouge to her cheeks. Either that, or she was very flushed and the redness gave her a clownish appearance.

"Hi, Mam. Are you OK?" Jenny spoke softly, so as not to startle her.

Sue slowly turned her head. Her eyes looked brighter today, her expression easy and relaxed. She smiled at Jenny. Not a smile of recognition, a smile of welcome.

"Come in, dear. Are you here for the key?" She pointed at her bedside locker. "It's in my drawer over there beside the bed."

"What key would that be, Mam?"

Her mother tutted and shook her head. "The key, dear!" she scolded.

Jenny changed the subject. "Look, Mam? Look who's come to see you?" She placed Lucy's chair close to her mother's.

Lucy was awake for once, sucking away on her knuckle as her big eyes stared up at her great-grandmother.

Her mother's expression changed from surprise to delight as she gazed down at the baby girl. She clasped her hands together. "Oh, would you look at the little nipper!" She leaned over in her chair.

"Careful, Mam." Jenny reached out to stop her mother from falling over.

Her mam slapped her hand away. "I can manage, I'm not an invalid."

"I know that, Mam." She gently laid a hand on her mam's shoulder. "Do you want to hold her?"

Her mother looked confused by the question – but this was followed by a slow smile.

Jenny unlocked Lucy's belt and carefully lifted the child out of her chair.

"Sit back in your seat, Mam."

Her mam frowned and Jenny gently pushed her back into her chair with her free hand. She smoothed down the fluffy blanket and carefully placed Lucy into her mother's arms. Her mam smiled as she cradled the little baby, gently caressing her soft cheek with her thumb. Suddenly Lucy hiccupped, followed by the cutest gurgling sound.

Jenny looked on and felt the tears fill up her eyes, tears that had threatened to break for the last few days but she had stubbornly held them in until today. Today she was broken. Watching her mother, her favourite person in the whole world and the one person she could always count on, but now lost to a terrible disease, holding her great-grandchild with such love in her eyes. Three generations in the same room, yet the fourth one missing. The tears spilt onto her skin. She couldn't stop the floodgates even if she tried.

Her mother looked up at her, the confusion returning.

"What is it, Jenny?" she said in the softest voice.

Jenny stared at her mother in shock. *What did she just say?* She was overwhelmed. Her mother hadn't said her name in ages. She had resigned herself to the fact that she had two mothers. The one before the disease and the one after.

What the hell did it matter? She might as well tell her mam, offload what she was going through. The woman might be having a moment of clarity but it would be gone again soon. "Clara is missing, Mam. She gave me this baby, Lucy, and then she left. Nyah is gone to England to find her, somewhere in London. Pimlico."

She looked at her mam then to see if the mention of the area triggered something in her memory. It didn't appear to but her mother was watching her intently, her eyes focused.

Jenny's voice sank to a whisper. "Nyah found the flat she was staying in, but Clara wasn't there ... they found ... " She couldn't say the rest. She pulled a tissue out of her pocket and wiped her nose.

Her mam didn't interrupt – she just continued to observe her, a strange look in her eyes. She was biting her lower lip, a thing she used to do in the old days when she was deciding whether to let Jenny stay out late with her friends, or attend a dance.

"Why don't you try the key?"

Jenny sniffed. She had lost her again. She pushed away her irritation. "What key, Mam?"

Those moments of clarity, they were cruel almost.

Her mam pointed at her locker again, as she had done before.

Her mam became agitated and Jenny took Lucy from her, cradling the child in her arms. "She's probably hungry, Mam, I'll feed her." She rummaged in Lucy's bag and found a bottle of formula. She teased Lucy's lips and the baby sucked greedily as she locked eyes with Jenny. In a matter of minutes her lids became heavy with sleep.

Suddenly Sue grabbed her walking stick and began to push herself out of her chair. Jenny instinctively wanted to help her but she didn't want to wake Lucy.

"Be careful, Mam! Wait! Can I get something for you?"

Sue ignored her and shuffled slowly around the bed, before sitting on its edge. She then opened the top drawer of her locker and started moving things around inside.

"Are you alright, Mam?"

Her mother returned and sat back in her chair. She held out a closed fist, a strange look in her eyes.

"What is it, Mam?" Jenny frowned.

Her mother didn't reply. She unfolded her hand. A silver key attached to a keyring with the initial C dangled from her finger – *C for Clara.*

CHAPTER 26

"Why were you in Jeff Baker's flat, Nyah?"

Lana and Nyah had been escorted to the police station. For questioning, the police had said, just routine. They were sitting at a metal table in an interview room with a police officer standing at the door when a detective walked in.

Nyah hadn't spoken since they had arrived, not one word. He looked at Lana now, his complexion ashen. His eyes were red, his mouth moved but no sound came out. He was in shock – it's not every day you see a dead body.

Lana took the lead.

"It's a long story, detective. Nyah's sister, Clara Doyle, is missing."

He opened a file on his desk and started writing. "How long?"

"For three days. We know she travelled to England and ..."

"Excuse me – how do you know that?"

"I work as a private investigator back in Ireland. I have a source who works at the airport. He confirmed that someone bearing Clara's identity boarded a plane to Stansted airport three days ago." She looked him straight in the eye.

He frowned, probably not too impressed with Lana's methods. She tried not to roll her eyes – it was unlikely he played by the book all the time himself.

"Why Pimlico?"

Lana looked at Nyah. He was staring at his hands resting on his lap.

"Nyah has family connections in Pimlico. It was as good a place to start as any."

He wrote something down in his notebook. "What happened when you got to Pimlico?"

Lana filled the detective in on the series of events that had occurred over the last few days – the visit to the house of Nyah's granduncle's ex-girlfriend, Audrey, which led them to the Old Rose pub and the barman's information about Clara and Bella and where they were staying.

"The barman, Jeff Baker, told me that Clara and Bella were both bunking down with him, temporarily. He told me that he used to date Bella, on and off. That is why he was helping her out."

The detective sat back in his chair. "Quite an odd gesture, don't you think?" He addressed this question at Nyah.

Nyah shrugged, but didn't look up. "What?" His voice was quiet, barely audible.

"To let your casual girlfriend and her friend stay with you?"

Nyah looked up this time. "I don't know anything about this girl Bella, only that she worked in the Old Rose pub and that she knew my sister and she found a place for them both to stay. That's it, that's all I know about Bella. Clara has been living in Belfast – she was going to university there until recently. She never mentioned a Bella. They can't have known each other for long." He sounded angry.

The policeman standing at the door took a step forward.

"Nyah," Lana cautioned.

"No, Lana. They're wasting time here." He pointed his finger at the detective. "My sister was in that flat. Her jacket was hanging off a stool. She was with that girl Bella and now that girl is dead. Clara must be petrified. And now she is out there somewhere and nobody is looking for her?"

"They *are* looking, Nyah," said Lana.

Nyah was watching the detective. "*Are* you?"

The detective looked like he was deciding whether to tell Nyah something. He cleared his throat. "We checked Bella's phone. They knew each other. Clara and Bella. They have been friends for several months at the very least. We are still going through Bella's messages but they seem very familiar with each other. Are you sure you never heard of Bella before?"

Nyah shook his head. "No. I don't understand any of this. How would they know each other? My sister led a quiet enough life back home in Limerick until she moved to Belfast seven months ago. She attended university ... unless she met Bella there but she never mentioned her, not at any time when we talked on the phone or messaged each other ..." He stopped. Should he tell them about the tattoo?

"What is it, Nyah? Anything you can tell us could help find your sister, anything at all?"

"There is a baby. My sister had a baby. My mother was worried about my sister because she wasn't contacting her so often, which was unusual, so she made a surprise visit to Belfast. When my mother arrived at her flat, there was a baby. Clara said it was hers."

"Where is the baby now?

"She's with my mother. Back in Ireland."

"Did you know your sister was pregnant?"

Nyah shook his head. "No."

His guilt was evident to Lana. She could see it written all over his face.

He leaned forward in his chair. "But I found a photograph of her, one she posted on her Instagram page a few months ago at Christmas. She was out with some friends. Here – look."

He took his phone out of his pocket and showed the image to the detective.

"The baby was born on New Year's Eve, she said. The photo was taken on the 23rd of December. Look at her stomach. It's completely flat."

"Maybe it's an old photo and she only posted it recently?"

"No – my mother bought that dress for Clara last Christmas. It's new."

"Have you read through any of the comments?"

"A few. There's nothing of interest. Just other friends admiring the girls' outfits, that sort of thing."

"Do you know the other girls in the photos with your sister? The more recent photos?"

"The two girls she shares with. Well, I don't know them but Clara has mentioned them a few times. She's been sharing a flat with them since last September."

"But you have never met them?"

"No, I haven't."

The door opened and a female police officer entered. "Detective, may I have a word?"

The detective stood and left the room.

The other police officer remained at the door. He didn't engage with Lana or Nyah. The small room was suddenly very quiet.

Lana sipped her tea. It was cold and she resisted the urge to spit it back into her paper cup.

"That could have been Clara. Whoever murdered that girl ..."

"I know, Nyah, I know ..." She reached out and took his hand. "We *will* find her, Nyah. I promise you ..."

"She was somebody's daughter, Lana. Someone will be wondering where she is right now. Someone is probably worried sick about her. Like we have been about Clara. Supposing Clara ..." He stopped. "Supposing things end up like that for my sister?"

"Nyah, don't ..."

"Or worse? Supposing we never find her?"

She turned towards him and closed her fingers around his. "*Nyah, look at me.*" He did as she asked. "We'll keep looking until we find her. We'll keep going. OK?" She lifted his chin.

He nodded. "OK."

"And the police here will find out who Bella was – and hopefully other information that will help us."

He nodded. "Lana ..."

"Yes?"

"There's something else I haven't told you."

"What?"

He took a deep breath. "She had the swan tattoo on her arm. The same design as my father's. She was the girl on Clara's Instagram photo."

Before Lana could react, the door opened and the detective returned. He had a strange look on his face.

Again, Lana took the lead. "What is it, detective?"

"Your sister took a flight to Shannon airport in Ireland. This afternoon."

Nyah pushed back his chair and stood. "*What?*"

"Sit down for a moment, Nyah." The detective gestured towards the chair.

Nyah sat.

"There's something else. We just heard back from forensics. Bella was examined briefly at the scene."

Nyah moved to the edge of his chair. "*And?*"

The detective sighed. "There's a scar on Bella's mid-section, her abdomen. Her wound opened and bled a little during the attack."

They waited.

"It's still too early to tell but the pathologist thinks the scar is recent enough."

"So? She must have had surgery or something." Nyah had a confused expression on his face.

But Lana knew what the scar meant. At least she thought she knew. She'd had her suspicions for a while and, if she was right, it would explain everything. She suspected that Nyah was in denial.

"The scar is from a caesarean section," the detective said.

Nyah stared at him.

"As I said, the scar is recent – the pathologist will have to run further tests but he estimates about three months. The wound wasn't fully healed."

CHAPTER 27

The weather had turned foul. The rain pelted against the front window of the car and the wipers were barely able to clear the screen. It was almost impossible to see. Jenny was coming up to the intersection of the city's largest public park as the lights changed to amber and then to red. Jenny slowed to a stop, idly drumming her fingers on the steering wheel as she waited.

She wondered what significance the key had. Of course, it could be nothing. Clara might have dropped it when she visited her grandmother, but Jenny felt that wasn't the case. She felt sure that Clara had left it in her grandmother's locker drawer for a reason. She just didn't know what that reason was. She had stayed in her mam's room longer than she had originally intended, now and then gently questioning her mother to no avail. Then searching for something, anything that did not belong to her mother. She found nothing – just the key with Clara's initial.

She glanced at the lights, urging them to change. *Come on, come on, change already!* The detective would probably be pulling up outside her house any minute and if she wasn't there he would leave. She really needed to see him. She noticed movement outside the park. Christ! Who was out in this rain? They'd get drenched. When the wipers cleared the window she caught sight of a cream trouser suit, blonde hair and a pair of high heels. The wipers cleared the glass again and even though it was just a fleeting glance, she knew who it was. Megan Carmichael. The woman was standing at the entrance to the park, her wet hair pressed against her skin. She turned and hurried in through the gate, her movements awkward in her high-heeled shoes. What the hell was that about? Apart from the fact that Megan was out in the pouring rain, what was she doing in the park? Jenny knew that inside the gate there was a bandstand that Megan could use for shelter but ... it was still a bit odd, wasn't it? A public park wasn't the kind of place you would expect to find Megan Carmichael, even on a dry day. And there was something else that seemed odd. Megan had been standing outside the park, just standing there in the pouring rain. Was she waiting for someone?

The lights turned green and Jenny moved forward, glancing quickly at the park entrance as she passed by. Generally, the gardens would be busy with people walking their dogs or strolling with their families, runners out for a jog and of course the odd wino. But not today. In this downpour, it appeared deserted. She felt confused about what she had just seen. The more she learned about the Carmichael family, the more peculiar they appeared. Between Megan, Ned and Alexis, she couldn't make sense of their behaviour.

By the time she reached the turn-off to her road, the rain had eased off. A moment later Jenny turned into her drive.

There was a dark car parked out front, a man sitting in the driver's seat, watching her as she approached. When Jenny came to a stop he climbed out of his vehicle and straightened his jacket.

His hand was extended when she got out of her car. "Mrs. Doyle? Thank you for agreeing to see me."

She nodded. "Come inside."

She carried Lucy's car seat around the corner of the house, fumbling in her pocket for her keys, the edge of the seat cutting into the side of her knee. Suddenly she was overcome with tiredness and she was glad she was still outside in the cool air as she felt a hot flush creeping up her neck.

"Here, let me help you?"

He took the car seat and she unlocked the door leading into the kitchen. She badly needed a cup of tea.

"Thanks. She's only a baby but she seems to weigh a ton."

Jenny filled the kettle and placed two mugs on the counter. She popped two tea bags inside.

"I'm sure," he said. "I remember that stage very well."

"You have children?"

"Two girls. Well, young adults now. They're in their twenties, living their best lives. Not asking for money from me anymore. Well, most of the time anyway." He laughed.

"Good for them." The kettle boiled and she poured water into two mugs. She placed the drinks on the table.

"It must be strange looking after a baby again. Especially when you didn't know the child existed?"

Jenny smiled. "I'm enjoying it actually." She spooned the tea bags from the mugs and placed them on a saucer. She found a half-full pint of milk in the fridge and poured some into her own. She passed the carton across the table to the detective – she couldn't be bothered with a jug.

"Sugar? Or a biscuit?"

He shook his head. "No, thanks."

"Do you miss your daughters?"

"Yes, of course. But as long as they're happy, I guess that's all that matters. Young people are very much protected from the difficulties of life while they are still in school. It's when they move away from home and venture out into the real world that they see how easy they had it."

Suddenly she had enough of the charade. "What brings you here, detective?"

The detective reached into his pocket for his notebook, taking the hint. "The two girls that shared a flat with your daughter? You texted me their full names and addresses."

"Yes, after I visited you at the station. What about them?"

"What do you know about them?"

Jenny shrugged. "Not a lot really. Just their first names, Becky and Emily. And that they knew each other before college. They had a three-bedroom flat close to the university and they were looking for a female student to share. Clara found their advertisement online."

He scribbled away. "So, she found this accommodation herself?"

Jenny nodded.

"And what? You paid a deposit?"

"Yes. She was searching up links connected to the college website all the time. Everything she enquired about had been already taken. We were worried she wouldn't find a place. And Belfast isn't exactly somewhere she could commute to."

"How did you pay?"

"That was online too. Clara got the IBAN and I just did a transfer every month."

"What name did you put on the transfer? You always have to input the name of the account holder along with the IBAN and the amount when you make a transfer."

"Yeah, yeah, I have it saved in my phone, hold on." She reached for her phone and scrolled down through her notes, then stopped and looked at him. "I'm sorry ... why are you asking me all this? What has it got to do with anything?"

"I'll explain. Just answer the questions, please. Tell me ... did you ever actually visit the flat? Like when she moved in?"

"No. I didn't need to. Clara took the train up that first weekend."

"The train?"

"I went with her as far as Dublin. We had lunch and then she caught the Belfast train and I came home. It was close to eight months ago, detective."

"Did you visit after that?"

"This week was my first time. Look, I know this sounds pretty loose, like I didn't care. But it wasn't like that. Clara and I, we talk every day. Several times. It was only lately that she had grown distant. Like, in the last few months."

"I'm not judging you, Mrs. Doyle. I'm just trying to establish what you knew about Clara's life in Belfast ... "

"I saw photos, Clara seemed to be happy. She liked the girls she was sharing with, they got along."

"But did you actually meet them? When you visited this week. Emily and Becky?"

"No. I didn't. But Nyah has received messages from one of them – Emily, I think. They weren't there when I visited. Emily had gone on a trip and Becky had gone home to her parent's house for a few days. And there are photos. On Clara's social media accounts. Lots of photos." Jenny narrowed her eyes. "What's all this about, detective?"

The detective sighed. He closed his notebook. "They don't exist, Mrs. Doyle."

Jenny frowned. "*Excuse me?*"

"When you sent on the girls' contact details I got one of my colleagues to check them out on our data base, their addresses and so forth. We found nothing, but that is not unusual. Belfast is out of our jurisdiction. So, we contacted our counterparts up north to pay a visit to their homes. Again, they found nothing. An elderly couple live at the address you gave us for Becky. They have been living there for over forty years and they have one child, a son who recently moved to Australia. The address for the other girl, Emily, is registered as a derelict building – nobody has lived there for years."

Jenny sat at the table, speechless. She put down her phone. She reached for her tea, cradling the mug. She needed to warm up her hands as a chill crawled up her spine.

"The police in Northern Ireland also went to the flat. Where Clara has been staying."

"And?"

"The place is empty. There was nobody there."

"But who owns it? I can show you the IBAN I sent the rent to." She reached for her phone again. "I have it saved here somewhere."

"We will need that, yes. And our investigators in Belfast are looking into all of that for us."

She found the name and number and presented the screen to the detective.

"Ah, yes," he said, as if he recognised or expected the account holder's name or details.

He jotted the information into his notebook.

"What is going on, detective?"

He finished writing. "At this stage we're still making enquiries. But, as you probably know, a young girl has been found murdered in a flat in London?"

Jenny nodded.

"Your daughter was in that flat at some point over the last few days. We have reason to believe the murdered girl was living with Clara in Belfast."

Jenny couldn't believe what she was hearing. The past eight months had been a lie. Clara, her beautiful daughter, whom she thought she knew better than anyone, had been lying to her about everything.

CHAPTER 28

Their flight was being called as they gathered up their belongings from security.

"Hurry, Nyah, we don't have much time." She pointed at the tray on the shelf. "Look at all your stuff! Jesus!"

They had just come out the other side of security and the queue had been long. She pulled on her jacket and felt for the buckle of her belt. She watched as Nyah stuffed his personal items into his holdall. She quickened her pace as she slung her bag over her shoulder and zipped up her jacket. She felt Nyah's presence behind her.

"I'm right beside you, Lana."

"Where the fuck is the bar?"

He smiled as he shook his head.

"What?"

"It's so odd to hear you swear."

"I get a bit weird when I have to catch a flight. I told you this already. The last time we travelled together I had time to take a little relaxant. This time I don't have that luxury. So, ignore me. That's an order."

"We will be in the air for less than an hour. Fifty minutes max. An Irish wedding ceremony goes on for longer."

"I am aware. But those fifty minutes are hell for me. The entire time I am in the air I think we are falling, Nyah. Falling out of the sky. And I checked the forecast in Ireland. Lots of rain. Which means a wet runway."

"But you know it's perfectly safe, right? I mean, it's safer to fly –"

"Yeah, yeah, I know – it's safer to fly than drive and all that. I know I am completely irrational but my fear takes over my rational. That's why I always try to take some form of anaesthetic, to dampen down my anxiety a little and to avoid the embarrassment."

"Embarrassment?"

"People staring at me. It's embarrassing."

"I don't get it. You were fine on the way over!"

"I had wine! Two big glasses! And the weather conditions were good and there was zero turbulence!"

"I'll hold your hand."

"Fuck off, Nyah!"

Nyah laughed. "For the entire journey!"

"No, thanks. In fact, I would prefer if we didn't sit together. That way only strangers get to witness my distress."

"Too late. I already checked us in, side by side." He gave a small smile. "You'll be fine, Lana. I'll distract you."

Their gate was announced.

"Oh Christ," Lana muttered.

"Come on, I think it's this way."

They took off in the direction of the boarding gate.

Nyah was quiet as they walked.

"Are you OK?" Lana asked.

He nodded.

He was still in shock, she knew that. To have thought that he had seen his sibling's dead body, not to mention the news about the baby. She wasn't sure if he was relieved or disappointed not to be an uncle after all. Though that was still to be proven. And from what he had told her about his mam's bonding with the baby, Jenny would be upset too.

Lana stopped to look at the large screen listing flight details and quickly scanned the information. "Shit, the gate closes in four minutes. Let's make a run for it."

She took off down the corridor, Nyah following right behind her. They trailed the directional arrow and climbed the stairs. They then descended another flight of stairs, before ascending another. Heathrow airport was an actual nightmare. Unfortunately, they couldn't get a flight from any of the other London airports at short notice so they had to go with what was probably the busiest one in Europe. Plenty of flights to avail of in Heathrow, but plenty of legwork needed. They arrived at their gate just as the steward was about to close the door leading into the tunnel.

" *Wait!*" Lana yelled. She had her documents ready as she reached the steward.

The girl checked her passport and boarding pass before handing them back, then did the same with Nyah's. "Just in time. Enjoy your flight."

Lana and Nyah walked through the tunnel that led to their plane.

Lana could feel the dread creep up again as she stepped onto the aircraft, noticing droplets of rain on the door as they passed through.

Soon, that door would be closed and she would be locked inside. Her breath quickened, her hands became clammy. *Please don't happen now, not here, not in front of Nyah!* It had been months since she had suffered a panic attack.

There was another steward smiling at them, hand extended for their boarding passes.

Breathe, Lana, breathe! She tried to ignore her rapidly beating heart as she shuffled down the aisle, her legs like jelly. A moment later she found her seat. Nyah sat in beside her. They fastened their seat belts as the stewards closed the overhead baggage areas and the flight began to taxi down the runway. They were moving already.

Wow, they really had only made it by the skin of their teeth.

Frantically, Lana rummaged in her pocket and with trembling fingers she found her headphones. She quickly turned on some music from her playlist, something easy to listen to so she could drown out the sounds of the plane. She sat on her hands, leaned forward so that her forehead rested on the back of the seat in front of her, closed her eyes and tried to imagine she was somewhere else. Jesus, she would never be able to relax on a plane! Every time she flew, she felt more and more terrified. Enclosed environments brought on her anxiety.

After a moment, she was aware of something gently massaging her back. She opened her eyes. *Nyah.* "You don't have to ... "

He shook his head and continued the circular motion as the plane picked up speed on the runway. A few seconds later she felt the familiar flutter in the pit of her stomach as the plane left the ground. All the time Nyah kept up the gentle massage, the movement both relaxing and distracting.

She felt the plane level off. She lifted her head and opened her eyes. Glancing at the surrounding passengers, she saw they were reading their newspapers or books, sleeping, playing video games on their iPads or phones. She envied each and every one of them, with their carefree attitude to this form of travel. She wished she could be like them.

She reached up and felt for Nyah's hand on her neck. "You can stop now."

He raised an eyebrow.

"No, seriously. Thank you, though, it really helped." She pulled out her headphones.

He smiled and took his hand away.

The seat-belt sign turned off and the steward walked down the centre aisle of the plane, handing out magazines. Everything was perfectly calm, no reason to panic, her breath returned to normal. For now.

"When did it start?"

"What?"

"Your fear of flying?"

"*Em*. It's a combination of things to be honest. I have a fear of enclosed spaces. An irrational fear. If I feel like I am trapped or I have no control, I panic." She hesitated. "Also ... something terrible happened a few years back that left me severely traumatised." She glanced at Nyah. His expression was full of concern.

"I'll explain another time, yeah?"

Nyah nodded and she was relieved.

Lana had worked for the Office of the Director of Public Prosecution for five years. While preparing for the trial of a domestic violence case, she had grown particularly close to one of the victims, a seven-year-old girl named Chloe Long. The child was living in a safe house with her mother Zara. Lana's role was to help them prepare for the trial against Zara's husband who had knifed them both during an unprovoked attack. Lana had taken to the young girl and according to Zara the feeling was mutual. Lana had come up with a code for Chloe and Zara to use if it ever happened that she called to the house and somehow one of the husband's family was inside, having found out where they were living. They were to use the word *stranger*. And Chloe had used the word *stranger* one day when Lana called by for a pre-arranged visit. For some reason, Lana hadn't picked up on the signal. Maybe it was because it was coming from Chloe – she thought she was kidding around. But she wasn't. Chloe answered the door and warned Lana not to come in, that she couldn't let a *stranger* in. Her father's brother had found them. He had murdered Zara Long and Chloe too, not long after she answered the door to Lana. A young girl had died because of her negligence.

She wasn't prepared to explain her mistakes to Nyah. Not on a plane. Besides, he had his own worries to deal with. The detective had continued to interrogate Nyah but it was clear that he didn't know anything about the dead girl. Nyah answered their questions about his missing sister and Lana corroborated his story. The police had checked with the Dormund Hotel and the manager, Pam Yeboah, had confirmed that Lana and Nyah had been at the hotel that morning. Luckily, Clara was reported missing in Ireland and the English police were able to validate the fact by making a couple of phone calls. The detective said they had managed to unlock Bella's laptop. Someone had been looking up flights to Ireland for that afternoon. Had both girls been planning to travel back to Ireland? Lana guessed as much. When they'd arrived at the apartment, Lana had noticed a suitcase just inside the front door. She would hazard a guess that the bag belonged to Bella. Clara had just a backpack. There was no sign of this in the apartment, just Clara's jacket. She wondered if Clara had left the apartment briefly for some reason and, returning, found Bella's body and in a panic ran.

The police had informed Lana and Nyah that they could travel home to Ireland but they might need them for more questioning.

Lana checked her watch – they were ten minutes into the flight. Forty to go.

"Why has she gone back now, Lana? After all that?"

"I don't know, Nyah.

"That makes sense about the baby, I get that. She belongs to Bella, not Clara. But we don't know what the connection between them is. And why one minute Clara is telling me to go home and the next she is going home herself. Of course, something must have scared them both."

"I agree. They must have realised that they weren't safe in England anymore. I'm guessing she ran. That she found Bella, panicked and ran. That would account for the jacket being left behind."

"Yes. But why leave Lucy with Mam in the first place?"

"She knew Lucy would be taken care of. She may have contacted your dad, if he is still alive and living in London – or his uncle David Miller who we know has some connection with the Old Rose pub – and Miller might have put a word in for her, got her a job. Then you show up asking questions. She tries to warn you off but probably knows that you won't listen."

"But Mam says she hasn't contacted her and –"

"I know that, Nyah. Look, I don't have the answers. I'm just saying what I think might have happened, but of course I could be wrong. Like, I have literally nothing to go on here."

"Again, my fault. If I hadn't asked questions in the bar we might have found her last night."

Lana didn't reply to that. It was true. Nyah had acted rashly and it had cost them time.

"Tell me about that key again, Nyah. What your mam told you."

"Just that Nana started fussing about a key left in her bedside locker drawer. Asking Mam 'Are you here for the key?' And then produced it and gave it to her. It has Clara's initial attached to it. Mam bought her the keyring when she moved to Belfast."

Lana didn't know what to make of that. Nyah's grandmother had dementia, hadn't she? She checked her watch again: twenty-five minutes in. Almost halfway there. She took a breath and glanced over her shoulder down the aisle. A woman a few seats back was wrestling with a toddler, trying to get him to sit quietly. Good luck with that, she thought. If there was one thing that turned her off having kids, it was watching their behaviour on a plane. The cutest of children turned into monsters when trapped on an aircraft. Maybe they secretly didn't like flying any more than she did but they didn't possess the etiquette to hide it. The little boy was slapping his mother across the face now. Lana looked away.

She felt the plane jolt and the seat-belt sign went on. Her heart leapt inside her chest. The toddler started to cry and Lana felt like joining him. The captain announced that they were experiencing some turbulence and asked that everyone remain seated with their belts fastened. The plane bumped along, repeatedly. Lana took a deep breath and leaned forward in her chair. Her head felt heavy as blood rushed around her body. She felt Nyah's fingers again, their rhythmic movement kneading into her back. The plane jostled around for another thirty seconds and then everything went smooth again.

Lana realised she had been holding her breath. She slowly sat up in her seat, feeling light-headed. "

"It's fine, see? Just a bit of turbulence, that's all. Potholes in the sky."

He smiled and she felt like crying at the warmth in his eyes. They reflected honesty and kindness. He had been through so much and he was looking out for her and her stupid phobias.

"Peter and I, we started a relationship," she blurted out. "Last summer."

"You don't have to explain anything to me, Lana. Your private life is your own business."

"You have been honest with me, Nyah, and besides I want to." She played with a loose tread on the sleeve of her jumper. "It was pretty intense from the beginning. I had just lost my mother and he was still grieving for his brother." She turned to look at Nyah. "Peter's brother died in a drowning accident in Castle Cove over twenty years ago – did you know that?"

Nyah shook his head. "No? Jesus, that is shit. I didn't know that. Poor guy."

"Yeah, and he told me that he suspected foul play, that it wasn't an accident. And I was investigating the near-death of that girl on Mutton Island at the time, so that brought it all back to him. But I made a few enquiries and got my hands on the coroner's report on his brother. It was definitely an accident, death by drowning. I showed him the report." The thread came away from her jumper. "So, I guess the document sort of re-ignited his grief, if you know what I mean? Brought it all back to him, the memory. I don't think he had dealt with it properly at the time. He had suppressed everything for years by focusing on what he imagined had happened that night instead of accepting that it was an accident. So, we bonded in our grief in a way. Dad died years ago, but Mam had been fit and healthy, at least I thought she was. So it was a huge shock when she passed away. Suddenly, I was an orphan. To lose one parent is pretty hard to deal with but to lose two, it's heart-breaking, and I don't have any siblings. I felt completely alone in the world. Peter was there for me, and we became close. I started spending more and more time down in Castle Cove, on weekends, that sort of thing. He never once came to Limerick but that was OK with me because I wanted to get away from the city on my time off. And, besides, you've been to Castle Cove, right? It's a beautiful part of Ireland."

Nyah nodded. "That's for sure."

"A few weeks back, I was due to give evidence for a case I had been working on. I remember it was a Thursday. The circumstances surrounding the case had been difficult, domestic violence, and everyone was tired, emotionally drained as well as physically. I was due to go on the stand and present my findings, but the judge decided we would re-adjourn until the following Monday. So, I had three days off. I had all my prep done so I was at a loose end, and I decided to head to Castle Cove that evening, to surprise Peter. Turns out, I'm the one that got the surprise."

Nyah frowned. "What happened?"

"Peter's van was parked outside his house when I arrived, but he wasn't there. I remember it was after seven in the evening so I guessed he was at the local pub having a few pints with the other fishermen. I parked and walked down to the village to look for him. There is a small boutique hotel on the main street. I stayed there once – it's really beautiful and there is an incredible view from the terrace."

"I know it."

"I decided to pop in for a glass of wine and just sit outside and just chill for a while. As I said, the weeks had been draining, and that view, it would cure any kind of stress. So, I ordered at the bar and carried my drink outside. Peter was there. And he wasn't alone."

"Go on?"

"He was deep in conversation with a guy called Gary Duke. Gary used to run the local boat hires, until the Department of the Marine shut him down due to negligence. It's a long story."

"So, Peter was having a drink with another guy, what's the issue with that? Wait? Were they together?"

"No, nothing like that. The girl who was found on Mutton Island – she had fallen off a boat. It was one of Gary Duke's boats."

"OK?"

"Something else was going on. There is this summer house, The World's End – it's just past the pier?"

"Yeah, I know it. Pretty luxurious-looking property."

"And then some. Well, a party had been planned at the house, the same weekend the girl was found on the island. The hosts had invited investors."

"To invest in what?"

"Women."

"*No way! The World's End summer house?*"

"Yeah."

"I don't get it – what does Peter have to do with the house?"

"Nothing. But Gary Duke does. He was under investigation for supplying the boats transporting the girls to the house. A young woman from Estonia, Eva Mroz, went missing over a year ago. The Gardaí believe she was trafficked to Ireland. There is a connection with one of the guys who organised the party at the house – the authorities found electronic evidence of correspondence on the girl's laptop. They believe she was lured to Ireland under false pretences, a promise of work. She hasn't been seen since she left her home town. Forensic tests were carried out on one of Duke's boats. The investigation is ongoing."

"So, you think Peter ...?"

"I don't know what to think. They both looked up when I walked out onto the terrace. Gary Duke scowled – natural enough – I'm not his favourite person. But Peter looked guilty of something, like he had been caught out. He knew how I felt about Gary Duke, and everything he represented. I'd told Peter things about the case, things I shouldn't have shared. I trusted him. I mean, Duke is under investigation for people-smuggling and Peter is sitting there, drinking beer with him. I was so angry. I hadn't let anybody into my life in ..." She threw her hands in the air. "When Dad died I immersed myself in my career. I don't trust easily so it was a big deal for me to commit. I saw red that evening. Peter tried to talk to me but I kind of went from zero to one hundred in a matter of seconds. I felt so let down. I ran back to his house, got in my car, and drove back to Limerick. We haven't spoken since. Until he called me last night."

"What did he say about this Gary Duke guy?"

"Just that they had randomly bumped into each other. He said he was enjoying a beer on the terrace when Duke arrived out and joined him."

"I take it you don't believe him?"

Lana narrowed her eyes. "I don't know. Peter never drinks in that hotel. I only know about the place because I stayed there once. So, why was Peter even there? Either he had planned to meet Duke or it was just a coincidence like he said but ..." She shrugged.

Nyah took a moment before asking his next question. "Do you love him?"

Lana shook her head – the request was too intimate to answer. "I can't respond to that, Nyah. I really can't. But I do need to talk to him. He said that he wants to explain things, and I owe him that much." She looked at Nyah. "What happened last night, Nyah, between you and me? I'm sorry ..."

"Lana, don't ..."

"I can't start anything with you, not now. I probably need to be on my own for a while, to get over Mam's death and come to terms with that loss. She was my best friend."

Nyah smiled, trying and failing to hide his disappointment. "I understand. But if you want to talk, when all this is over, you know where I am, right?"

She smiled back. "Yeah. I know where you are."

The captain announced they were about to make their descent. My God, she had actually forgotten she was in the air. She took a deep breath and stuck her headphones back in. Closing her eyes, she leaned forward, once again resting her forehead on the back of the seat in front of her. A moment later, she felt his fingers on her back.

Lana smiled as her plane came in to land.

CHAPTER 29

The detective had shocked Jenny when he'd told her about Clara's flatmates. The two girls that she thought her daughter was sharing a flat with in Belfast did not even exist. So, who were the girls in the photos Nyah had seen on Clara's Instagram? Just a couple of college friends maybe, on a night out. And that poor girl Bella had stayed with Clara in the flat in Belfast. The detective didn't know how long for but there was evidence she had been there, whatever that meant. Jenny tried to remember her time in the flat in Belfast. The flat had been sparse of furnishings, though a bit messy, with clothes thrown on the couch and dirty ware in the sink. Jenny hadn't thought anything of it, though – they were students after all and she had been focused on her daughter and the baby. Looking back now, she remembered that she didn't have to persuade Clara to come back to Limerick with her. Her daughter had readily agreed. In fact, Clara couldn't get out of there fast enough. She had appeared pale and drawn, as if she hadn't slept for days.

She was thinking now that some crisis must have led Bella to suddenly leave for England and that Clara must have wanted to join her. However, the baby would have been a problem. Without a passport, she wouldn't have been able to travel. What would Clara have done if Jenny hadn't turned up when she did? Where would she have left the baby? And why did she visit her grandmother, and leave a key? The bigger question was why did the two girls run off in the first place? Someone had found them in the flat in London, someone they were afraid of. Who was Bella and why had she been murdered? Was Clara meant to have been the victim? Her head was spinning from it all.

Her phone rang. Checking the caller ID she saw Megan's name flash across the screen. *No way*, she thought – she wasn't answering a call from that woman again. The last thing she needed now was another running commentary about how amazing her daughter Alexis was and the mistakes Clara had made. Jesus, would she ever just leave her alone? And the woman hadn't an ounce of sincerity in her. A memory came to her of a time in primary school when Megan had teased her about her shoes – Jenny's mother had bought her new shoes, red patent with silver buckles on the front. Jenny had been mad about them until she had arrived in to school and Megan called her "that Dorothy one off the telly". Everyone had laughed. Megan had started singing *Follow the Yellow Brick Road* in a high-pitched voice and the other girls had joined in – sheep, the lot of them doing Megan's bidding. Jenny had run home crying to her mother. She remembered again what her mam said: "*There are mean girls everywhere, Jenny – you just have to figure out a way to look through them.*" Megan Carmichael had been a mean girl, and it was almost impossible to look through her. It still is, Jenny thought. Admittedly, she was curious about seeing Megan at the park earlier and her reasons for being there, but she wasn't going to lose sleep over it. She let the phone ring out as Lucy started to fidget in her chair.

"You must be hungry, *eh*? Poor little mite. What will we do with you at all?" She scooped formula into a bottle and used the warm water from the kettle to make up Lucy's feed. She lifted the baby from her seat and went about changing her. When she was freshened up, she laid her into the crook of her arm. The baby gazed up at her, eyes wide, her lips pursing as she sucked on her bottle, her little hand grasping at the empty air, not quite able to coordinate her movements. She smiled at the child that had captured her heart.

She was worried sick about Clara, and whatever it was that she had got herself involved in. Why couldn't she have told her? Why didn't she feel like she could confide in her own mother? Was she that unapproachable? She had always done her best for both of her children, and in desperate times she had taken desperate measures. She had always protected them and encouraged them to stand up for themselves, and they had been close as a family. Very close. That fact was probably what hurt the most, that Clara hadn't been able to trust her. Was this her fault? Because she hadn't been entirely honest with them about their father? She felt the tears sting the backs of her eyes for the umpteenth time since she had arrived on Clara's doorstep in Belfast. The tears spilled over and once they started, she couldn't stop them. The little baby gazed up at her. She looked concerned, worried, her eyes searching Jenny's, and then the little hand reached up again, this time finding Jenny's skin. Jenny swallowed hard. This young child was comforting her, a woman in her fifties. It should be the other way around. She made a decision there and then, that she would look after this child. She would take care of her. She would raise her, she would nurture and care for her. She would give her every opportunity that she deserved. Whatever happened, this child would be in her future. They needed each other.

She glanced out the window at her back garden, the garden she had spent all her free time in until recently. Gardening had been her retreat when her marriage fell apart. When she finally returned to the house after staying so long with her mother, she had immersed herself out there in the garden. Rotating, planting, grooming, and pruning. It had taken years to get it to the stage it was at now and Jenny enjoyed spending time there. She would sit on the green bench and she felt peace. *Safe*. She never felt afraid out there, because the scariest thing for her had already gone. A fleeting image of the dark car with the UK registration came to mind – she quickly pushed it away.

Her phone beeped and she flipped it with her free hand. There was a text from Megan. My God, would the woman ever let up? She leaned forward to read the message.

Jenny, can you come over? I haven't been entirely honest with you.

No fucking way, Megan! She threw the phone on the table.

CHAPTER 30

Nyah offered his passport to the woman behind the Perspex. She barely glanced at his face and photo ID before scanning the passport and handing it back to him. He tucked it into the front pocket of his jacket. Lana was on the phone, having passed through before him. She had received multiple messages from her assistant when she had turned on her phone after they had landed – it must have pinged about twenty times, one after the other. She had started returning calls as they exited the plane. For him, there was nothing from Brad Fulham – the man's silence did not bode well for his future with the company. He pulled his phone out of his pocket and dialled his mother's number. As he waited for her to answer, he thought about what he had to tell her about Lucy: the fact that she wasn't Clara's child. He had held back that piece of information when he had told her about Bella. From their conversations over the last few days, he gathered his mam had become very attached to the baby. He wasn't sure how she would take it when she found out there was no blood relationship between them. The only problem was that his mam wasn't picking up her phone. He tried her again now and it went straight to voicemail. Sighing, he tucked his phone into his pocket – she was probably busy changing the baby or something and would call him back when she noticed the missed calls.

He was gasping with the thirst, and he realised that he hadn't had anything to eat or drink all day. His breakfast had been cut short when he was presented with Clara's note at the hotel. He caught Lana's eye and signalled a drinking motion with his hand. She gave him the thumbs-up as she chatted away, her expression serious. He nodded and left her alone. The airport was busy and he drifted with the crowds until he found a café where the queue wasn't too long. He grabbed a couple of pastries and used the self-service to pour some coffees. He stood in the queue to pay and he thought of Bella, the young girl with the swan tattoo on her arm, whose dead body he had found only a few hours earlier. Her whole life cut short. Then he realised that, embroiled in the recent traumatic events, Lana and he had lost sight of one vital question: why was Bella's tattoo the same as his father's?

The queue shifted and that's when he saw her. A girl with long blonde hair slipping out the back door of the café. She wore a pair of blue skinny jeans and a black hoodie. A purple backpack was slung over her shoulder. *Clara.* He abandoned the drinks and rushed after her, bumping into a waiter holding a tray piled high with crockery on his way. The dishes rattled but thankfully, nothing fell. "*Sorry!*" he called back. He reached the back door just as it slammed shut. *Damn.* He pushed hard on the bars and eventually the doors gave way, opening outwards onto a yard lined with bins and crates. He scanned the laneway but there was no sign of Clara. *Where the fuck did she go*? He heard a roar in the sky and turned to see a plane coming into land just over the back wall behind the café. It was close, close enough so that he could read the writing on the underbelly, **Aer Lingus**. One part of the yard was a dead end, the other leading out onto a road. He realised he had entered the maintenance area of the airport. Had Clara spotted him in the café and made a run for it? From where he stood, he could see a taxi drive past. He ran up the yard and emerged onto the main arrivals area with a row of taxis parked with their engines running, hoping for a quick pick-up fare. A small queue of travellers formed along a wide path as drivers loaded luggage into their boots before driving off. There was a group of Americans piling their bags into a taxi bus, the older woman of the party loud and pushy as she directed where everyone should sit. He found himself surrounded by lots of extremely long bleached hair, white teeth, designer jackets and Ugg boots. The group were making such a fuss about their expensive bags, wanting to keep some in the car and others in the boot. The driver appeared irritated with their requests, and also they were taking up space on the path, holding up everyone else in the queue.

Nyah craned his neck to see past the Americans. And then he saw her again, throwing her purple backpack into the back seat of a taxi. She looked really skinny, thinner than the last time he had seen her for sure, but it was definitely Clara. He saw her ease herself into the back seat of the taxi and reach out to pull the door closed.

"*Clara!*" he shouted.

She looked out, turning her head towards him, a look of surprise on her face, followed by something else. Fear? He wasn't sure.

"*Clara! Wait!*"

She shook her head and gave a small smile before closing the door. The vehicle moved away from the kerb.

"*Shit!*"

The Americans were scattered in front of him as they continued to discuss their baggage, their accents loud and brash. "*Out of the fucking way!*" he roared. They parted like the Red Sea. But when he emerged from the crowd, his sister was gone.

His phone rang and he pressed it to his ear as he watched the taxi turn out of the carpark. "Lana!"

"Nyah! Where did you go?

"I'm out front."

"I thought you were picking up some drinks?"

"Come out to arrivals, the taxi area. Hurry. I'll explain when I see you." He hung up.

He dialled Clara's number but the call went straight to voicemail. He tried his mother again but this time it rang out. There was an empty can on the ground and he kicked it in anger and disappointment. He had missed her again – his little sister was just out of his reach every fucking time. When he spun around, Lana was standing outside arrivals watching him, a strange look on her face. He ran his hand through his hair and strode over to her.

"Clara was here."

"*What?*"

"She just got into a taxi." He gestured at the Americans. "Those bloody idiots are taking up the whole path – I couldn't get through."

"But she caught a plane hours ago!"

"She was here, Lana." He pointed at the pavement. "*Right fucking here.*"

"OK, OK. Let's go, Nyah."

"We don't know where she's gone."

"Probably your mam's is a good start?"

"She's not answering. My mam."

"You're sure it was Clara?"

He gave her a withering look.

"Sorry, come on, let's go." She hurried across the carpark towards the short-term parking area. "I think it's this way. Bay C."

Five minutes later, they were heading out of the airport and driving towards the motorway. "Try your mam again."

He dialled his mam's number and listened before shaking his head.

"I don't know why she isn't answering but you're right – Clara must be heading there first. There's nowhere else for her to go."

"Did you check to see if her phone is switched on? Clara's phone?"

He nodded as he dialled her number again and a voice said the number was not available.

Lana was quiet. Her hands gripped the wheel as she stared straight ahead.

"What is it, Lana?"

She kept her eyes on the road. "What do you mean?"

"I can tell by the look on your face."

"What look?"

"You're *thinking* look?"

"We'll talk at the house. First, I need to have a chat with your mother. Check Clara's Snap Map."

"I already checked. She's turned her phone off. Lana, I have had enough lies and subterfuges these past few days. I am not in the mood for this shit. Tell me what you are thinking?"

She sighed. "Last night, when I got off the phone to Peter, I put in a call to Ella – my assistant. I asked her to look for someone for me."

Nyah frowned. "Who?"

She turned towards him, a look of something in her eyes – he wasn't sure what.

"Your dad."

"*And?*"

"Well ..." She stopped.

"Go on, tell me. What did your assistant find out?"

"She got your dad's social security number and she put in a call to the Gardaí. They ran a trace on the number. Nobody has used it since that day he assaulted you, Nyah. Nobody."

"So? He could have used a different number?"

"How? Unless he had money that he could access, how would he survive?"

"Maybe he went abroad?"

"Again, he would need money. You said he didn't work, that your mam was the breadwinner in the family. You said he was always complaining about being broke. How would he get out of the country without any money?"

"Lana, I don't think those are strong arguments. People disappear all the time. Maybe he *had* money. Or someone lent him some. It doesn't take much to get to London. Maybe he had planned it in advance? People like David Miller in London are wheeler-dealers – they know how to get false papers, how to pull strings. Who knows?"

She glanced at him. "Well, the one thing we *do* know is that he *hadn't* planned it in advance. He wouldn't have gone anywhere if he hadn't tripped on that doll."

That silenced him.

"Nyah, your father vanished that day, the day he attacked you. Without a trace."

"You think he's dead, don't you?"

"Yes."

"Why would Clara go to London then? And what about the Old Rose pub? And my dad's uncle, David Miller? And Bella with the same tattoo as my father? What would take Clara over there? Why is she so scared that she can't take a minute to talk to her own brother at the airport?"

"I think Bella is the connection. I don't know why yet. But everything leads back to her. She gave birth to Lucy, and she lived with Clara in Belfast. They were together in London."

Nyah didn't answer. This whole shit-show was totally fucked up. He could picture Clara climbing into the back of a taxi, the uncertain smile flickering across her face when she realised it was him calling out to her.

"You are sure it was her?" Lana asked again.

"I know my own sister, Lana."

"So why did she hang out in the airport after her plane landed?"

"Maybe she was waiting for someone? Had met someone." He sighed. "Why wouldn't she talk to me? She saw me. She smiled at me. Kind of."

"Did you see anyone else? Around her? Following her?"

He looked at Lana, suddenly alarmed. "I didn't think to look. Do you think someone was watching her?" He glanced at the side mirror.

"Let's get to your mam's."

Lana indicated and took the exit for the motorway. As she merged into traffic she picked up speed.

He was sure there wasn't anyone following them but every now and then he checked the side mirror.

The motorway was quiet and it wasn't long before they were taking the exit route to the small village Nyah had grown up in. He could feel his heart beating faster the closer they got to their destination. He wasn't sure what was waiting for him. He hoped it would be his mam, Clara, Lucy and some answers.

They were turning the corner when it came to him that the four of them would be in the same place, together for the first time. He kind of liked the idea. The only one missing would be Nana.

He lifted his hand and signalled left. "It's here, Lana."

She didn't reply.

When he looked at her, she was smiling. "What?"

"I know where your house is, Nyah."

"It was a long time ago. When you were here last."

"I remember it."

She slowed and turned into the narrow driveway and a moment later they pulled up at the side of his childhood home.

"Looks like she isn't here," Nyah said. "No car."

"But maybe she's parked around the back?"

"I don't think so. She always parks right here at the side of the house. She thinks it presents a deterrent for potential intruders – you know, rather than the car being out of sight."

They got out of the car and walked around to the back of the house. No car.

Nyah gazed around – he felt that something was off. Nothing had changed since he'd left three days earlier – but why had he thought anything would? There stood the green bench that hadn't been painted in years, blending in nicely with the style of the garden, flowers were beginning to bloom, trees and shrubs were flourishing. There was lots of vibrant colour. His mam had green fingers and she spent a lot of time out here planting, weeding and pruning – but it was more than that. She had a creative talent – the garden was like a secret garden, with lots to explore and discover.

He peered in the kitchen window, framing his face with his hands. "There's a half-empty baby bottle on the table."

"Have you a key?"

"Back in my apartment. *Shit.*" He ran his hand through his hair. "Hold on."

He ran to the green bench, struggled to lift one of its legs and then moved his free hand around the undergrowth. A moment later he looked back at Lana, grinning, holding a key aloft.

"The spare key. God knows how long it has been there." He stood up. "Looks a bit rusty, but it might work. I don't think Mam has moved that bench in years, not as long as I've been alive I'm sure. It would barely budge."

He went and inserted the key into the lock and tried to turn it. No go. He wiggled it gently from side to side. Then it engaged and the lock shifted.

He entered the kitchen, Lana following close behind.

"*Clara!*" he shouted. "*It's Nyah! Are you here?*"

Silence.

He hurried out into the hallway and walked down to the back of the bungalow, pushing open doors as he went. Every room was empty.

He returned to the kitchen. "No-one here," he said to Lana.

She pointed to the bottle on the table. "That's still warm. Your mam can't have gone too far."

"Maybe Clara came back and they went out somewhere together?"

"Try your mam's phone again."

He dialled Jenny's number. It started to ring in his ear. It also started to ring in the kitchen. "Her phone is here. She must have left in a right hurry. Mam always has her phone with her." He spotted the device on the windowsill. He picked it up. Five missed calls from him.

"Can you unlock it?"

He nodded. "Yeah. She has the same password for everything. The month I was born followed by the month Clara was born. 1002. No secrets in this house." He typed in the number and the screen opened.

"Check her more recent messages."

He opened the messages, feeling a little uncomfortable invading his mam's privacy.

"What's this?" Lana had picked up the framed picture on the windowsill.

"Ah, Clara painted that when she was in primary school. It's just a bunch of farm animals. She won a prize for her work and the school had it framed. Been on the windowsill for years."

"Find anything on the phone?"

"The last message is from someone called Megan."

"Who's that?"

"The name seems familiar but I don't know."

"What does it say?"

"'*Jenny, can you come over? I haven't been entirely honest with you.*' That's weird."

"When did she send it?"

"Twenty-five minutes ago." He shoved his fingers through his hair. "There are missed calls too from this Megan, whoever she is."

Lana was still studying the picture – the horse drinking from a trough, cows lazing in the field, a dog and a cat playing in the yard. The perfect animal family on one side of the picture, and then, a mixture of torture, horror and misery on the other.

"This is an unusual piece of work. Very advanced for a young girl."

"Yeah, I suppose."

"She's quite talented."

"Yes, she's gifted at drawing and painting. But that picture tells you more about her personality. She loves animals, unity, and happiness. This last year, her behaviour is everything that she doesn't embody." He frowned. "I think she painted this around the time the boy died. Luke. The title is written on the back. *Animal Farm*."

Something flickered across Lana's face. "Luke – the brother of Clara's friend Alexis. Who fell down the stairs and broke his neck."

"Yes, him. *Oh!* Actually, I think the mother's name is Megan."

Jenny's phone rang in Nyah's hand. He checked the caller ID. **The Spring Park Nursing Home** flashed across the screen. He frowned.

"Something up?"

"Nana's nursing home."

"Answer it."

"I don't know if I should. They're obviously looking for Mam."

"Is it normal that they would ring her?"

He shrugged. "I don't know. I haven't been here much since I moved out last year. But, yeah, I guess they'd ring if they had to ask permission for something or if she injured herself or ..."

"Answer it."

Nyah pressed the green button. "Hello?"

The woman on the other end asked if she could speak with Jenny Doyle.

"This is Nyah, Jenny's son. My mam's out at the moment. Can I help you?"

The voice talked for a few moments.

Then Nyah hung up. He put the phone down on the counter.

"What is it, Nyah?"

"My nana, she's had a fall. They don't think it's anything serious but they want to have her checked out by a doctor. They've called an ambulance."

"Maybe that's where your mam is gone? Maybe she already knows about your nan somehow and is on her way there or to the hospital?"

Nyah shook his head. "It just happened, Lana. So Mam couldn't have known." He bit his fingernail as he looked around the kitchen. "What should I do?"

Before Lana could answer, they heard a car pull up outside.

"That must be her now." Nyah peered out the kitchen window but saw that it was a black car. "No, it's not her."

He moved to the back door and opened it.

A man was approaching, a man who was familiar to him but he couldn't comprehend why. He came to a stop.

"Can I help you?" Nyah asked.

"*Nyah! Wait!*" Lana hissed from inside.

He stepped out to meet the man, glancing over his shoulder. "*Just a minute, Lana!*"

He felt the first blow as he was turning back towards the man. It dazed him and he stumbled a little forward. The second blow sent him falling. He reached out to grab something but there was nothing to hold on to. He tumbled forward, his face hitting the gravel. Then came a kick in the stomach, and then another, and another. He curled up into a foetal position to protect himself, just like he had done all those years ago when his father had attacked him. The man continued to throw kicks into him.

He was facing the green bench as the man continued to strike with his foot, the bench where his father used to sit, when the moods were better. A memory came to him.

The sun was shining, the sky was clear blue, not a cloud to be seen. Clara was wearing a white dress – bare arms with ruffles over her shoulders. The sun seemed to illuminate the white of her dress, streaks of gold shone in her hair. Their dad was sitting on the green bench, his arm around Clara's waist as she stood beside him. Nyah was lying on his stomach on the grass in front of her, his chin resting on the palms of his hands as she chatted away. She had a wand in her hand as she pointed at the different plants and attempted to name them. Nyah envied her, her ease in their father's company. He didn't possess that – his relationship with the man wavered from calm to angry, hot to cold. Nyah never quite knew where he stood with his dad. His sister's hand swirled around in the air as their father looked on proudly until Clara pointed at Nyah and stopped her chatter for a moment.

"Look, Daddy," she said then. "Nyah is sad. Look at his face!" Her eyes were full of concern as she peered down at her brother. "Come up here, Nyah – come up here with us!" She reached a hand out to him.

As he pushed himself off the grass their dad had laughed, a nasty cackling sound. "Leave him where he is, petal. He is a useless lump, your brother. Not like you, my princess!" He squeezed her waist and pulled her closer to him.

She looked at Nyah then, her brother, older than her by eleven years. She was so young and naïve and confident in her father's love. But at that moment she recognised something, and he could see it. Something obvious and heart-breaking and disappointing. Their father had no love for Nyah. Clara stayed where she was on the bench, afraid to annoy their dad, but she continued to look at Nyah. *She knew*. She knew that their father loved her and not her brother, and her brother knew that she would protect him, and he would protect her. A silent vow to each other.

Nyah hoped Lana was gone somewhere safe. He was losing consciousness as the green bench wavered in front of him, his vision distorted, his little sister in her white dress, gesturing with her wand … and then, everything went blank.

CHAPTER 31

Alexis knew something. Jenny was sure of it. There had been something unsettling about the girl, the way her eyes had darted around the showroom when Jenny walked in the door. As though searching for a means to escape. She decided she would pay her another visit. She was not going to see Megan. To hell with that woman and her demands. She would mention Bella's name to Alexis and see if there was a reaction. She slowed as she drove along the outside railing of the dealership carpark. She turned into the yard and found a spot near the front door so that she could listen for Lucy.

Switching off the engine, she sat for a moment. What should she say to the girl? She chewed on a fingernail as she observed the showroom. There was not a customer in sight, both inside and out, nobody viewing cars or even looking around the lot. She wondered again how they made money in this place – surely a car lot with no customers couldn't be good?

She had thought Nyah would have called her by now. She patted her pocket for her phone to check for messages, but she couldn't feel the device. She searched inside the driver's door pocket, but again there was no sign of her phone. *Shit*. She must have left it in the kitchen. She had left the house in a rush, distracted by the detective's information. It didn't matter, she wouldn't be gone for long. She just needed to speak to the girl, press her on a few things, and then she would head home. Glancing over her shoulder, she noticed Lucy was fast asleep. The baby had been a little fidgety after her bottle but the motion of the car had sent her into a deep slumber.

She opened the car door and climbed out, quietly closing it behind her. She had left the window open halfway, letting in plenty of air. She crossed to the entrance and advanced up the steps. When she stepped inside the showroom, there was no one around, nobody behind the desk. She did a full three-sixty of the room, but there was no sign of life. Everything was really quiet, there wasn't a sound. She frowned as she scanned the showroom. Who was handling the shop? Was Ned outside with a customer and maybe she had missed him? But there was nobody in the carpark, she was sure of it

She walked around the table. There was a desktop monitor with a keyboard in front, a couple of glossy catalogues advertising cars and a bunch of papers – invoices. A name caught her eyes on the bottom of one: *Ned Carmichael*. She flipped through the other invoices, each one signed by Ned. Why was his name on the bottom of the invoices? He didn't own the business, did he? She scanned the desk and her eyes rested on a yellow Post-it stuck to the side of the monitor. She hadn't brought her glasses with her so she leaned in close to read the name on it. Her heart leapt out of her chest.

It read: *Call David Miller*. Her husband's uncle. *What the fuck*? Who was that message for? Ned? Had Alexis taken the call?

She hit a key, activating the screen. The headline of a news item appeared: **Young Girl's Body Found in London Flat**. She stepped back from the screen, her heart starting to race. Someone, maybe Alexis or Ned, was reading about Bella's murder. There was a telephone number scribbled beside the name on the Post-it.

She heard a cry and realised she had forgotten all about Lucy. Grabbing a pen, she wrote David Miller's number down on the back of her hand. She quickly turned and banged her knee as she made her way around the desk. A sharp pain shot up her leg. *Ah Christ!* She limped the rest of the way out of the showroom and down the steps to her car. Lucy was crying hard now, hungry no doubt. She hadn't taken much milk earlier. She felt a pang of guilt. She knew she was neglecting the child, wandering around the place playing detective. But she had to find her daughter, for Lucy's sake as well as her own.

She opened the back door of her car and eased herself along the seat, unstrapping Lucy's belt. She lifted her out of her car seat. "There, there, little one ... it's alright, it's alright ... " She patted the baby's back and Lucy began to settle. "Good, girl, you are so good ... " She ran her hand up and down Lucy's back, the little face hot with tears pressing into her own. "I'm sorry, pet, I'm so sorry about everything ..." She reached into the child's bag and felt around for a bib and one of the bottles she had made up before she left the house. She uncapped the lid, tucked the bib under Lucy's chin and began to feed her. Lucy guzzled the warm milk, her tiny fingers pressed against the side of the bottle, her eyes staring into Jenny's soul. "Take it easy, Luce!" she whispered as she dabbed at the dribble around the baby's mouth with the bib. A few minutes later, Lucy pushed away from the teat. Jenny recapped the bottle and held the baby against her chest, gently rubbing her back.

She was still massaging her back when she heard a car approach. It stopped outside the entrance of the showrooms and Alexis jumped out. She quickly ran up the steps. Outside the entrance she stopped and took her phone out of her pocket. She looked terrified. She peered down at the ground, her phone pressed close to her ear as she listened. She started to cry, shaking her head and wiping her nose with the back of her hand. Jenny held her breath as she moved along the back seat to get closer to the open car door so she could hear what Alexis was saying. She carefully pushed at the handle with her hand. Please don't cry, Lucy, she silently pleaded.

"I don't care anymore, Dad!" Alexis suddenly screamed into her phone. "I'm sick of all the lies. I'm not doing it anymore. I hate you! I fucking hate you both!" She put the device into her back pocket and entered the showroom, slamming the door behind her.

What was that about? Jenny wondered if it had anything to do with the David Miller message. Lucy broke wind so she carefully placed her back in her car seat and fastened the belt around her small frame. She searched the baby's bag for a soother and found one in the side pocket. She gently teased Lucy's lips with the teat and the baby suckled greedily on the rubber. She got out of the back seat and climbed into the front. Starting the engine, she turned out of the parking space, passing the car parked outside the front door. *A black car*. In her rear-view mirror, she noticed something else about the black car. The registration plate had a yellow background. What the hell? Was it the same car that had called to her house the night before last? When someone had fumbled with her back door? Was that someone Ally or Ned? Most likely Ned. And if so, why? The Carmichael family were showing a lot of interest in her lately.

She decided to pay Megan a visit. The woman had invited her over after all. And maybe she would have some answers. She estimated it was about a fifteen-minute drive from the car dealership to Megan's house. She glanced at Lucy in the rear-view mirror. The baby was wide awake now, her eyes dancing around as she watched the countryside pass by.

Jenny realised her hands were trembling as she gripped the wheel. So, Ned had called to her house and tried to get inside and he was in contact with David Miller. That was the most alarming part. How was all this connected and why was Clara involved? If the tone of Alexis' call was anything to go by, Ned was very angry with his daughter right now. The chilled-out, nerdy, placid man was nowhere to be seen.

She needed to talk to Megan. Megan would have some answers. She'd have to take Lucy with her but at this stage it was time to come clean, and it appeared Megan had more explaining to do than she had anyway. People who lived in glass houses shouldn't throw stones.

She heard the sound of a horn and she swerved just in time to avoid a van. The angry driver waved a fist at her as he flew past. *Get a grip*, she told herself, there was no point in killing someone.

Lucy whimpered in the back seat.

"It's OK, sweetheart. I just have one more visit to make and then I'll get you home for a warm bath and a nice long nap," she murmured soothingly as she turned onto the road where the Carmichaels lived.

A few moments later, she pulled up outside the two-storey home. The house had been built about twenty-five years earlier, approximately two miles outside the city centre. A row of detached houses with open-plan front gardens, uniform in appearance, lining each side of the road. Twenty years ago, the open-plan front garden was all the go, a very American style promoted to develop Irish real estate. But, as the years had gone by, the owners got tired of opening their front door and looking at the face of their neighbours on either side and across the road. Plenty of shrubs and trees had been planted to maintain privacy. Megan and Ned had done the same. Tall evergreens surrounded the front and sides of their house. The trees looked like they hadn't been trimmed in a long time – they almost blocked the small wooden gate at the front. There was a wider gate to the side of the house which was closed. No doubt Megan and Ned parked their cars behind this gate.

It was the middle of the afternoon but Megan was a stay-at-home mum. She enjoyed her lunch dates with her girlfriends but generally she was footloose and fancy-free. Well, that was the impression she gave Jenny anytime they had met. Even though Jenny had seen her at the park earlier, she guessed she was back at the house now, and she had as much as summoned her over, hadn't she?

Jenny climbed out of her car and approached the house, Lucy's chair tucked under her arm. Peering in over the wooden gate she could see Megan's silver car in the narrow driveway, the driver's door wide open. Megan must have been going out somewhere and forgotten something in the house. Or else she had left the door open in a hurry to get inside and change her clothes – she must have been soaked right through when she arrived home. Either way, Jenny thought it best to move fast if she wanted to catch her. She pulled aside some of the overgrown tree branches and turned the handle on the gate but, as she tried to push it open, she realised the tree had actually grown around the wood from the other side. The gate wouldn't budge. The family obviously didn't use this entrance. She moved to the larger gate and noticed it was electronically controlled – she would need a zapper to open the lock. She sighed. Megan was forever full of her notions – electronic gates outside a semi-detached? There was a small intercom attached to the pillar supporting the gate. Jenny contemplated pressing the button to alert Megan to her presence, but something told her that the element of surprise might work best here. It would give her the upper hand. She decided she would see if there was another entrance before using the intercom as a last resort. She had come here to confront Megan and warning her would give the woman a chance to prepare. Jenny didn't want that, not after everything that had happened. She was tired of the game-playing. Today, she wanted answers.

Megan's house was located on a street corner and the hedge ran all the way around the side of the property. She turned the corner and walked along the path at the side of the house, and right at the end she came across a gap in the hedge leading into the back of the house. It was just big enough to allow a small person to squeeze through, but it would be awkward with the baby's chair. She would have to release Lucy and carry her. She looked through the gap to see if there was anyone in the back garden but there was nobody in sight. Whatever Megan was doing, she must be inside the house. She returned to the car and carefully unbuckled Lucy. The baby didn't protest as Jenny lifted her out of the chair and held her close to her chest. There was a hood on her playsuit and Jenny pulled it up over her head. The baby looked around in amazement at her new environment. Jenny left the seat in the back of the car and walked around to the gap in the hedge.

"You've had quite the adventure in your short little life, haven't you, Lucy?"

She pressed the baby close to her body and held her hand at the back of Lucy's head as she crouched down low before pushing through the gap. The garden was small, another feature that came with these houses. The builder wanted to maximise the use of space, get as many built as possible. Borders and perimeters took up space and space meant money. It appeared Megan wasn't a keen gardener – she may have made a bit of an effort in the front but the back was neglected and completely overgrown. She tried to remember what it had been like when Clara used to visit Alexis. She was sure the garden hadn't been overgrown back then. Not the case anymore. The grass was high now with no path visible.

She could see the kitchen window and patio doors leading outside but, again, there was no activity. She advanced up through the tall grass, the bottom of her jeans getting damp from the earlier rainfall.

Suddenly, she heard a sound. It was so faint she wasn't sure if she had imagined it. She didn't move. Lucy's big eyes stared up at her, sensing something was different. And then she heard it again. A cry. It was coming from the house. Had Megan fallen? She might need help. She hurried towards the patio door and tried to slide it open but it was locked. She went around the side of the house to the front door. It was ajar. She listened for any sound but whatever it was that she had heard earlier had now stopped. What to do? She wasn't sure if she should just barge right in. She pushed the door open a little with her foot. The hallway was wide with black-and-cream check-patterned marble tiles, whitewashed walls and minimal furniture, a stark contrast from the cluttered and overgrown gardens outside. A crystal chandelier hung from the ceiling. A staircase opened out onto what appeared to be a landing, the wall lined with art deco. It was years since Jenny had been in this house. Not since that time, when the boy Luke had died. She didn't remember it looking like this. The Carmichaels must have had it renovated at some point. It appeared almost unlived in now.

She stepped inside the hallway. There was a cream marble table inside the door with a large vase filled with dying white lilies, their orange pollen sprinkled along the surface of the table. A white framed photo stood beside the vase, showing a much younger Ned, Megan, Luke and Alexis posing for the camera. There was something odd about the picture, Jenny thought. Their postures were stiff, their smiles forced. But that wasn't it – most families looked uncomfortable when posing for photos. She leaned in closer and realised what was wrong with the image. It was the eyes, the children's eyes. There was something unusual about them both. They were staring into the lens, their mouths turned up slightly at the edges, but closed to hide their teeth. Perhaps they were missing a few. But they appeared odd sitting against Megan and Ned, who were both smiling wide behind their children. It looked like a photo taken for two different occasions – a happy one and a sad one.

The house was completely still now, not a sound to be heard. Lucy's head rested against her chest, her soft little mouth blowing warm air onto her skin. Fast asleep again. Seriously, the baby could sleep for Ireland. She moved past the hall table, resting her hand on the bannister. Everything was white, blindingly white, except for the odd splash of colour emanating from the paintings.

Jenny glanced down at the floor at the bottom of the stairs and realised that Luke's body had been found right at the spot where she was standing. She knew because Clara had told her. Alexis had gone into great detail, describing how Luke had met his fate. His head had been at an odd angle facing the door and his eyes were wide open. A shiver ran down Jenny's spine.

The door at the end of the hall was half open. She advanced towards it now, though something caught in her chest. *Fear*? She could hear a humming sound the closer she got, sort of a vibration, like a phone on silent ringing on a hard surface. She took her time as she made her way down the hall. The sound became louder. The fear grew in her chest – she didn't know why. It was only Megan and, yes, she was a royal pain in the arse but she wasn't dangerous, was she?

She pushed open the door leading into a kitchen and, again, everything was white. The kitchen units, the counter top white marble, the floor tiles white, everything white. There was something very clinical about the room. There was certainly no warmth that you would generally feel coming from a family kitchen. It was more like a laboratory. The humming sound was louder in here and Jenny knew then what it was. A microwave. Something was heating up or defrosting. So Megan must be in the house somewhere. Jenny felt foolish now. Why had she just walked in the front door with no clear plan? What was she even doing here? And squeezing in through the hedge was ridiculous. What had she been thinking?

She turned to leave, and that's when she saw it.

A purple backpack. Clara's purple backpack.

Her mouth felt dry. Her heart jumped into her chest. She rubbed at the fine hair on Lucy's head as her breath caught. What was Clara's backpack doing here? The microwave continued to hum. Lucy stirred in her arms, sensing her alarm. Was Clara here?

She remembered buying her that backpack. The week before she started college. Clara was always so particular about her bags. She couldn't care less how she dressed, but her bags had to be on point. Each new school term she had to have a new bag, and shopping for one was an arduous task. She would take forever to decide which one she wanted and Jenny would slowly lose the will to live. She had been no different when she was prepping for college. The purple backpack was one of five that she couldn't make her mind up about. She eventually settled for it when she realised her mother was losing patience. Now that bag was sitting under Megan's kitchen table. She reached down and pulled it out with her free hand. She slipped back the zip. It was packed full of clothes and other belongings of Clara's – in fact, the things she had packed in Belfast to take home to Limerick. She thrust her hand into the rucksack's various pockets. A jumble of stuff – her passport, documents, make-up, a set of tangled headphones. And in one, a ticket stub with today's date.

It was from a plane flight taken this afternoon. So, she had flown home. And come here to Megan's house. *Why?*

The microwave pinged and she jumped in fright.

She heard movement upstairs. Her heart began to hammer in her chest. Something told her to hide. There was a door at the side of the fridge. She quickly opened it to reveal a walk-in pantry with rows of shelves stacked with spices and tinned foods. She stepped inside and gently pulled the door towards her. She could hear someone coming down the stairs and then footsteps in the kitchen. The microwave door opened and closed. She could hear the sound of plates and cutlery moving around as food was scooped into a bowl. The scent of something cooked with tomatoes and herbs filled the air. The smell drifted into the pantry and Lucy shifted her position. She started to move her head against Jenny's chest, no doubt searching for a nipple in response to the aroma wafting around her nostrils. When there was nothing forthcoming, she searched more frantically.

No, please, Lucy, don't let me down, not now, not here!

She searched her pocket for a soother but there was none there. She must have left it in the car or dropped it somewhere. The baby let out a small cry and the movement in the kitchen stopped. Jenny held her breath. Lucy was quiet again.

Please stay like that, Lucy, don't make a sound.

Jenny continued to hold her breath. There was no movement in the kitchen now but that didn't make her feel confident. She slowly exhaled just as the pantry door swung open. Jenny let out a scream. Lucy gazed up at her, eyes wide open now.

Megan looked surprised at first, and then she gave a slow smile. She had changed out of her wet clothes into a pair of black jeans and a cream jumper. Her hair was pulled back from her face, which was free of make-up. Jenny didn't think she had ever seen the woman without a fully made-up face. She had a carving knife in her hand.

Megan tilted her head to the side. "Well, this is cosy, Jenny. What are you doing here?"

Jenny was stuck for a reply. She didn't know what to say. "You asked me to come over."

"Why are you hiding in my pantry?" Megan was unable to mask her amusement.

Jenny smiled awkwardly. "I have no idea. I saw the front door was open and I thought I heard someone shout so I came inside. I called out for you but when I didn't see anyone in the house I made for the kitchen." She smiled weakly. "I stupidly thought this was the back door. My mistake."

"How did you get in through the front gate? I didn't hear the intercom."

Jenny didn't know what to say to that. She made to move out of the pantry but Megan held the door in place, blocking her.

"And who is this?"

"What?"

Megan nodded at Lucy.

"Oh, the baby. She's just, *em* ..."

"You're not going to try and tell me it's your boss's niece again, are you, Jenny? Because that would be a bit rich, wouldn't it? For a boss to ask you to mind his baby niece for three days?"

"She's not my boss's niece."

Megan nodded, still with an amused look on her face.

"She's Clara's baby."

Megan continued to nod.

"Can you move aside, Megan? I really need to get her home."

Megan opened the pantry door wide. "By all means, Jenny, you can go if you please. But I did ask you to come over here for a reason." She moved back to the empty bowl on the counter and carried it to the sink.

"What reason?"

"Clara." She didn't look up as she rinsed the large container in the basin.

"What about Clara?"

Megan dried her hands, turned and lifted the plate of lasagne from the counter and walked to the kitchen door. "She's here."

CHAPTER 32

From Jenny's kitchen Lana could see the man repeatedly striking Nyah with his foot. She could also see that he had a gun in his hand. *Jesus Christ!* Her hands trembling, she fumbled with her phone as she dialled 999 for emergency. In soft but urgent tones, she explained to the operator her location and what was happening. She had to leave – she needed to get to Megan Carmichael's house immediately. She had realised something as she examined Clara's painting. "*You can't tell Nyah – promise me, Lana – he must never know about Animal Farm.*" The title of Clara's drawing – *Animal Farm*. Clara had told her a terrible secret but not the whole truth.

A few years back Lana had been working on a case where a young child had witnessed a murder. The girl, nine years old at the time, completely blocked out what she had seen, which turned out to be her grandfather sticking a breadknife into her grandmother's back during an argument while she was standing at the sink. After the attack, the man turned to his granddaughter and pressed his finger to his lips. At the same time, he ran the forefinger of his other hand across his throat. It was a threat to shush her up. He told the Gardaí that his wife had suffered an assault from an intruder and, even though the authorities had their suspicions, there had been no material evidence to contradict the man's story and the little girl, the only witness, wouldn't talk. Children lack the life experience to understand and process traumatic experiences vocally. But there are other methods. The young girl had refused to talk about the attack and so a counsellor had worked with her, using art therapy as a means to express what she had witnessed. The girl had drawn a room with a table and chairs in the centre, a woman standing at the sink, a man behind her. The man's arm was raised and he was holding a knife. In Clara's picture, she had shown what happens to animals when they are neglected. If you don't look after them, they become sick, malnourished and they die. Alexis and Luke were neglected children. From what Nyah had told her, the two children had suffered. Lana was convinced of this, and Luke most likely didn't fall down the stairs and break his neck. If Clara had spent time in their house as a young girl, she had sensed the truth and, rather than confiding in someone, she had painted it. And, all those years ago, Clara had told her about a boy who had assaulted her. She had never mentioned his name, but Lana was now quite sure that boy had been Luke. She said the assault happened in "Animal Farm" – and now Lana knew why she had chosen that significant name.

Lana realised she couldn't do anything for Nyah other than call the emergency services – the man had a gun – and she urgently had to get to Megan's house. She was now sure that Clara had gone there when she got off the plane and, judging from the message on Jenny's phone, she had headed over there too. Jenny was in danger and maybe Clara too. All she had was a name, Megan Carmichael, but she would call her assistant, Ella, and get her help locating the property. It couldn't be too far from Jenny's house if the daughters were friends and attending the same primary school. And didn't Nyah mention that he had collected Clara once and that they had walked into town to meet their mother? But first, she had to get out of Nyah's house without the man seeing her.

She ran out to the hall and tried the front door. *It was locked.* And there was no sign of a key, either in the keyhole or hanging on a hook nearby. She couldn't hear anything from outside, but she knew she didn't have long – the man would enter the house once he was finished with Nyah. She raced down the hall towards the bedrooms. She remembered the layout from her stay years before, remembered that Jenny's room was located at the end of the hall and that the room had a large window facing the back garden. If she could get there, she had a chance. She found the room and opened the window. She stood perfectly still, pressing her body against the wall. She needed to make sure that the man was inside the house and that she wasn't going to bump into him out here. He would know she was in the house – he would have heard Nyah call back to her as he left the kitchen. Nyah would never make an investigator – he had alerted the intruder to the fact that he wasn't alone.

Lana held her breath as she listened and after a moment she could hear someone moving around inside the house. Now she had to make a run for it. She climbed out the window.

Her heart gave a sickening jolt as she saw Nyah lying on the ground. He wasn't moving.

She stopped. Her whole body trembled. *She couldn't leave him.* He needed immediate medical care. Then she remembered the gun. *Keep going, Lana! You can't help him if you get yourself killed. The ambulance and Gardaí are on their way. And Jenny and Clara are in danger.*

She rounded the corner of the house, ran to her car and leapt in. She started the engine, tugging the old gear stick into reverse. She reversed quickly and turned. In her rear-view mirror, she could see the man come around the corner of the house. She accelerated down the drive and saw him running after her, gun raised.

She turned the corner onto the road and, with one hand on the wheel, she dialled Ella's number. The girl answered immediately.

"Ella?"

"Lana, where have you been? I have been trying to reach you. This guy called about your garden and –"

"Ella, I need your help. Life and death."

She filled Ella in quickly. Ella told her to stay on the phone while she found the address for Megan Carmichael. A minute later, she was back on the line.

"OK, there are three Megan Carmichaels in Limerick. One is a retired teacher in her seventies and another a 4-year-old child. The third is in her 50's, living on the North side of the city, a housing estate. Brookhaven Drive. Actually, I think I know it."

"That's got to be the one. Can you drop-pin me her full address?"

She could hear Ella clicking away.

"There, you should have it now. I'm going to meet you there, Lana. Don't enter the house until I get there. Stay on the phone, don't hang up on me, Lana."

Lana gripped the steering wheel as she glanced in her rear-view mirror. There was no sign of the black car but if he figured out where she was heading, it was only a matter of time before he was behind her.

"Are you still there, Lana?"

"I'm here."

"Are you alright?"

"Yes."

Suddenly tears were rolling down her cheeks, tears for Nyah. *Please let him be OK, please let him be OK.* She felt distraught leaving him behind, and something else too, she wasn't sure what ... she wiped at her face with the back of her hand. Stay focused, she warned, help is on its way for Nyah. You have a job to do.

She rounded the corner and slowed her pace as she searched the road for Megan's house. There was a red car parked on the footpath a little way up the quiet street. Nyah had mentioned his mam drove a red car. Lana hung up the call. Ella would not be impressed, but there was no way she could wait for the girl or the Gardaí to arrive. She passed the red car and turned at the corner, parking on the footpath a little bit further down the road. She climbed out of the car and walked back to where the red car was parked. She glanced in the window and noticed a child's car seat in the back of the vehicle. She glanced over at the house, surrounded by tall trees. She crossed the street and peered over the small gate at the front of the property. She could see a silver car parked in the drive, the driver's door wide open. Her eyes moved to the front door of the house. It was also open.

She debated what she should do. She knew the smart thing would be to wait for Ella. Her assistant had called the Gardaí, and Megan's house was only a short distance from the city. They wouldn't be long, she was sure of it. Having said that, the man who beat up Nyah might be here any minute. She had to get inside, find Jenny and Clara, and warn them – get them out somehow. She tried the small gate but it wouldn't budge. The electronic gates were shut. She rounded the side of the house and found a small gap in the hedge. Crouching down, she pushed her way into the back garden. There was a small pink baby soother lying on the grass. She picked it up and turned it over in her hand. It appeared clean, she was sure it hadn't been out here for long. Had Jenny come this way before her, with the baby? She wondered why she would have come this way and not just rung the intercom.

The grass was high in the back garden – but some of it had been trampled recently, leading up to the back patio door. Someone *had* come this way very recently. She peered into the kitchen. The microwave door was open but, other than that, the room was in perfect order and spotlessly clean. There was no sign of life. She tried the patio door but it was locked. She had started to make her way around to the front when she heard a car pull up close by. The house was a corner house at the end of a one-way street so there wouldn't be any traffic coming down this road, unless someone had taken a wrong turn. Whoever it was intended to visit. It must be the man in the black car. It had to be. An image of Nyah's lifeless body flashed in front of her. She pushed it away. Now was not the time to let emotions get in her way.

She pressed herself against the wall as she waited. She heard the sound of a beep and the electronic gate opened, followed by footsteps. And then the front door closed. If it was the man who had attacked Nyah, he had a gun. She edged around the corner of the building, crouching down to pass the window until she got to the front door. There was a black car parked in the drive now. She couldn't hear a sound from out here. There was a glass panel with a white wooden frame at the side of the door. She stole a glance inside – the hall was empty. She took a breath and carefully tried the front door. It opened wide. She could hear voices, angry voices, people arguing, at least two.

She entered the house.

CHAPTER 33

Clara was lying on the floor on her side. Her wrists were tied behind her back and there was a gag around her mouth. She started to struggle when she saw her mother and baby Lucy. Jenny ran to her.

"*Aw*, isn't that cute!" Megan sneered. "Mother and daughter reunited!"

"Clara, are you OK?" Jenny pulled at Clara's gag.

"Don't touch it, Jenny – stupid girl bit me on the hand."

Jenny stopped. "Clara?"

"And I was only trying to help you, Clara, wasn't I?"

"Megan, what is going on?"

Megan laughed. "You still don't know? You haven't been able to figure it out?"

"What is Clara doing here? Where is Alexis?"

"Don't worry about her. Useless child, always giving me trouble. Now, my boy Luke, he was different, he had potential. But you put a stop to that, didn't you, Clara?" She walked right up to Clara and pushed at her foot with her own. "He was only being kind – friendly. And you had to make up lies about him." She stooped down and hissed close to Clara's ear. "*Complete and utter lies!*" She placed the bowl of steaming lasagne on the carpeted floor near Clara's feet.

The hairs on the back of Jenny's neck stood on end as she glanced from Megan to her daughter. Clara started whimpering behind the gag, shaking her head, her eyes darting around the room, terrified.

Jenny recalled a conversation she had with her daughter only last summer.

Jenny was walking down the hallway past Clara's bedroom. The door was open and Clara was getting ready to go out, piling on the make-up. She had stopped and leaned against the doorframe, watching with amusement as Clara applied lipstick. Clara was such a beautiful girl but she really didn't know it herself. She had very low self-esteem. She wore her long blonde hair loose around her face like a comfort blanket where she could hide away from the world. It was one of the main reasons why Jenny had embraced Clara's decision to enrol in university in Belfast and live away from home.

"Off out?"

"Yeah."

Jenny observed her for a moment as her daughter worked away with pencils and brushes.

"I met Beverley Mahon from your class in primary school – remember her?"

"Yeah? Think so, haven't seen her in years though."

"She was always a nice girl, Beverley."

"She was alright." She peered into the mirror, inspecting her work. "I remember she had a hard time in school."

"Did she?"

Clara wrinkled her nose. "She didn't fit in. The girls gave her a rough time. You know what kids can be like."

"She's nearly a lesbian now."

"*Mom!*" Clara stopped mid-stroke, her mascara brush in her hand. "You can't say that someone is *nearly* a lesbian."

"Well, you know what I mean."

"No, I don't!" She resumed her primping.

"Are you?"

"Am I what?"

"A lesbian? Or maybe you are bisexual? Or polyamorous?"

Clara stopped what she was doing and turned to observe her mother. "Why are you asking me questions like that, Mam?"

"Beverley seems very happy." No response. "It's just that you have never shown any interest in boys." She ploughed on, digging deeper and deeper. "So it's OK, if you are – lesbian, I mean. You can tell me."

She remembered the way Clara had looked at her, with great sadness in her eyes. Her head had dropped slightly. Jenny had regretted bringing it up at the time and now she knew, didn't she? Had Luke Carmichael done something to her daughter in this house? Had his sister Alexis found out? Did Megan know about it? In the painting, *Animal Farm*, Clara had drawn animals, happy and suffering. She had painted *Animal Farm* not long after Luke's death.

"You can quit the innocent act now, Jenny. Tell your daughter what happened to her father."

"What are you talking about, Megan?"

"Oh, come on! You don't think people believed it when you said he just left one day, do you?"

"I don't know where he is."

"I think you do, Jenny. Danny Doyle is like a bad penny – they always turn up. I learned that the hard way. But that man hasn't been seen in years. Where is he, Jenny?"

"*Megan. Untie Clara and let her go*."

"You see, we had a thing. Years ago. Now, I know Danny could be fickle, but what we had was special. He wanted to move back to London. And he was taking me with him. We had it all planned. And suddenly he just vanished."

"I don't know where he is, Megan," Jenny replied firmly. She knew that Clara was watching her. She had her father's eyes. She stole a glance at Clara. Something passed between them. What did Clara know? Jenny had only told one other person what had happened that day.

Rays of sunlight came through the gaps in the blind, revealing particles of dust swirling around the room. Baby Lucy lay asleep in her arms – oblivious to what was going on around her.

Clara had stopped crying, her body was still, but she wouldn't look at her mother now. Suddenly, Jenny felt exhausted from keeping her secret about Danny from her children. But she could never tell them the truth. *Never.*

When she had returned to the house that day, once she had the kids settled in their grandmother's, the day he attacked Nyah, her husband

Danny had already started drinking. She found him lounging on the sofa in the living room, his arm sprawled across the back, a half-empty beer bottle on the coffee table in front of him. The television was on – the volume turned up high. He was focusing on some match – a football game. The commentator got excited about whatever was happening on the pitch and Danny leaned forward in his seat, his fist pumping the air, and then a moment later, slapping his hand on his thigh in disappointment.

"*Fucking idiot! Offside, you fucking wanker ref!*" he roared at the screen.

She hated him in that moment, with every fibre of her being. He had just beaten up their chid, his only son, and the bastard cared more about a football match?

As if sensing her presence, he had turned in his seat, a look of surprise on his face – surprise that she had come back? He appeared bemused by her somehow. He slowly stood, brushing past her as he stumbled out to the kitchen. She heard him open the fridge. She followed him, facing his back as he pulled out another bottle of beer. He turned as he twisted the cap and fired it onto the floor, before taking a long drink, observing her over the top. He came closer, his eyes menacing, until he was right in front of her, his breath stinking of beer. She wondered how many he'd had before she arrived. She could smell sweat on his body and something else – she couldn't put a finger on what. Lavender? It was an odd combination. He had been out the night before, all night. She had no idea what he had been up to but she suspected there was a woman somewhere, a woman that smelled of lavender. She didn't know what had prompted the beating, but either Nyah or Clara had annoyed him in some way, unintentionally. However, the reason never mattered. It didn't take much to provoke him, especially when he was hungover.

Then he reached up and grabbed her by the throat with his free hand, his faded tattoo with its strangled swan apparent, pressing his fingers into her throat.

"*You fucking hurt me earlier, my beautiful fucking swan!*"

"*You attacked our son!*"

"What brought you back, Jenny? *Huh?* What are you looking for? A bit of rough, is it? Is that what you want?"

He pushed her back towards the kitchen sink. Jenny couldn't breathe – her eyes grew wide as she observed his face, inches from her own as he continued to squeeze. Tears stung her eyes. Tears for her, for her children, for the life that she had suffered since the day she had met him. He would never stop the abuse, the control, the lying and manipulation – she knew that in her heart. This hell would never be over as long as he was alive. He was fumbling with the button of her jeans with his free hand, pushing them down over her hips as he pressed himself against her. No, she thought, not anymore, she couldn't live like this anymore. Today, he had crossed a line. He had hurt Nyah.

She reached behind her, feeling around for something to hit him with as he continued to push at her jeans, until eventually her hand found the knife block. She knew there were six knives in the block, the sharpest on the top row. She pulled one out of the block and before she could change her mind, she plunged it into his neck. Blood spurted out like milk pouring from a carton. She searched his eyes. He was stunned. He grabbed the side of his neck as he stumbled back, his mouth opening and closing. One step, two steps, he went down on the third. Her heart was pounding – she couldn't believe what she had just done. Blood was gushing out of his neck, his body quivered as he tried to stop the bleeding with his hands. He looked at her and for the first time since she had met him, she saw something different in his eyes, something that he must have seen many times in hers. *Fear*. Danny looked scared. Really scared. A moment later, his hand slipped away from his neck and he stopped moving. He lay still on the kitchen floor, staring up at her. Jenny knew that he was dead.

She had to move fast.

She zipped up her jeans and tied the button as she stepped over him, before running out to the shed in search of a shovel. Glancing around the garden, she spotted the green bench. She walked over to take a closer look. It was close to the hedge, pushed up against a high wall and a nice bit away from the house, the perfect place to bury a body. It stood on metal legs with a seat and backrest made from wood. She had painted it the previous summer but exposure to the harsh winter elements had caused some of the colour to peel at the edges. She moved the bench and started digging stealthily and a few hours later she stood back, sweat dripping down the sides of her face. She had dug a six-foot hole, big enough and deep enough to take a man's body. She went back to the kitchen. Danny was exactly where he had fallen, perfectly still. His eyes were still open wide, glaring up at her. She leaned over and closed the lids, before dragging him out of the kitchen and across the yard, stopping several times to catch her breath. When she got to the side of the shallow grave, she tipped his large frame over the edge. She was exhausted. Wiping her forehead, she shovelled soil in over his body. She got herself into a rhythm. *Keep going*, she told herself, *you can't stop now*. Jenny marvelled at herself. She had no remorse, not for a second, as she continued to fill the hole with earth. *Just get the job done, and get back to Nyah and Clara.* That's all she thought about – her two children. When she was finished, she levelled out the soil and pulled the green bench over it.

She checked in with her mam about the kids and told her that she wouldn't be much longer. Fatigue took over but she had to keep going. She wasn't finished yet. She ran back to the house and started cleaning up the kitchen. There was blood everywhere and this took a lot longer to mop up than she had expected. She washed the floor several times and sprayed bleach on every surface. She cleaned up the sink and put the bottles of beer in the rubbish. After, she showered and changed her clothes, stuffing her soiled items into a plastic bag. She piled Danny's clothes into an old suitcase and found his passport in a file where they kept all their documents. She put the passport in with his clothes, packed separately to her own. She locked the door and left the house, driving directly to her mam's.

Nyah and Clara were fast asleep when she had arrived and she was grateful she didn't have to answer any of their questions, but her mam was awake and Jenny sat down and told her everything. She cried. They both cried. She remembered she was shaking so much that her mother held her in a firm embrace. She had handed her neat whiskey which she gratefully accepted. Jenny then went out to her mam's back garden and lit a fire. She piled Danny's clothes and passport onto the fire and they both watched them burn. She decided that she would talk to Nyah and Clara in the morning and tell them everything. But the next day her two children didn't ask about their father. As the weeks turned into months and they still didn't ask, Jenny decided they might have forgotten about him or blanked him out of their minds and memories.

When eventually she felt strong enough to bring the family back to the house, Nyah unexpectedly asked if his dad was going to be there. Jenny had just shrugged and said that he was gone, and he had accepted that. He even looked relieved.

They got on with their lives. She had planted grass seeds over the earth and the grass had grown under the green bench. *Never look back*, she had told herself.

Had her mother told Clara what had happened during one of her more lucid moments? She was the only person in the world that Jenny had confided in. Megan couldn't possibly know anything. She was trying to stir the pot and doing a very good job of it.

They all heard a shout coming from downstairs.

Megan looked towards the door leading out onto the landing. "Don't move, Jenny. And keep that baby quiet." She crossed the room and closed the door behind her.

Jenny heard the distinctive sound of a key turning in the lock.

Jenny waited a moment. When she was sure Megan had gone downstairs she carefully laid the sleeping baby Lucy on the carpet and untied Clara, pulling the gag down over her chin. Clara sat up and rubbed her wrists. She reached out for Lucy. The baby peered up at her, wide eyed, her little fingers reaching out to grab a strand of Clara's hair.

"Hey, hey, hey, little one! That hurts." She snuggled Lucy into her neck. "I've missed you so much." She closed her eyes. Tears escaped, tumbling down her cheeks.

Jenny noticed the plate of food. "Are you hungry, Clara?"

Clara shook her head. She held on to Lucy as if her life depended on it.

"Tell me about Bella?"

Tears continued to pour down Clara's face. "I'm so sorry, Mam."

"Who is Bella?"

"I can't believe she's dead."

"Clara? Who was she?"

"She was my half-sister," Clara sobbed.

Jenny was stunned. "*What?*"

"Last summer, just after my school exams, and a few months before I was due to start college, I came across this website about finding your family through DNA. I almost ignored it and then I thought about Dad." She looked at Jenny, her expression asking for approval.

Jenny didn't react.

"I wanted to meet him, to see if he would talk to me. Do you understand?"

Jenny nodded.

"I completed the questionnaire and nothing happened for ages and I forgot about it until one day I got a phone call from a girl. Her name was

Bella. She said she was my half-sister and that we shared the same dad. Danny Doyle was her dad and she too wanted to meet him." She glanced at Jenny again. "I couldn't ask you about him, Mam, you … the look on your face whenever I brought him up. Nor could Nyah."

Jenny was confused. "But you never did ask me about him!"

"That's because we knew it hurt you."

"What did you do?"

"I went to see Nana."

"Nana?"

Clara nodded.

"But why Nana? She doesn't remember anything!"

Clara smiled sadly. "She does remember some things. She told me Dad was dead."

"What else did she tell you?"

"Just that he was dead and I had to trust her about that. I was so angry, Mam. You never said he was dead. *Ever*."

"I'm sorry, Clara. But you can't really believe what Nana says."

"She was very definite, Mam. And I believe her. Anyway, Bella and I became friends and we really got on well together – like, we talked all the time. About everything. I told her about school, that I was finishing soon and thinking about college. She said she was thinking about college too and wanted to go to Belfast. She said she had a granduncle who had a flat there. That if I went to Belfast I could stay with her. Pay rent, of course, because she would have to get someone to share with her. That was the deal with the granduncle. But it would be just the two of us. I was desperate to meet Bella and spend time with her. I mean, I had a sister.

And I desperately wanted to get away from home. And from you. For lying to me." Her eyes filled with tears again. "I was so angry with you."

"Go on."

"So I started researching for courses in Queen's and I submitted an application. Like, it's much easier to get started up there. The point system that we have down here in the South? It doesn't exist in the North – the entry requirement is not as demanding as it is down here. It is expensive, though, but Bella said she would help with my fees until I got a part-time job. She said her uncle was loaded. I talked to you and I started making plans. You were busy with Nana. It was easy to tell you that I had everything sorted because Bella had done everything for me."

"But what about Emily and Becky?"

"They don't exist. Bella and I made them up, their names and address. I'm sorry for lying about them, Mam, but I couldn't tell you about Bella. I thought if you knew about her, you wouldn't let me go. Because she is Dad's daughter. And, she is practically the same age as me, which means …"

Clara didn't need to finish her sentence. Jenny knew what she meant. Danny Doyle had got some other poor girl pregnant around the same time as Jenny. She wasn't surprised – she had always guessed he was playing around and he would often visit his uncle in London when Nyah was small.

Lucy's head snuggled into Clara's neck.

"So, the girls in your photographs. On your social media?"

"Just a few friends from college, nobody interesting. They were doing the same course as me and we would go out as a group."

"What happened to Bella's mother?"

Clara shook her head. "Dead. According to Bella, she was an alcoholic. That's what her granduncle told her. She died when Bella was a small girl. She didn't raise Bella – her granduncle did. And his on-off girlfriend – whenever he was inside, that is. Audrey something-or-other. The man was in and out of prison regularly. Bella was terrified of him. He was obsessed with her, she said. She told me that he used to make her feel uncomfortable, that he would touch her sometimes ... inappropriately. She said he was sick."

"Jesus!"

"She was desperate to get away from him."

"My God, that was a heavy burden for you to bear! But you seemed fine at Christmas. Remember we had that Facetime after dinner? And you were in great form when we talked on the phone."

"That's because I *was* in great form. For the first time in years, since what had happened to Luke in this house. I had got a job in a local bar. I hated my course but I was going to stick it out, at least for a year. There was this option to change then, once you had completed your first year."

She smoothed her hand over Lucy's back and looked away from Jenny.

Jenny waited, sensing there was more to come.

Clara looked back, directly at her. "When I arrived at the flat last September Bella told me she was pregnant."

Jenny felt like she had been punched in the stomach. She looked at Clara and then at Lucy. Their bond was undeniable but ...

"Lucy is Bella's child?"

Clara nodded.

"Who is the father?" The question came out as a whisper.

"She wouldn't say. I still don't know. I don't think she did either."

"When did she give birth?"

"New Year's Eve, as I said."

"That's why you didn't come home for Christmas?"

"I couldn't leave her on her own, Mam. Her granduncle was putting pressure on her to go back to London for the holidays. If he had seen her bump, he would have gone crazy. He behaved as if he owned her, as if she was his possession, she said. He had even warned her, fairly explicitly, that she was not to get involved with any boy. I guess he wanted her for himself."

"Poor girl!"

"So she told him she was keeping me company because I was on my own and I told you the same thing."

"So her granduncle lives in London?"

Clara hesitated. "Yeah."

"What's his name?"

"David Miller."

"David Miller. Of course." Jenny felt sick. She gazed at little Lucy. Lucy who had become *her* baby in such a short time. But wasn't hers. Who wasn't even Lucy's. A thought struck her. "Had Bella named the baby Rebecca?"

"Yes, after her own mother. She is registered as Rebecca Miller. But when Bella left for London she wanted to change that. She was freaking out and said the granduncle might find out about her existence someday, when she was older. She was going to change her name to protect her identity. Maybe call her Jane. We talked about it in London when I went to stay with her, before she, before ..."

Jenny stared at her daughter. She had spent her whole life protecting her children from their father. She thought the younger years might be the most vulnerable for them and that once they grew older they would have forgotten about him, but she had been stupid and naive to think that. Then it dawned on her. The billing name on the IBAN for Clara's rent – Arabella Miller. Bella.

"Bella went into labour. I had just come off the phone to you when she had her first contraction. She had been feeling off all day. A couple of hours passed and then she started screaming in pain at the contractions. I had never heard anything like it. I didn't know what to do. Then her waters broke. I called an ambulance. She was in labour for hours and hours. It didn't go well and in the end she had to have a caesarean. But the baby was fine and Bella recovered well afterwards."

"Why didn't you call me?"

"I wanted to tell you so many times, Mam. I was planning on coming down in February for my birthday and I was going to tell you everything then – but I was called into work in the pub. And then I kept putting it off. It was easier not to say anything because if I told you about the baby then I would have had to tell you about Bella."

"Clara ..."

"As I said, Bella couldn't tell her granduncle. She told me some other things about him, Mam. She found photos on his computer when she lived with him in London, photos of children. Apart from her fears for herself, she feared that her baby would have been in so much danger if he knew about her." She held Lucy a little closer.

Ugly images sprang unbidden to Jenny's mind. She shuddered. David Miller. An evil man. She tried to shake off the horror she felt. She must try and understand where the Carmichaels fit into all of this, if she was to have any hope of dealing with Megan.

"Clara – where do the Carmichaels come into all this?"

"Alexis sent me a message. Out of the blue. It was the middle of December. I mean, that girl barely talked to me in secondary school. After ... what happened with her brother Luke, she kind of withdrew or something into herself. She didn't talk to anyone. Anyway, I was living in Belfast nearly four months and she sent me a message asking if she could come and visit. I didn't know what to say."

"What did you do?"

"I told her to come up." Clara hesitated. "I told Bella everything, Mam. So she knew about Alexis. And Luke."

Jenny looked away. She still didn't know what had happened in this house the day Luke died, but she had a fair idea. "What did he do to you, Clara?"

Clara hung her head.

"Just answer me this? Did he hurt you?"

Clara nodded.

"Once? Twice? More than that ..."

"Once. He was a little prick, Mam. He was always passing comments about me, my clothes, my hair, that sort of stuff. But I was well able to stand up for myself. One day, I was here playing with Alexis. We were baking in the kitchen. Her mother had bought ingredients. I remember we were dipping strawberries in melted chocolate and my hands were all sticky. There wasn't any soap at the kitchen sink so I went upstairs to the loo to wash them and ... when I came out of the bathroom Luke was standing there. He had this weird look in his eyes. I tried to get past him and the next thing I know he is dragging me into his room and ..." Clara sniffed. "I can't tell you what he did to me, Mam. All I know is that I froze." She took a deep breath. "Alexis came looking for me. She found us in his room. She just lost it. I mean she completely lost it. She was yelling at him with tears streaming down her cheeks, flinging clothes and shoes around his room. Anything she could get her hands on. I ran out of the house and left them arguing. I don't know what happened after that. The next thing I find out Luke is dead."

Jenny let this new information sink in. She couldn't believe that something so evil had happened to her daughter in this house. She swallowed the lump rising in her throat.

"Please, Mam, I can't talk about this now ..."

Jenny put her arm around her daughter and smoothed her hair away from her face. "I understand, love."

"Thanks, Mam."

"What happened when Alexis arrived in Belfast?"

"I met her at the train station. She was OK. Still a bit quiet or something, but I was expecting that. That first night we all went out but Bella left early. She would get tired easily, you know, and she was heavily pregnant at this stage. Alexis got really drunk. She told me her dad was working for this guy in England, and he was trouble. Her dad had told her to come spy on me for this English guy. That she was to find out about the girl I was living with. *Bella*. Somehow, he knew about her and our connection. Alexis felt awful about everything ... about Luke." Clara dropped her head. "She told me she wasn't going to tell her dad anything. She'd say there was nobody called Bella living with me. She gave me a key to the safe in their house. She said there was paperwork there, about things her father was involved in, incriminating evidence that he wouldn't want anyone to see. She asked me to safeguard the key."

The key in her mother's locker at the care home with Clara's initial attached.

"Alexis went home and told him she wasn't doing his bidding anymore. He was furious with her. And the mum, Megan, heard them arguing."

So, that was why she had called her. She had been trying to figure out if Jenny knew anything.

"Two weeks after Alexis went home, Bella went into labour. She had to stay in the hospital for a few days after the birth and then she was allowed to bring the baby back to the flat."

"How did you cope with a new-born? I mean, how did you even know what to do?"

Clara smiled. "Google. And the hospital staff were really helpful. A community nurse called every day for the first couple of weeks. We managed." She nodded at Lucy. "She just slept a lot. Bella tried breastfeeding for a while but I fed her the bottle too. To give Bella a break." Her expression clouded. "But, her granduncle, he was putting pressure on Bella to go back to London for a visit. One morning he phoned and demanded that she go home. I was beside her when she took the call. He was threatening that he was getting on a flight to Belfast. Bella was so upset. Then, I told her about Alexis – the real reason for her visit. She completely broke down. She was terrified. She was sure her granduncle was behind everything. And she didn't trust Alexis not to tell her dad about the pregnancy. She asked me to look after the baby and she called her granduncle and told him she was catching the next flight over. The next day she left for England. She said she would stay with a friend in London and work in the Old Rose pub until she figured out what to do. She said that would calm the uncle down for a while at least. And so, she left us."

"What happened next?"

"You knocked on my door."

"Why did you let Lucy with me? Why did you leave?"

"As I said, if David Miller had found out about the baby, there could have been horrific consequences – both for Bella and for the baby. When you arrived at my door in Belfast, you thought she was mine and I played along with it while I was trying to figure out what to do. When we stopped at Connolly Station in Dublin I texted Bella and she said to let you take Lucy home, that she would be safer with you."

"But why did *you* go to England?"

"I wanted to help Bella. Try get her out of there. But Jeff betrayed her. He's another one of David's henchmen. He told him everything."

"Who drove you to the airport?"

"Alexis."

"Did she collect you from the station in one of her dad's cars?"

"Yeah."

The black car, with the English registration. "I saw you talking to someone on the phone on the platform in Dublin?"

"I called her."

"So you knew you were leaving, when we were on the train?"

"Yeah."

"And did you ring Alexis a few weeks ago? And ask her for a car?"

Clara frowned. "No? Why would I do that? I can't even drive. I only called her while we were waiting for our connection in Dublin."

So Megan had made that shit about the car up. What else had she lied about?

"I saw Megan this afternoon. Standing outside People's Park."

"She asked me to meet her there. So I took a taxi from the airport. She said she wanted to talk about Luke, that she wanted to apologise for what he had done."

A thought struck Jenny. "Bella had a tattoo on her arm."

Clara gave a small smile. "Last summer, when Bella and I started talking she asked me if I had any pictures of dad so I sent her a copy of the photo of the two of you in the living room. When I arrived in Belfast, she had the same tattoo on her arm."

Jenny was stricken with pity for the girl. Longing to meet her father, copying his tattoo to feel closer to him. Not realising he too was a monster like his evil granduncle.

"Oh, I see." She couldn't share her feelings about that tattoo and its inventor with her daughter. "We were so puzzled by it all, Nyah and I've both been worried sick."

"I know, Mam. I'm so sorry."

They heard a door slam somewhere in the house and then footsteps on the tiles in the hallway below. Lucy stirred. Clara reached for her mother's hand and they both waited for Megan to return.

CHAPTER 34

Lana froze at the bottom of the stairs. The argument she had heard when she was outside the house had turned into a shouting match.

"*She told him where I am, Megan. It's only a matter of time before he gets here or sends one of his heavies!*"

"I can't leave the house, not now."

"*Why?*"

"Upstairs. Jenny and Clara. And some fucking baby."

"*What? Are you serious?*"

"Clara knows, Ned. What happened to Luke."

"I know she knows."

"*You knew? Why didn't you fucking tell me?*"

"She came to the showroom. Threatened to go to the Gardaí about what he did to her."

"And Alexis overheard you both?"

"Yes. Always sneaking around, that girl."

"When I heard you arguing about Clara you told me that she was looking for a car!"

"I lied."

"You're a stupid fool! You should have told me. We could have got rid of Clara before any of this happened."

Lana glanced up the stairs. She could make it if she moved now. *Right now.* The voices stopped in the kitchen, and then she heard footsteps approach. *Shit.* Whoever it was would be entering the hall any second. She spotted a door under the stairs and quickly opened it and stepped inside. It was a downstairs toilet. *Please don't let any one of them decide that it's time to use the loo!* A moment later, she heard the kitchen door open and footsteps on the stairs.

She counted to ten and slowly opened the door. She could hear voices coming from upstairs. She quietly entered the kitchen and looked around for a weapon. Where were Ella and the Gardaí? They were taking far too long. The station was just across the bridge from Brookhaven Estate. She spotted a carving knife lying on the draining board. She quickly grabbed the knife and moved back out to the hall.

She could hear muffled voices coming from above. She couldn't see clearly from where she was standing but she guessed the door must be closed. What was she going to do? She looked at the knife in her hand. Would she be able to use it if she had to? She remembered the man and what he had done to Nyah – the gun dangling menacingly at his side. He didn't appear to be holding back so she had better be ready to use the knife if she was going to confront him. She felt a vibration in her pocket. Pulling out her phone, she could see Ella's name flashing across her screen. The device stopped vibrating and started again a moment later. She couldn't answer her. Not now. She couldn't risk the people upstairs hearing her conversation.

She silenced the call and quietly climbed the stairs. The wide landing was carpeted a deep pile, cream in colour. There were five white doors, all closed. There was nowhere to hide here. If that man or whoever opened a door, she was in plain sight.

She could hear their voices more clearly now, coming from the door at the end of the landing. A baby started to cry. She couldn't imagine how unsettled the little child must be – she had been through a whirlwind of change the past few days, and she was only a few months old.

Lana crept along the landing, the knife held out in front of her. She tried the door next to the one at the end. It was open. She slipped inside.

"What the fuck is going on, Megan?" He pointed the gun towards Jenny, Clara and Lucy. "What are they doing here in my fucking house?"

"I'm trying to fix your mess, Ned."

"*My* mess? It seems like you've created a mess all of your own."

Megan laughed sarcastically. "You've got to be kidding me! All I have ever done is try to protect this family."

Ned laughed harshly. "Well, that's a fucking joke! This family? This was never a family, Meg. Never. Oh, we pretended as if, in front of your friends." He waved the gun at Jenny. "But it was all for show. That idiot son of yours could never shape up. He was a fucking useless piece of –"

Megan slapped Ned across the face. *Hard*. Her expression was like thunder.

Ned laughed. She went to hit him again and he grabbed a hold of her wrist, his nostrils flaring.

"Don't you ever disrespect our son again!" Megan warned.

"He was a useless piece of shit and you know it!" He nodded towards Clara. "Interested in little girls. His death was a blessing."

Jenny winced. She glanced at Clara who appeared to be in a trance. She vaguely wondered if this was the room where the assault had taken place. It was empty except for a single mattress on the carpeted floor.

"*Don't say that about Luke!*" Megan screamed. "*He was our son!*"

"He was *your* son. *Not mine!*" he snarled.

Megan rolled her eyes. "You're just talking shit, Ned."

"Go on then? Let's see you deny it, shall we? Luke wasn't my kid. *He was yours and that Doyle idiot's!*"

There was silence in the room. Nobody moved.

"Did you think I didn't know about your little affair, Megan? I've known for years. And guess what? Two can play that game."

Megan took a step back from Ned. She glanced frantically at the people in the room, her expression panicked.

Ned pointed the gun at Clara. "*So our son tried to have sex with his little half-sister!*" he yelled.

Megan charged towards Ned in a rage.

Clara screamed.

Then the bedroom door burst open.

Lana had heard the scream. Followed by a door opening and then someone was running up the stairs. *Who the hell was that*? She was sure it wasn't Ella – the girl would never enter a strange building on her own. It didn't sound like the Gardaí – they would alert the occupants in the house of their presence. She tried to see through the crack in the door. She could just about make out a shadow on the landing, but that was it.

And then, she heard a shout.

"*Alexis, no!*"

A thud, followed by a cracking sound and then more shouting. Lana emerged from the room to see a man tumbling down the stairs, the same man who had just beaten up Nyah, and he was falling, his hand outstretched to the girl standing above him. A moment later, he landed hard on the marble tiles. Lana glanced at the girl – she was holding a rock in her right hand. The girl started to cry, great big sobs. A woman emerged from the room next to Lana's. She tried to take hold of the rock from the girl but she wouldn't let go. They didn't notice Lana standing there with a knife in her hand.

"What have you done, Alexis?"

The girl looked startled. "He tried to push me, Mum, I swear."

The woman glanced at the rock in the young girl's hand, panic in her expression.

Lana could hear sirens now, getting closer.

"Alexis, let go of that!" the woman ordered. "*Now*!"

The girl dropped the rock on the carpet and the woman grabbed it and ran down the stairs as the girl continued to stare at the man on the floor below, her hand cupping her mouth. She was crying and shaking.

Lana took a step forward and laid a hand on the girl's shoulder.

She turned to Lana as if noticing her for the first time.

"Are you OK?" Lana asked.

Fresh tears filled the girl's eyes. "I killed him. I killed them both." She ran down the stairs and knelt beside the man just as the emergency services filed in the front door.

Lana walked into the bedroom at the end of the landing.

Jenny was sitting on the floor, her arm around Clara, the baby cradled between them. They looked up as she entered.

"Jenny? Clara? Are you OK?"

Jenny narrowed her eyes.

"It's Lana."

Jenny nodded. "I know who you are. Where's Nyah?"

Lana didn't reply.

EPILOGUE

Jenny was sitting on the green bench, watching Clara play with baby Lucy on the grass. Clara's blonde hair shone like gold against the early-summer evening sun. A few months had passed since the incident at the Carmichaels' house and life had moved on – as best as it could. It wasn't the same, but they were all coping in their own way. Clara hadn't returned to college in Belfast – not too surprising. She had submitted a strong portfolio to the Limerick School of Art and Design and she was hoping to secure a place the following autumn. She should have chosen the Art College in the first place but, if she had, then she wouldn't have met Bella and if she hadn't met Bella then the family wouldn't have met Lucy.

Clara looked up at Jenny, a smile playing on her lips and something passed between them, an unspoken message.

When Megan had left them both alone in that room, Clara had asked Jenny what really happened to her dad and in that moment Jenny contemplated telling her daughter everything, coming clean and finally sharing her secret, the one she had kept for many years. But she didn't. She told Clara the same thing that she had always told her. That when she returned to the house that afternoon, Danny had already left, and that she didn't know where he had gone. And that, yes, he could be dead. Clara had simply nodded. Whether she accepted this explanation or not, she didn't comment either way, and she didn't bring up what her grandmother had said. Hopefully, she realised that Sue's mind was not reliable anyway. Who could believe the ramblings of an old woman suffering from dementia?

Jenny now knew that Danny had been seeing Megan around the time he attacked Nyah. God only knows how long their affair had been going on but, if Ned were to be believed, Danny was Luke's father.

Nana was back in the nursing home again after her fall. She had sprained her wrist and the staff were watching her carefully but she was recovering really well. Jenny was going to bring her out on the weekend to spend some time with Lucy. Nana absolutely adored the little girl. Her face lit up whenever they visited.

Nyah emerged through the back door and slowly limped across the garden. He was using a cane during the last few weeks, having taken his first few steps without a walking frame since the beating. He had almost died that day and if Lana hadn't called an ambulance, he probably would have. He had suffered a collapsed lung, several broken ribs, a dislocated shoulder and his leg was broken in three different places. The surgeon had also removed his spleen. Ned Carmichael had meant to kill him. He nearly had.

Slowly, Nyah made his way across the lawn and came to sit with his mother on the green bench.

"How do I look?"

"Why are you wearing a tie?"

"Don't you like it?"

"Who are you trying to impress?"

"Nobody."

"Lana," Jenny said. It wasn't a question.

"Does it look alright?" He rubbed the back of his neck, a grimace flickering across his face. He still got regular spasms, and every day he suffered chronic pain and muscle cramps. His consultant said they would fade away in time, but might never go completely. He would have discomfort for the rest of his life.

"It looks formal."

"Lana is making dinner."

"At her house. I don't think she expects you to wear a tie for dinner in her house, Nyah."

"But what if she is wearing a dress?"

Jenny smiled slowly. "You still really like her, don't you?"

"What do you mean by *still*?"

Jenny laughed. "I remember the way you used to look at her, Nyah. When you were in college and you brought her down to visit. Like there was nobody else in the room."

"That obvious?"

"That obvious." She ruffled his hair. "The tie looks great."

Clara approached with Lucy resting on her hip. She sat on the bench. "What's with the tie?"

"That's it, I'm going." He grabbed his cane.

Jenny touched his arm. "Not yet. Let's just sit here a while. All of us. It's not often we get to sit together."

"Mam, I moved home. So did Clara. And Lucy lives here too. The house has never been so busy."

"I know. Just, give me a minute." She took a deep breath, as she scanned the garden, in full bloom at the height of the summer. Danny Doyle's presence was everywhere. "Your dad, he could be difficult ..."

"Mam ..." Nyah started.

"No, let me finish. I haven't told you everything. And you deserve to know. You do. Both of you. He was your father." She took a deep breath. "He was difficult. I think we all know that. But he loved you both. He did, in his own way. He didn't show it very well." Jenny looked at Nyah. "Particularly with you, Nyah. Being the boy, I guess he was tougher on you. But he did love you both. And I'm sorry you didn't get to see him before he left."

She was crying now. She couldn't stop herself. All the years of holding it in, not being able to discuss their father with them. And she knew she would never tell them the whole truth. But she could tell them that he loved them. For their sake, not his, and even if it wasn't exactly the truth. This would give them some sense of closure.

Nyah put his arm around her shoulder. Clara rubbed her hand on the other side. Lucy stared, her big eyes moving from one to the other, sucking vigorously on her little thumb shoved into her mouth.

"It's OK. I am OK. I'm just, I'm sorry. That you didn't get to say goodbye."

They sat there like that for a while. Nobody uttered a word, each of them lost in their own thoughts. Jenny would never tell her children what she had done to their father. Some things were better left unsaid.

But in a weird way, they were all together with him now. She had said her few words, and she would move on. *Never look back.*

A taxi pulled into the driveway and stopped at the side of the house. "Right, well, I'd better get going." Nyah used his cane and the arm of the bench to pull himself up. He leaned over to kiss his mother. "See you later, Mam." He ruffled Clara's hair, blew baby Lucy a kiss and limped across the garden.

Jenny shouted after him. "Have you got your key?"

He waved his hand in the air.

He hobbled into the back seat and the car turned and disappeared down the drive.

Clara scooted down the bench closer to Jenny. She leaned in to her mother and Jenny put her arm around her. She smiled at baby Lucy, the absolute joy of all of their lives. Poor Bella was lost. But they had rescued her little treasure. David Miller was a nasty bastard. She had often wondered why he didn't come looking for Danny. But now she knew, didn't she? He mustn't have wanted him to know about Bella. He must have wanted to keep her for himself.

David Miller was no longer a threat. He owned Skater Car Dealership and Ned was his employee, but the business had been a ruse for his criminal activity. Ned had evidence to incriminate Miller – he kept it in the safe at his house. Alexis had found the key to the safe and given it to Clara for safe keeping, and Clara had hidden it in a place nobody would ever look. In the locker of her nana's bedroom at the nursing home. David Miller had been arrested at Heathrow airport on his way to Spain. He had a number of offences to account for, child-trafficking and pornography among them.

When Bella found out that she was pregnant she got out of London fast. She was in constant fear that he would find her and punish her and take her baby away. Bella had found Clara and dragged her into her corrupt world. Unbeknownst to Clara, her half-sister was in way over her head. David had killed Bella in the London flat that day. He had found out about the pregnancy through Jeff in the Old Rose and demanded to know the whereabouts of the child. He was furious with her for lying to him about the baby. But she wouldn't tell him where Lucy was. He had controlled Bella her whole life and now she was finally standing up to him. He slit her throat for her efforts, his own grandniece. Clara had left the flat that day in order to buy them both sandwiches in the local deli. Bella stayed behind to search up flights to Ireland. When she had arrived back, she found Bella's body. If she had been there, he probably would have done the same to her.

Jenny had only seen Megan Carmichael once since the events that took place at her house. Instead of her usual overbearing bullshit, the woman had crossed the street to avoid her. Megan told the Gardaí that she was the one who hit Ned with the rock, even though Alexis had confessed to what she had done. The girl wasn't talking now and Megan was claiming self-defence. It would be up to the Gardaí to decide what happened next. They were preparing a book of evidence for the Director of Public Prosecution. Jenny thought about Luke, and what he had done to Clara. Clara had disclosed some information, but she wasn't ready to talk about it yet, neither of them were. It was a difficult pill to swallow, realising that your child had endured a sexual assault while in her best friend's home.

"Come on, Mam – let's get this little one to bed." Clara stood. She extended her free hand to Jenny.

Jenny took her daughter's hand and they both walked across the lawn towards the house. Away from the green bench.

Nyah straightened his tie and smoothed it into his collar. Maybe he shouldn't have worn a tie. His mother had teased him, his sister had teased him. The porch light was on. Would he have time to take it off? He could just about make out the inside of the hallway through the frosted glass. The lights inside the house were dim. It was the middle of May and there was a long stretch in the evenings. It was a few minutes after eight and dusk was just about settling in. Nyah rang the doorbell. *Take off the tie, Nyah*, a tiny voice warned inside his head. He started pulling at the fabric around his neck. A moment later, he could see movement in the hallway and then the door swung open. Lana stood on the other side, her slender arm holding onto the latch. Her face was devoid of make-up, her hair had grown and the brown tresses rested over one shoulder. She was wearing a white T-shirt with the phrase *I'm from the 061* printed across the front in green letters – the Limerick area code. Faded jeans with a rip on the right knee and bare feet, toenails painted a pale-pink colour. She looked gorgeous just standing there, her weight resting on one foot as she leaned into the doorframe. *Not formal.*

She smiled up at him. "You're wearing a tie?"

Own it, Nyah. Why did he always feel like a schoolboy around Lana Bowen?

"Felt like wearing a tie." He offered the bottle of wine he had stopped into the off licence to pick up. It was a white Sauvignon Blanc, from New Zealand. "You were drinking this one at the airport."

She smiled as she took the bottle from him. "At the airport I drink anything. But thank you." She opened the door wide. "Come on in!"

He stepped inside the narrow hallway. Shedding his jacket, he popped it on the coat rack attached to the wall.

"We're out on the patio."

She took off down the hall and disappeared into what he guessed was the kitchen.

We? Who is we? He thought it was just the two of them for dinner. He pushed aside his disappointment as he followed her down the corridor, his cane in his hand. The kitchen was the colour of primroses. LED lights dappled pale shadows onto the white granite counter tops. There was an island in the centre and a bowl filled with lemons and limes. He glanced out the window at the fairy lights scattered around the garden, illuminating the colourful undergrowth. He could hear voices as he followed Lana out to the patio area.

Peter Clancy was sitting at the table, a glass of red wine in his hand. He was dressed in a pair of faded blue jeans and a white T-shirt, his dark hair a stark contrast to his tanned skin. *Not formal.*

Nyah's heart sank.

Peter stood, extending his hand when Nyah approached.

"Nyah? How are you, man? It's been a while?"

"Good, yes, very well." His reply came out terse, more formal than intended but Peter didn't seem to notice. He settled into the chair opposite Peter.

Lana appeared at Peter's side, resting her hand gently on his shoulder. There was something very intimate about the gesture.

Nyah steadied his heartbeat.

"Drink?"

"Ah, yeah, a beer is fine, thanks. Whatever you have."

She smiled and walked back inside.

"So, Lana told me what happened. Pretty rough. How is everyone doing?"

He didn't know why but he was suddenly annoyed with Lana. Why did she feel the need to tell this man what had happened to him and his family? And what exactly was he doing here anyway? It was a Friday evening and Peter was a couple of hundred miles away from his home in Castle Cove with a drink in his hand. Which meant he had to be staying somewhere. Was he staying here? With Lana? The sinking feeling rose again. He shouldn't have got his hopes up when Lana had texted asking him over for dinner. He really shouldn't. In that conversation they had on the plane, Lana told him that she needed time alone. He'd hoped she had changed her mind. And it seemed she had, about Peter at least. He decided he would finish his beer and leave, get the hell out of here and go find a bar and drown his sorrows. He couldn't go home and face his mother and Clara, not yet. But no – he had been invited to dinner. He couldn't just walk out. He'd have to stay. Grin and bear it.

He glanced around the garden. It looked great. The grass was freshly cut and the hedges were trimmed back. Someone had given the place a bit of attention. He doubted that it was Lana herself that had carried out the work – she had complained about the state of the place while they were away.

"Yeah, quite rough. Everyone is fine now though. Thanks to Lana. Thank you for reconnecting us. I had no idea that ..."

Peter grinned. "That she was a shit-hot private investigator?"

Nyah glanced at Peter and something passed between them – an acknowledgement that they liked the same girl. Peter nodded as Lana returned with Nyah's beer.

She sat, tucking her feet up beneath her. She sipped on her white wine.

"Right, I'm off." Peter finished his drink and placed his glass on the table.

"Do you want a coffee? Or a refill?"

"Nah, I'm driving, thanks. I shouldn't really have had this one." He nodded at Nyah. "Nice to see you again, Nyah."

"I'll walk you out." Lana followed him back into the kitchen.

He was going? Nyah could hear her soft laughter inside the house and then the front door close. A moment later, she was sitting beside him again.

"He didn't stay long?"

"How is Clara?" She ignored his question.

"She's doing better. It will take time though. She's seeing someone, a therapist, for what it's worth."

"That's good."

"It's hard to understand how all this happened."

"People lie, Nyah, all the time. And they cover up and they pretend that everything is OK."

"But what Luke did. To my sister. She was only a kid. And she kept it to herself all these years?"

Lana glanced away.

"And his mother and father knew. Megan tried to protect her son's memory by ghosting my sister. And then she came for her again, when Clara was planning to disclose what had happened ... because Bella was encouraging her ..."

Clara had confided in Bella during their time in Belfast. She had told her that she had been abused by her best friend's brother. It had only happened one time. One time is too many, Bella had said. She had encouraged Clara to talk to Luke's parents. Clara had gone to visit Ned at the showroom. He had always seemed like an easier person to approach so Clara had chosen him over Megan. Alexis had been at the showroom in the back office. She heard the entire conversation. She had kept Luke's secret once before. She wasn't prepared to do it again.

"It took three days to find my sister, Lana. And in the end, it was you who found her. If it wasn't for you ..."

"How is Lucy?"

Nyah smiled for the first time since he had arrived.

"She's a beauty. Honestly, she has brought so much light into our home. And Mam is besotted with her."

"How is the adoption process going?"

He shrugged. "Slow. That is to be expected. But our legal team don't think there will be any barriers, you know, objections. Mam has to do a medical and some other stuff. It's standard procedure for adoption. David Miller is the closest living blood relative the child has, and he is behind bars awaiting trial for Bella's murder. Nobody knows who Lucy's father is. Clara being her half-sister makes her the next of kin. So, hopefully Lucy will grow up in our home, legally. Mam will be her mother, on paper at least."

"That's really good news."

"It's weird that he bought Skaters, isn't it?" Nyah shook his head. "Like, what a coincidence."

Lana shrugged. "Not really. It served two purposes."

"What do you mean?"

"He found a place to hide his illegal activity. A quiet car dealership with a shady manager."

"And the second one?"

"Skaters is in Limerick – close to Danny Doyle's house, your dad's. Miller's nephew. Your dad must have been scouting properties for him and then Skaters came on the market. It's funny that your dad didn't get a job there."

"Mam says Skaters was up for auction about sixteen years ago."

"Just before your father disappeared."

They were both quiet for a moment.

"Why was Peter here?"

Lana sighed. "He came to explain about Gary Duke. He swore to me that he hadn't planned to meet him."

"Do you believe him?"

Lana glanced at Peter. "He travelled all the way from Castle Cove to tell me."

"That doesn't answer my question."

She nodded and glanced away. "Yeah, I believe him."

Nyah played with a crumb on the table. He didn't want to talk about Peter or Danny Doyle anymore. "Lana?"

"Yes?"

"What you said? On the plane?"

"Yeah?"

"Do you still feel the same?"

There was no point in waiting and hoping for something to happen between them. He may as well get it out in the open. Or else, every time he would see Peter or some other guy he would always be guessing. He needed to know how she felt. And if she didn't see any future for them both, then he would just have to accept it.

He could see that she was thinking. *Her thinking face.* She was watching the garden, lit up subtly by fairy lights, lanterns hanging from trees. It looked beautiful, magical. For a moment, neither of them spoke. He felt hot, his throat constricted. He pulled off his tie.

"When I left you that day, lying on the ground outside your mother's house, something happened to me, Nyah. I don't know what, but I felt like I was running away from my home. I don't know why ... but the feeling nearly broke me. All my years working as an investigator, I have never lost sight of the task. *Always keep your mind on the job, never lose focus,* that's what we are trained to do. But that day, seeing you there, I wanted to turn back. I nearly did. And, I realised something."

"What?"

She turned to look at him. She placed her hand on his, her skin warm.

"You, Nyah Doyle, you are my home."

THE END